## THE THRIE ESTAITIS

*Ane Satyre of the Thrie Estaitis* is a mid-sixteenth-century *tour de force*, the theatrical masterpiece of Sir David Lindsay of the Mount. Born about 1485, the son of a Fife laird, Lindsay served for most of his life at the Scottish court, as usher to the young James V, as Snowdon Herald, and eventually as Lyon King of Arms. His earliest surviving poems come from the end of the king's minority: he was already voicing strong criticism of the abuses of the contemporary Church. This is developed into a sustained attack in three later works: *The Tragedie of Cardinall Betoun* (1547), *Ane Dialog of Experience and ane Courtier* (1552), and *The Thrie Estaitis* (1552). While the nature and extent of Lindsay's commitment to Protestantism is a matter for debate, there is no mistaking the vigour of his condemnation of ecclesiastical misconduct, or the dramatic skill with which he brings his arguments to life. *The Thrie Estaitis* was successfully revived by Tyrone Guthrie, in an acting edition by Robert Kemp, for the Edinburgh Festival of 1948, and there have been several subsequent productions.

Roderick Lyall is Professor in Scottish Literature at the University of Glasgow. Born and educated in Perth, Western Australia, he taught English at Massey University in New Zealand before moving to a lectureship in Glasgow in 1975. He was appointed to a Titular Chair in 1987. He has published numerous articles on medieval Scottish literature, and has edited William Lamb's *Ressonyng of ane Inglis Merchand and Scottis Merchand* and (with R. D. S. Jack) Sir Thomas Urquhart's *The Jewel*.

*Sir David Lindsay of the Mount*

# ANE SATYRE OF
# THE THRIE ESTAITIS

*Edited with an Introduction and Commentary
by Roderick Lyall*

CANONGATE
CLASSICS
18

This edition first published as a Canongate Classic in 1989 by Canongate Publishing Limited, 17 Jeffrey Street, Edinburgh EH1 1DR. Introduction, notes and commentary copyright © Roderick Lyall 1989. All rights reserved.

The publishers gratefully acknowledge general subsidy from the Scottish Arts Council towards the Canongate Classics series and a specific grant towards the publication of this volume.

Set in 10pt Plantin by Hewer Text Composition Services from disc supplied by the editor. Printed and bound in Great Britain by Cox and Wyman, Reading.

Canongate Classics
Series Editor: Roderick Watson
Editorial Board: Tom Crawford, J. B. Pick

*British Library Cataloguing in Publication Data*
Lindsay, *Sir* David, c. 1485–1555
Ane satyre of the thrie estaitis
I. Title
822'.2

ISBN 0-86241-191-2

# Contents

# Introduction

The audience which attended the performance of *Ane Satyre of the Thrie Estaitis* at the Castle Hill, Cupar on 7 June 1552 were citizens of a deeply troubled nation. Eight years of intermittent war with England between 1542 and 1550 had left the country economically weakened and politically divided. Several Scottish fortresses were still garrisoned by the French troops who had been brought in to fight the English. Government was in the hands of the faction led by James Hamilton, earl of Arran and duke of Châtelherault, but his position was quickly deteriorating, and by the time the play was performed again at Edinburgh, probably on 12 August 1554, he had been replaced by Mary of Guise, mother of the Queen who was then only twelve years old and who had been absent in France, the bride of the Dauphin, since 1548. In the summer of 1552, a year after the treaty by which the Anglo-Scottish war was brought to an end, much of Scotland was in the grip of famine: and this 'derth' was, as we shall see, a recurring theme in Parliament and in the proceedings of the Council.

The privation which must have been the consequence of campaigns in Angus, Lothian and the Borders was exacerbated by other factors: there was economic exploitation, which had been complained of in the past, and there are hints that agricultural land was being enclosed in ways which were causing still more hardship. Much of this oppression was suffered at the hands of churchmen, not least in Fife where, in 1546, a group of lairds with Protestant sympathies had assassinated Cardinal Beaton, archbishop of St Andrews. The Council of the Scottish Church had attempted reform in 1549, but three years further on there was little evidence of substantial progress.

This is not to suggest that the government was unaware of the need for change. James Hamilton, archbishop of St Andrews and brother of the Governor, had convened another Council on 26 January 1552, which had among other measures agreed to the production of a catechism for the guidance of both clergy and laypeople.[1] An officially-sanctioned vernacular textbook of elementary theology went some way towards meeting the criticisms of the Reformers, even if its contents were to prove impeccably orthodox. By the time Lindsay's play was performed at Cupar, the *Catechism* must have been nearing completion. Its colophon is dated 29 August, and its four hundred pages must have taken the printer, John Scot, much of the summer to set up in type. Although the main point of its careful exposition of the Ten Commandments, the Creed, the Sacraments and the *Pater Noster* is the instruction of the laity, both the statute approving its introduction and, at some points, the text itself assert the need for reform among the clergy:

> The office of a Preist and Byschop is nocht to leive in idilnes, nocht to leive in fornicatioun and huirdome, nocht to be occupeit in halking and hunting, bot to leive ane haly lyfe, chaist in body and saule, to pray to God for the pepil, to offer giftis and sacrifice to God for the pepil, to preche the word of God to the pepil, and lyk lanternis of lycht to gife exempil to haly lyfe to the pepil, quhow thai suld contemne all inordinat lufe of carnal plesour, of warldly geir, and temporal dignitie and to leive a christin lyfe to the plesour of God.[2]

The provincial councils of 1549 and 1552 conceded that these duties were widely neglected, and to that degree there must have been common ground between Hamilton's reform party and more radical critics of the Church. On the other hand, the audience of *The Thrie Estaitis* saw churchmen resisting reform rather than embracing it, and this surely reflects Lindsay's conviction that the time had passed when the Church might succeed in putting its own house in order. Archbishop Hamilton's *Catechism* is a remarkable witness to the desire for a more spiritual Church in Scotland, but it was too orthodox to meet the objections of Lutherans and Calvinists on such matters as indulgences and the doctrine of Purgatory, the privileges of the ecclesiastical courts, and the cults of saints.

A week after the provincial council approved the preparation of the *Catechism*, Parliament convened. Here, too, ecclesiastical matters formed an important element of the business, and if the earlier meeting had implicitly recognised the validity of the Reformers' condemnation of clerical abuses, Parliament now appeared more concerned with reinforcing the laity's obligations to the Church. Stiff fines were imposed for swearing, for the disruption of the Mass and for attending Mass when under pain of excommunication, and acts were passed against bigamy and adultery. None of these problems was, of course, new; but taken together these measures might be seen as complementary to the campaign of better instruction which had been initiated through the *Catechism*. But the overwhelming concern of the 1552 Parliament was with the famine which had been developing over the previous two years. Despite previous acts 'for stanching of beggaris', it was noted that

> the beggaris daylie and continuallie multipleis and resortes in all placis quhair my Lord Governour and uthers Nobillis convenis swa that nane of thame may pas throw the streitis for raming and crying upone thame.[3]

The answer to this unpleasant and unwelcome situation was to reinforce the 1535 Act confining beggars to their parish of origin, a law which means that the Poor Man of *The Thrie Estaitis* is manifestly a criminal.

Other acts attempted to restrict the slaughter of lambs and the hunting of hares and young gamebirds, to insist upon the maintenance of 'ressonabill prices', and to control consumption through new sumptuary laws: archbishops, bishops and earls were to have no more than eight dishes at a meal; abbots, priors and deans no more than six; down to burgesses and other 'substantious' men, who were limited to three. A more practical measure, perhaps, was that imposed by the Privy Council on 9 February, which blamed the spread of famine on the export of food and banned the sale abroad of 'fische, flesche, nolt or scheip, cheise, butter, or ony uther kynd of victuallis or viveris'.[4] But this seems to have little effect, for a similar decision was made on 16 October.[5]

This, then, was the atmosphere in which the Cupar performance of *The Thrie Estaitis* took place. Fife had been spared the worst depredations of the English armies, but the rapid deterioration of the economic situation must still have been apparent. It is clear that economic factors contributed to the crisis in the Church, and there is evidence that Fife was an important centre of lay resistance.[6] The assurances of Diligence that 'we sall speik in generall / For pastyme and for play' may not be mere theatrical convention: in a highly charged political situation, Lindsay deals carefully but forthrightly with a wide range of issues, for even his position as an officer of state would not have saved him had he stepped beyond the limits of toleration. A decade earlier, a friar had been burned for producing heretical plays in Dundee.[7] We should not underestimate the force of *The Thrie Estaitis* in its own time, and I am convinced that its time is very precisely 1552.

## Date and Early Performances

Three possible dates have been suggested for the original composition of *The Thrie Estaitis*. The earliest, proposed by John

MacQueen, falls in the earlier fifteen-thirties.[8] No external evidence exists to support such an early date: it depends entirely upon textual similarities between the play and poems written by Lindsay between 1528 and 1530, and upon the identification of King Humanitie with the young James v. The latter point is more a matter of faith than of evidence, since the covert nature of the supposed allusion makes it essentially unprovable. I suggest below that Humanitie is both a type of the Young King (a familiar figure in advice literature) and a representative of human nature more generally, but I do not find any real basis for the view that he is also a contemporary portrait of the Scottish king. That there are parallels between the protagonist's experience and the politics of James' minority is both undisputed and unsurprising, but it does not follow that they were topical in the sense suggested by Professor MacQueen. The textual evidence is no more compelling. As Anna Jean Mill pointed out,[9] there is no reason why Lindsay should not have gone back to his poems of the early part of James' reign for material exposing the perils of dissolute kingship and corrupt advice; there is, in fact, a good deal of evidence that he did exactly that throughout his literary career. Nor does Professor MacQueen deal with the parallel between ll. 2965–74 of *The Thrie Estaitis* and ll. 414–20 of *The Tragedie of Cardinall Betoun* (1547), which is at least as close as those with the early poems. I believe that it is more likely that the *Thrie Estaitis* version is an expansion of the lines in the *Tragedie* than that the latter is a contracted version of the former; but even if the reverse were true it would involve, if Professor MacQueen's hypothesis were to be accepted, precisely the kind of long-distance retrospective borrowing he discounts in the case of *The Dreme* and *The Complaynt*. And if these lines are a later interpolation, how we can be confident that *any* particular passage survives from a supposed earlier version of the play?

In the case of the second possible date, we do at least have clear evidence of a dramatic performance. Thanks to a Scottish Protestant, who supplied 'Nootes' to the English ambassador, we even know a good deal about the nature of the play performed before James v and Mary of Lorraine at Linlithgow on 6 January 1540, and the affinities between this interlude and *The Thrie Estaitis* are striking enough for the former to be widely accepted as the original version of the latter.[10] It clearly involved a quasi-parliamentary framework, with a Poor Man lamenting his lot and blaming much of his misery upon the depredations of the Church. He was supported by the representatives of the Temporality and the Burgesses, and the need for reform roundly asserted. The parliament was presided over by a king, whose three courtiers were named Placebo, Pikthanke and Flaterye. But the differences prove, on closer inspection, to be as significant as the parallels. The action of the interlude was, obviously, much less complex than that of *The Thrie Estaitis*, and the role of the king, in particular, was almost entirely passive:

> Nexte come in a King / whoe passed to his throne / having noe speche to thende of the playe / and then to ratefie and approve as in playne parliament all thinges doon by the rest of the players.

There is no mention of Sensualitie, or of the Taylour / Sowtar episodes; there is no John the Common-weill; nor is there a hint of Divine Correctioun. There was only one trio of vices, one of whom has no parallel in *The Thrie Estaitis*. Although there was a further character called Solaice, moreover, he played the part of presenter, equivalent to that of Diligence in the later play, rather than acting as another vice. A major role in the interlude was played by Experience, 'clede like a doctour', who may have resembled Gude Counsall in some respects, but who more obviously anticipates the authority-figure of Lindsay's most unequivocally Reforming work, *The Monarche*.

Despite these many differences, Lindsay was most probably responsible for the Linlithgow interlude, especially in view of the substantial payment made to him by the king soon afterwards,[11] and there are some points in the 'Nootes' at which we seem to see the very words of *The Thrie Estaitis* reflected in the abstract. But there are other details which have no parallel at all, most notably in the remarkable play on the King's presence in the audience:

> And whene he [the Poor Man] was showed to the man that was king in the playe / he aunsuered and said he was noe king / ffor ther is but one king / whiche made all and gouernethe / all / whoe is eternall / to whome he and all erthely kinges ar but officers ..... And thene he loked to the king and saide he was not the king of Scotlande for ther was an other king in Scotlande that hanged John Armestrang with his fellowes / And Sym the Larde and many other moe .....

The neatness with which the dramatist manages simultaneously to compliment James upon his attempts to establish order and to remind him of his ultimate responsibility to God for his stewardship of the realm reveals a keen theatrical intelligence. We would not expect the retention of the whole passage in a performance at which there was no king present, but the dependence of temporal rulers upon divine authority remains a relevant commonplace, and it does not occur in the surviving text of *The Thrie Estaitis*. While it may well be that Lindsay wrote the Linlithgow interlude, then, the differences between this lost play and *The Thrie Estaitis* are so great that it would be extremely rash to associate any specific passage of the extant play with this earlier piece.

One further piece of evidence suggests that the version of *The Thrie Estaitis* performed in 1552 might have been a revision of an earlier text. In his *History of the Kirk of Scotland*, written about 1634, John Row refers to a performance of 'Sir David Lindsay his Satyre'

> acted in the Amphitheater of St Johnstoun, before King James the v, and a great part of the nobilitie and gentrie, fra morn to even, whilk made the people sensible of the darknes wherein they lay .....[12]

Since Row's father was Minister of Perth from July 1560 until his death on 16 October 1580 and the historian himself grew up in the town, this statement must be given some weight. On the other hand, the rest of Row's account of the impact of Lindsay's work relates quite clearly to the last years before the Reformation, after the poet's death,[13] and there is no corroboration for his story of a performance of the play in Perth nearly thirty years before his birth. Perhaps, as Laing suggests, Row substituted Perth for Linlithgow; while the reference to the length of the performance may reflect Charteris' description of the 1554 Edinburgh performance (even the reference to 'a great part of the nobilitie' echoes Charteris). At any event, there is nothing in the text of the play as we have it which compellingly substantiates Row's assertion.[14]

The clearest evidence we have is for performances at Cupar on 7 June 1552 and at Edinburgh, probably on 12 August 1554. The first can be established from the 'Proclamatioun made in Cowpar of Fyffe': the exhortation to the people of Cupar

> On Witsonetysday cum see our play, I prey yow;
>
> That samyne day is the sevint day of June,
>
> (271–2)

leaves little doubt about the date, since between 1541 and Lindsay's death in 1555 the only year in which Whit Tuesday fell on 7 June was 1552. But George Bannatyne, who copied the Cupar Proclamation along with substantial extracts from *The Thrie Estaitis*, knew of another performance, 'maid in the Grensyd besyd Edinburcht', at an uncertain date in the 1550s. It was presumably this occasion which was cited by the printer Henry Charteris in the preface to his edition of Lindsay's *Warkis* (1568), where he mentions 'the play, playit besyde Edinburgh, in presence of the Quene Regent and ane greit part of the Nobilitie'.[15] Mary of Guise was Regent between 12 April 1554 and 28 April 1558, but Hamer presents convincing arguments in favour of the identification with *The Thrie Estaitis* of a play performed at the newly-completed Greenside playfield, situated on the northern side of Calton Hill, on the Sunday before 18 August (i.e. 12 August) 1554.[16] Hamer goes further, arguing that the text copied by Bannatyne derived from the 1552 Cupar performance, while that printed by Charteris in 1602 came from the Edinburgh performance of 1554. This last point is much less certain, and it seems likely that the textual differences between the two witnesses are largely due to editing by the printers rather than to revision by Lindsay for a revival of his play.[17]

The natural question, then, is whether the text of the play as we have it shows signs of belonging to 1552. The answer is that in several respects it does: Mill convincingly demonstrates that ll. 4599–602 look back to the Anglo-Scottish war which ended in 1550, while 3593–6 and 4603–16 deal with the so-called Smalkaldic War of 1551–53, involving France, the Empire and the Papacy.[18] In his edition of Lindsay's *Works* (IV, 226–7), Douglas Hamer argued that the latter references were more probably to the conflict between France and Pope Julius II in 1510–11, but the immediacy of the statement that

All the princes of Almanie,
Spainye, Flanders and Italie
*This present yeir* are on ane flocht ...
   (4609–11)

and the occurrence of two further allusions to the war in *The Monarche*, which was unquestionably composed in 1551–52, surely indicate that it was the contemporary political situation to which Lindsay was referring. If this view is correct, then the statement that 'The Paip ... / Hes send his armie to the feild' could scarcely have been made before May 1551, when Julius III committed his forces to a campaign against the French in Parma. The involvement of 'the princes of Almanie [Germany]' began in the following September, and although France and the Papacy made a truce in April 1552, this was probably not known in Scotland by the beginning of June. Furthermore, Joanne S. Kantrowitz has more recently shown that ll. 4638–9 of *The Thrie Estaitis* are an allusion to the dispute in St Andrews over whether the *Pater noster* should be addressed to the saints as well as to God, which originated in a sermon by the English Dominican Richard Marshall. Since this controversy belongs to the latter part of 1551, this passage, too, supports the view that the Charteris text belongs to the period of the Cupar performance.[19]

Most of these topical allusions, it is true, are concentrated in the Foly episode, which might well have been added to the play at a late stage of its compilation. But the first reference to the Smalkaldic War is integrated in the discussion between Diligence and the First Licent which plays an important part in the argument of Part Two, so that the version of this which we actually have must also be attributed to 1551–52. Further corroboration is provided by ll. 2965–74 which, I suggested above, are probably adapted from a similar passage in *The Tragedie of Cardinall Betoun*. All of these passages *might*, of course, have been added at a late stage of revision, while corresponding lines specific to an earlier phase of composition *might* have been excised by Lindsay in the same process. Such conjectures, however, have little value, and it must be said that nothing in the text as it stands can be shown to survive from a date before 1551. And, for what it is worth, the *tone* of the play, and particularly of Part Two, seems to me to belong to the later period, after long years of a destructive war against England and in the atmosphere of growing polarization which followed the death of Beaton and the failure of the 1549 Council. While I do not exclude the possibility that *The Thrie Estaitis* may include passages from earlier plays by Lindsay – as his poems frequently echo one another – it seems safest to regard the text as we have it as very firmly belonging to the early 1550s, contemporary with *The Monarche* and in the final years of the author's distinguished career as a royal servant.

### Sir David Lindsay of the Mount

Although more is known of the life of Sir David Lindsay than is the case with most other sixteenth-century poets, much remains obscure. We know for certain that he was the eldest son of David Lindsay of the Mount, who died in or shortly before 1524; and it seems reasonable to conclude, with Hamer, that since the son received his grandfather's lands of Garmylton, East Lothian on 19 October 1507 he must then have been at least 21 years old.[20] This would mean that he was born, at the latest, in 1486. It is a matter of conjecture whether either the David Lindsay who matriculated at the University of St Andrews in 1508 or the 'one called Lindsay' who occurs as a groom of the stable of the infant son of James IV, also in 1508, was the future poet: what is clear is that these references can scarcely be to the same individual. Whatever the truth of this confusing evidence, a

David Lindsay who was almost certainly the poet was established at court by 1511, and one of the earliest references to him is, significantly enough, a payment for a blue and yellow taffeta playcoat 'for the play playt in the King and Quenis presence in the Abbay [of Holyrood]' in October of that year. That David Lindsay of Garmylton was settling in Edinburgh is confirmed by a notarial document of 22 March 1513, not previously noted, in which a John Wilson acquired the sasine of a tenement on the south side of the High Street 'in the name of David Lindsay of Garmylton'.[21] Shortly afterwards, he was allegedly present at Linlithgow when a mysterious, ghostly figure appeared to the king and warned him of the disastrous consequences of his proposed invasion of England; the story is told by Lindsay's kinsman, the chronicler Robert Lindsay of Pitscottie and (on Sir David's own authority) by George Buchanan, and if it has any substance may reflect some propaganda incident organised by the faction opposed to the impending war.

Within a few months, Lindsay had become a prominent member of a court recovering from the shattering catastrophe of Flodden. He was already usher to the infant prince before his father's death, and he occurs frequently in this role, which combined ceremonial duties with the administration of the household and something like surrogate fatherhood, between 1514 and 1523. The intimacy of his position is clearly conveyed in the poet's *Complaynt*, written in 1529-30, in which Lindsay, now temporarily out of favour, reminds the king of their former relationship:

> Auld Wille Dile, wer he on lyve,
> My lyfe full weill he could discryve:
> Quhow, as ane chapman beris his pak,
> I bure thy Grace upon my bak,
> And sumtyme, strydlingis on my nek,
> Dansand with mony bend and bek.
> The first sillabis that thow did mute
> Was 'pa Da Lyn': upon the lute
> Than playt I twenty spryngis, perqueir,
> Quhilk wes gret piete for to heir.
>      (85-94)

He tells a similar story in *The Dreme* (1528), in which he recalls the stories, songs and clowning with which he entertained his young charge. With the very doubtful exception of 'The Gyre-carling', a poem preserved anonymously in the Bannatyne manuscript which recalls the title of the 'plesand storye' Lindsay claims to have told,[22] nothing of this early period survives, and our knowledge of it is dependent upon terse references in the records and Lindsay's retrospection. What is clear is that the poet's circumstances changed in the later 1520s, perhaps as early as 1525 when he is described in the Exchequer Rolls as 'formerly the king's usher'. Although both Lindsay and his wife, Janet Douglas, remained at court, his displacement as usher may mark a political reversal; and it probably has to do with the seizure of power by the earl of Arran and the Dowager Queen Margaret in the summer of 1524.

In the complex politics of the minority, control of the king's person was an enormous advantage, and the placing of power in the hands of the twelve-year-old James v on 26 July 1524 was no more than a ploy to justify the termination of the governorship of the absent duke of Albany. It was, however, a ploy which backfired on its perpetrators. Within months it was Margaret's estranged husband, the earl of Angus, who controlled both the king's person and the government, and Lindsay was more firmly removed from influence. In the *Complaynt*, which reviews in detail the events of these turbulent years, Lindsay makes it clear that it was through the king's loyalty that he avoided worse suffering, and he continued to receive his pension despite the ascendancy of Angus and his Douglas kin. Janet Douglas, certainly, continued in her office as seamstress to the king, and both she and her husband may in part have been protected by her family connections. But that did not prevent Lindsay from launching a scarifying attack on the Douglas faction after the fall of Angus in July 1528, and from announcing joyfully that

> Now, potent prince, I say to the,
> I thank the Haly Trinitie
> That I have levit to se this daye,
> That all that warld is went awaye,
> And thow to no man art subjectit,
> Nor to sic counsalouris coactit.
>     (Complaynt, 373–8)

In the Exchequer accounts for that year, the poet again appears as a member of the king's household.

It is to this period of restoration that Lindsay's earliest surviving poems belong. Between 1528 and 1530 he produced three long works: *The Dreme*, *The Complaynt*, and *The Testament and Complaynt of Our Soverane Lordis Papyngo*. All three are built around themes which dominate Lindsay's major writings: the injustices of contemporary society, the need for good government, and the misconduct of the clergy. Even in *The Dreme*, Lindsay's portrayal of Hell dwells upon its ecclesiastical occupants, giving eight sharp stanzas to an analysis of their indiscipline and ignorance, their misappropriation of the patrimony of the Church, and their sexual misconduct. *The Complaynt* returns in passing to the same themes in a passage which manifestly anticipates the language of *The Thrie Estaitis*:

> The proudest prelatis of the Kirk
> Was faine to hyde thame in the mirk
> That tyme, so failyeit was thare sicht;
> Sen syne thay may nocht thole the lycht
> Off Christis trew Gospell to be sene,
> So blyndit is thare corporall ene
> With wardly lustis sensuall
> Takyng in realmes the governall,
> Baith gyding court and Cessioun,
> Contrar to thare professioun,
> Quhareof I thynk thay sulde have schame
> Off spirituall preistis to tak the name.
>                                        (309–20)

But it is in the *Papyngo*, first printed in December 1530, that the attack on the Church becomes most explicit, and begins to prevail over the other aspects of Lindsay's political analysis. Whereas the first part of the poem is a fairly conventional exposition of the perils of the court, offering James traditional advice on the principles of good government backed up by the disastrous examples of his predecessors, the final section shows its parrot protagonist beset by the magpie, raven and kite, who represent the Augustinian canons, the Benedictines and the friars respectively and who become the objects of the Papyngo's scathing criticism. They have few real arguments with which to meet the attack, and the greedy rapacity with which they tear the Papyngo's body to pieces after her death provides a grim image of the attitudes of the contemporary clergy.

Such scenes inevitably raise the question of Lindsay's doctrinal position at this period. On the Continent, the Lutheran Reformation was now well advanced. Luther's attack on indulgences and on other aspects of traditional theology had burst out of Wittenberg in the summer of 1517, and was followed by his banning by both Church and Empire in 1520–21. In 1523 Zurich adopted Protestantism under the leadership of Ulrich Zwingli, to be followed by Basel, Strasbourg and Nürnberg, and by 1530 several German states, including Saxony, Hesse and Braunschweig-Lüneberg, as well as the kingdom of Denmark, had officially become Protestant. The writings of Luther,

Melanchthon, Zwingli and other Protestant theologians were now widely circulated, and in July 1530 Melanchthon produced, in response to Catholic condemnations, the 'Augsburg Confession', a list of 21 articles of faith and 7 on rites, the core theological position of the Lutheran Reformers. It is clear that this upheaval did not take long to affect Scotland. By 1525 Parliament was prohibiting the importation of heretical works, but the close trading links between Scotland and the Continent made it inevitable that the infiltration of Scottish thought by radical criticism of the Church should continue. Patrick Hamilton, a graduate of the (in general) impeccably orthodox universities of Paris and Louvain, may have been influenced by the new ideas in St Leonard's College at St Andrews, where Gavin Logie was acting Principal Regent, between 1523 and 1527, for after only a few months of the latter year in the Protestant universities at Wittenberg and Marburg he returned to Scotland to launch a violent attack on the Church and to become the first Scottish Lutheran martyr when he was burned in St Andrews on 29 February 1528.

It is difficult to believe that the tone of Lindsay's early poems was unaffected by these recent events, although he never refers to them directly. He even includes a visit to Purgatory in the spiritual itinerary of *The Dreme*, though with a hint of scepticism which suggests that in the year of Hamilton's death he had already begun to respond to the Reformers' arguments:

> I se no plesour heir bot mekle paine,
> Quhairfor (said I) leif we this sort in thrall:
> I purpose never to cum heir agane;
> Bot yit I do beleve, and ever sall,
> That the trew Kirk can no waye erre at all.
> Sic thyng to be gret clerkis dois conclude,
> Quhowbeit my hope standis most in Cristis blude.
>     (344–50)

The apparent acceptance of the authority of the 'trew Kirk' is hedged about with qualifications, as Lindsay sets his faith in the power of the Atonement against the theologians' affirmation of the doctrine of Purgatory. Such equivocation was no more than prudent at that political moment, but even such theological discourse as this is unusual in Lindsay's poetry. In these early poems generally, as in *The Thrie Estaitis* more than twenty years later, the emphasis falls upon clerical misconduct rather than upon questions of doctrine.

By the beginning of 1529, Lindsay had acquired a new function, as one of the king's heralds. He may already have been appointed

Snowdon Herald at this time, although he is not given that precise title until 25 May 1531, when he was sent by James V on a diplomatic mission to the Emperor Charles V. This was, so far as we know, the first of a series of journeys abroad as an ambassador, for after this four-month visit to Brussels, Lindsay travelled on missions to Paris four times in five years, apparently spending fairly long periods at these foreign courts. In 1531, for example, he reported to the Secretary, Thomas Erskine, that he had 'ramanit in the court vij. owikis [weeks] and od dayis', and his first visit to France appears to have extended from February until November 1532. The cultural consequences of such prolonged stays abroad were, of course, potentially considerable, and it is not surprising to find that Lindsay's subsequent writings, including *The Thrie Estaitis*, contain clear evidence of the influence of contemporary Continental publications. We can only guess at the acquaintanceships he must have developed on these occasions, and on his visit to the English court in August 1535, when he stayed briefly in a society in the throes of Reformation. In many ways, Lindsay's position on religious matters can be seen as comparable with that of the Henrician reformers in England: he does not challenge the strictly theological doctrines attacked by Luther, Melanchthon and others on the Continent, but he is scathing in his criticism of the indiscipline and abuse of temporal power of the Church.

The evidence of Lindsay's literary activity during this period is understandably thin, and consists almost entirely of pieces of occasional verse: *The Complaint of Bagsche*, *The Answer to the Kingis Flyting*, neither of which can be dated with any accuracy, and the formal *Deploratioun of the Deith of the Quene Magdalene* (1537). The early death of James' first wife was quickly followed by his remarriage, to the daughter of the duke of Guise. Her arrival at St Andrews on 10 June 1538 was greeted with a 'trieumphant frais [farce]' devised by Lindsay, combining spectacular dumb-show with 'certane wriesouns [prayers] and exortatiouns ... quhilk teichit hir to serve hir God, obey hir husband, and keep hir body clene according to Godis will and commandement'.[23] Such presentations were a regular feature of state occasions, and Lindsay's role neatly blends his theatrical interests with his formal responsibilities as Snowdon Herald. The St Andrews pageant is known only from a description by the historian Robert Lindsay of Pitscottie, but two other short works by Lindsay survive from the latter part of the reign of James V, the burlesque *Justing betuix James Watsoun and Jhone*

*Barbour* (1538), and an attack on the extremes of contemporary fashion, *Ane Supplicatioun in Contemptioun of Syde Taillis*. Other poems may, of course, have been lost, and we have already noted that the interlude performed at Linlithgow in January 1540 may have been Lindsay's; but in general it is probable that his official duties denied him much time for literary activities.

Scottish politics were again thrown into confusion by the king's death at the end of 1542. His daughter was only six days old, and it was inevitable that there would be another long minority. Power quickly fell into the hands of James Hamilton, earl of Arran, who was appointed Governor on 3 January 1543 and who was sympathetic to the Protestant cause. Before the end of January, indeed, Arran had arrested the Chancellor, Cardinal Beaton, declared the Pope 'a very evil bishop', and commissioned a friar to preach in favour of the vernacular Bible.[24] But this shift towards a pro-English, Reforming policy was to be short-lived: the return from France of the Governor's half-brother John, the abbot of Paisley, in the first half of April brought a powerful new influence to bear, and the Reformers around Arran were edged out. Lindsay himself was out of the country when John Hamilton arrived, having been sent to England with the late king's insignia of the Garter, not returning until the end of May. The following spring, he was sent to the Emperor Charles v with the Order of the Golden Fleece: he thus remained in office and was entrusted with diplomatic duties, but his absences from Scotland would inevitably have restricted any influence he might have had on the policies of the Governor.[25]

Nothing better illustrates the complexity of Lindsay's position than his role in the events of 1546–47. Several of his friends were involved in the assassination of Beaton on 29 May 1546, and yet the Lord Lyon (as Lindsay had become towards the end of 1542) was certainly acting for the Governor in the temporarily successful negotiations with the rebel Reformers in December. Arran himself, of course, was in a difficult situation: Beaton had long been his enemy, but his half-brother, who would soon succeed the murdered Cardinal as Archbishop of St Andrews, was firmly identified with the clerical party. Lindsay was therefore a natural spokesman in some respects, although it could have been no part of his brief to call upon John Knox to take up the Protestant ministry, as Knox himself tells us he did when again in St Andrews on government business in July 1547.[26] By this time, moreover, Lindsay had written the *Tragedie of Cardinall Betoun*, a dream vision in which the 'cairfull Cardinall' is made to confess the whole range of crimes of which he was accused by the Reformers. The affinities between this savage attack and the charges made against Spiritualitie in *The Thrie Estaitis* are numerous, and clearly indicate the extent to which the political climate had hardened over the past few years. The date of the lost first edition of this work of controversy, probably printed in St Andrews itself by John Scot, is conjectural, but it is difficult to believe that it was as early as March 1547, as Hamer suggests: even in the confused atmosphere of those months, Lindsay could scarcely have been employed by the Governor to negotiate with the rebels if he had publicly associated himself so incontrovertibly with their position. References to Lindsay in the official records are thereafter fairly intermittent, and it may be that after the appearance of the *Tragedie* he was regarded as less reliable than before. Pitscottie notes that 'Schir Dawid Lyndsayis buike' was condemned and burned by a Provincial Council of the Scottish Dominicans, and there is merit in Hamer's suggestion that this may have happened in 1549 rather than in 1559 (the date given by the chronicler).[27] But, whatever the truth of this, Lindsay was still entrusted with an embassy to the Protestant king Christian III of Denmark in 1548–49, and he continued to exercise the powers of the Lyon Herald until shortly before his death early in 1555. During the last half-dozen years of his life, however, he produced three substantial works, *The Historie of Squyer Meldrum* (c. 1550–53), *The Monarche* (1553), and *Ane Satyre of the Thrie Estatitis*. Of these, the latter two are in some respects closely related, since both deal in detail with the misconduct of the clergy and the need for reform. But while *The Thrie Estaitis* is a lively and entertaining play, *The Monarche*, the full title of which is *Ane Dialog betuix Experience and Ane Courteour, of the Miserabyll Estait of the Warld*, is a long and scholarly account of world history, drawn from a variety of sources and developing over 6300 lines Lindsay's view of the perversion of the Christian tradition by the Catholic Church. The dialogue structure is a thinly-maintained fiction, and the poem belongs in the medieval tradition of world histories like *Cursor Mundi* despite its partial reliance on Melanchthon's edition of Johannes Carion's chronicles and its often controversial tone. *Squyer Meldrum*, on the other hand, is a remarkable and generally attractive work, an application of the romance tradition to the life-story of one of Lindsay's personal friends, the Fife laird William Meldrum. It plays delicately with the conventions of medieval romance, but it never quite abandons the real world, and the sense of tranquil acceptance of the pains of human existence with which the poem ends makes a fitting epitaph not only for Meldrum but for the poet himself.[28]

## Sources and Analogues of The Thrie Estaitis

The most obvious range of influences upon Lindsay's drama is unfortunately the least visible. There is ample evidence of a flourishing theatrical tradition in Scotland before 1550, but it is a tradition virtually unsupported by surviving texts. Of the Candlemas and Corpus Christi plays in Aberdeen, not to mention the mysterious 'ludus de Belyale' mentioned in 1471, the only trace is in the various burgh records which refer to plays from 1440 on; and the same is true of the religious drama which evidently existed through the later fifteenth and early sixteenth centuries in Perth, Edinburgh, Dundee, Lanark and elsewhere.[29] How far these performances, which generally seem to have followed European tradition in taking place at the feast of Corpus Christi, developed away from procession and mime into full-scale plays is uncertain, but it seems that in Aberdeen at least, and probably in other burghs, there *were* genuine religious plays on Biblical themes and on the lives of saints. Officially designated 'playfields', certainly, occur in Edinburgh in 1456, Dundee in 1553 and in Glasgow in 1558, while a similar function was presumably fulfilled by the site at Wyndmilhill in Aberdeen, mentioned as early as 1440. But these burgh plays were only one element in a rich dramatic tradition which also included plays of Robin Hood (a kind of May game celebrating the arrival of summer), interludes and other performances at the royal court, and clerks' plays at the universities of St Andrews, Glasgow and, no doubt, Aberdeen.

There are some indications, moreover, that Lindsay was not the only Scot with Reforming opinions who turned to the drama as a vehicle for political or doctrinal debate. According to Knox, a dissenting Dominican named Keiller was responsible around 1535 for the performance at Stirling of a *Historye of Christis Passioun*, a work of heresy which eventually led to his execution in 1539. A little later, James Wedderburn, brother of the principal author of the *Gude and Godlie Ballatis*, itself a important avenue for the arrival of Lutheran ideas in Scotland, is said to have presented a tragedy of *Johne the Baptist* and – somewhat improbably, perhaps – a comedy of *Dyonisius the Tyrane*, both of which were Protestant in tone.[30] It is one of the great ironies of Scottish literature that, despite this early application of the stage to religious controversy, the Reformers were resolute, and ultimately successful, in eliminating Scotland's lively traditions of medieval drama, leaving a lacuna which remains only partially filled even today.

Since we have no texts of any of these plays, we have no way of knowing how far Scottish theatrical tradition had evolved away from, or been influenced by, foreign models. We do, however, know that Lindsay himself had ample opportunity to witness, and to read, plays in France, the Netherlands and England, and it is likely enough that he borrowed from these sources in writing *The Thrie Estaitis*. Given his position at court and his evident interest in theatre, he must, for example, have witnessed some dramatic performances during his stay in France in 1532, and there is little reason to quarrel with A.J. Mill's contention that he was 'steeped in the conventions of the contemporary French stage'.[31] Mill is, on the other hand, rightly sceptical about the evidence of influence of any *particular* French text on *The Thrie Estaitis*, and it is much easier to demonstrate the general affinities between French theatrical traditions and the Scots play than to show Lindsay using specific sources.

There are in essence three distinct but interwoven French theatrical genres which are reflected in *The Thrie Estaitis*: morality play, farce and *sottie*. The most distinctive of these are the *sotties*, the fools' plays which employed characters dressed in the costume of the fool and which were based upon the assumption that 'folly, not reason, is the governing principle of [the author's] world'.[32] This widespread French tradition is most obviously echoed in the Foly episode with which Lindsay ends his play; Foly's sermon is very firmly a *sermon joyeux* of the kind widely used in the *sotties*, and it is probably his awareness of this lively, anarchic but ultimately corrective genre that we owe his superficially somewhat bizarre decision to subvert the positive tone of the reforming Parliament with a reassertion of the power of vice.[33] The extent to which the rest of the play is influenced by the *sotties* is a more difficult issue, and is rendered more difficult still by the reinterpretation of the *sotties* themselves which has recently taken place. Some *sotties*, certainly, included criticism of contemporary political abuses, although the reign of Folly is generally seen in broader social and moral terms. It is true that Flatterie identifies himself as 'your awin fuill', and that he invokes the Christian festivities which were the traditional occasion, in France particularly, for the Feast of Fools. And the theme returns forcefully towards the end of Lindsay's play, when the lords of Spiritualitie are shown to be 'bot verie fuillis' when they are stripped of their ecclesiastical garments. Much of the same spirit of folly runs through another French tradition, that of the farce.[34] There are, however, significant differences: whereas the *sotties* portray fools who often perform the roles of ordinary people, the farces characteristically show ordinary people behaving like fools. The characters of farce, while they fall into a number of stock categories, are usually individualized by their names, and there is little attempt to generalize – or to moralize – from their misadventures. In this respect, the farce proper, as represented by pieces like *Les Femmes qui font refondre leurs maris*, is a dramatic relative of the *fabliaux*, poems which employ stock figures like the lecherous priest or friar, the young wife married to an old man, the deceitful craftsman, and so on. Unlike the *sottie*, the farce was well established in England by the sixteenth century, and there are definite French analogues for such manifestations of the English farce tradition as the plays of Heywood. The clearest instance of the influence of the tradition of farce upon Lindsay is the so-called Cupar Proclamation, the short play used to advertise the 1552 performance [see Appendix]. But there are traces of the world of farce in *The Thrie Estaitis* itself, in the episodes with the Taylour and the Sowtar and their wives and, very probably, in the role of the Pardoner. In this latter case, indeed, it seems likely that we can trace the influence of a particular farce.[35]

Some farces combine the traditional plot elements of deceit, trickery and low-level violence with characters who represent abstract ideas, institutions or social types. These '*farces moralisées*' therefore stand midway between the farce proper and the morality play, in which such characters are, of course, universal. While the moral world of the *farce moralisée* is marked by the cynicism of all farce, the morality play sets folly and sin within the larger context of a Providential order: the protagonist is seen suffering the consequences of his sin and making a spiritual recovery through the exercise of reason or the operation of Grace. This is a characteristic shared by the morality traditions in France and England, though in other respects there are distinct national developments, particularly in the relative length of the English moralities. Even in the sixteenth century, most French moralities are very short and dramatically undeveloped, and again it would be difficult to demonstrate that any individual play had a marked effect on Lindsay. Even a piece like *Les trois estatz reformez par rayson*, which deals with similar themes to those of the Scots play, bears little resemblance in detail; and several other French plays use the morality form to attack abuses among the Estates, plays like *L'Eglise, Noblesse et Povrete qui font la Lessive* (written by

1541) offering criticism of the Church as scathing as Lindsay's without containing any remarkable parallels.[36]

In addition to the possible influence, however general, of these interwoven French traditions upon Lindsay's dramatic methods, we must consider the English morality tradition, which was equally strong in the fifteenth and sixteenth centuries. Although *The Thrie Estaitis* is unusually long and elaborate even by English standards, there are greater structural similarities between Part One of Lindsay's play and such well-known English moralities as *The Castle of Perseverance*, *Mankind*, *Mundus et Infans* and *Youth* than can be demonstrated in the case of the French plays. Part One, indeed, follows the characteristic pattern of the English morality, with a young, inexperienced protagonist falling prey to the blandishments of the vices and only recovering through Divine intervention. Some elements of Lindsay's action, moreover – the disguising of the vices, the incarceration of the virtues – are stock devices of the English morality tradition.[37] Furthermore, we see the development in England, fairly early in the sixteenth century, of moralities with a political dimension: Skelton's *Magnyfycence*, for example, is probably not as topical as was once believed,[38] but its protagonist is, like Lindsay's Humanitie, a young prince who combines the specific weaknesses of undisciplined kingship with sins which have a more general application, and the vices are, like Flatterie and his 'brether', courtiers who represent in particular the duplicity of their kind.

*Magnyfycence* is sometimes seen as an analogue to *The Thrie Estaitis*, but the personal themes of Part I are parallelled more closely by R[ichard?] Wever's *Lusty Juventus*, a Protestant morality in which the protagonist is advised by Good Councell and Knowledge (of Gods Veritie), seduced by Hypocrisie (who adopts the disguise of Frendshyp), Felowshyp and a wanton called Abhominable Living, and ultimately brought back to his Christian duty and rewarded by Gods Mercyfull Promyses. Although it is relatively crude in both dramatic structure and doctrinal argument, *Lusty Juventus* anticipates Lindsay's play in its adaptation of the morality structure to the Protestant interest. Hypocrisie, for example, is given a long elegy for the passing of Papist 'vaine zeales and blynd intentes' (390–443), and there are frequent references to the reform of former ecclesiastical abuses. The date of Wever's play is uncertain: that usually accepted is around 1550, but its most recent editor has persuasively associated its doctrines with the 'Royal Catholicism' of the last years of Henry VIII rather than with the more evangelical Protestantism of Edward VI's reign.[39] This, too, is suggestive in the content of *The Thrie Estaitis*, for we have already seen that the theological ambiguities of Lindsay's position have something in common with the eclecticism of Henrician reform. If *Lusty Juventus* was indeed written in the mid-1540s and printed in the earlier part of the reign of Edward VI, Lindsay might well have been aware of it, either in performance or through a printed text. It is, then, possible to find parallels for many of the elements of *The Thrie Estaitis*, although there is little evidence for the influence of any particular source. And the *combination* of those elements to produce a single, complex whole, now morality, now farce, now *sottie*, appears to be Lindsay's distinctive achievement, one of the high points of late medieval theatre.

## Structure and Allegory

As previous critics have pointed out, there are significant differences between the two Parts of *The Thrie Estaitis*. It is in Part Two that the motif of the Estates becomes central, and Lindsay now adopts the model of parliamentary procedure as the controlling element in the action. As an obvious link between the two halves of the play, the Parliament which will dominate Part Two is called at the end of Part One. But this is more than merely a structural device: the purpose of the new Parliament is reform, and it is clear that this political change can only be undertaken when the underlying moral conditions are appropriate. The cleaning-up of the Court which is achieved by Divine Correctioun in the closing scenes of Part One is, therefore, a necessary precondition for the wider political action of Part Two; ideologically, the shift in focus which Lindsay makes is consistent and carefully thought out. An inevitable consequence is that Part Two is more discursive than Part One, where the scheming of the vices and the incarceration of Veritie and Chastitie produce some elements of theatrical action. But a more important difference lies in the nature of the characters who play the central roles: whereas the dominant figures in Part One are truly allegorical, representing moral forces such as Wantonnes, Sensualitie, Gude Counsel and Chastitie, those who dominate Part Two are essentially social types, such as the representatives of the Estates and their supporters, and John the Common-weill and the Poor Man. To understand this difference is vital to an appreciation of the relationship between the two stages of Lindsay's argument.

His concern in Part One centres on the court of King Humanitie, which is, although it represents the locus of kingship in general and draws upon medieval traditions of satire against courtiers, specifically a *Scottish* court. But Humanitie occupies a strikingly double role: he is both a Young King, illustrating through his seduction, fall and subsequent recovery the intimate connection between private virtue and public prosperity, and a representative of humanity itself, the lineal descendant, as we have seen, of Mankind, Everyman and other protagonists of the morality tradition. It is, perhaps, a Protestant touch that the agent of his reform is not Grace but Correctioun, introducing the reformation which we are promised in Diligence's opening speech. But Lindsay's development of the morality genre is more radical than in such shifts of emphasis, for the regeneration of the young king is simply a prelude to the play's real subject, the political revolution which is set in train once the king's moral revolution has been completed.

The allegorical significance of Part One at the socio-political level is fairly easy to grasp. Humanitie demonstrates through his opening prayer that he is well-intentioned, but he is fatally dependent upon his pleasure-seeking courtiers, Wantonnes, Placebo and Solace. He offers no resistance to their proposal that Sensualitie should be introduced into the court, and he quickly succumbs to her advances. Gude Counsall scarcely has time to lament his exclusion from the political process before the second group of vices appear, sharply changing the tone of the action and introducing a decisive new threat, duplicity. While the courtiers are devoted to the life of the senses, they are almost pathetically honest; as their names emphasize, Flatterie, Falset and Dissait are united by their mendacity. Besotted as he is by sexual pleasure, the king is unable to perceive their disguises, and he promptly elevates them into positions of responsibility within his household. The inevitable consequence is that Gude Counsall is forced into retreat and Veritie and Chastitie are attacked and placed in the stocks: in anticipation of the predominant themes of Part Two, Spiritualitie and his supporters play a leading part in their persecution, illustrating the alliance between the vices, who are after all disguised as clerics, and the Church. But the consequences of the moral collapse initiated by the arrival of Sensualitie extend throughout society, a fact which is emphasized by the scene in which the Taylour and the Sowtar entertain Chastitie until she is driven away by their wives; Lindsay skillfully manages to have things both ways in this riotous but entirely relevant exchange, ridiculing the craftsmen for their impotence but equally attacking the wives, whose own bawdiness is underlined by the way in which they set upon Chastitie under the impression that she is a whore.

The placing of Chastitie in the stocks alongside Veritie marks the lowest point in the fortunes of virtue and of the king, and is immediately followed by the arrival of the varlet announcing the impending entrance of Correctioun. The reform which God's agent will undertake is explicitly political, and the Varlet warns us that

> He sall reforme into this land
> Evin all the Thrie Estaits.
> (1492–3)

The immediate consequences of his arrival are the flight of the vices, taking with them the king's money-box, the restoration of Gude Counsall and release of Chastitie and Veritie, and the expulsion of Sensualitie, although she only departs as far as the benches of the Spiritualitie. This cleansing of the court is, as we have already seen, a necessary preliminary step, making possible the much more complex task of eliminating political abuse from the country at large. The courtiers who initiated the king's downfall, it is interesting to observe, are treated with some leniency, forgiven by Correctioun and permitted to engage in harmless entertainments provided that they do not again lead Humanitie from the path of kingly virtue.

But this political sense of Part One is intermingled with another level of meaning, springing from the other dimension of King Humanitie. His fall as a king illustrates the dependence of the state upon the probity of its rulers, but as Humanitie his susceptibility to sin is a mirror for every member of the audience. At this level, the initial blandishments of Wantonnes and his companions signify the mortal danger that the soul is put into by the invitation of the senses, while the introduction of Sensualitie leads naturally and inevitably to the overthrow of reason, represented here by the more obviously political Gude Counsall. This action, however, is familiar from many late medieval works, among them Dunbar's *Goldyn Targe*. The battle is for control of the human soul, and the victory of Sensualitie paves the way for the intrusion of the vices of duplicity. Only with the direct intervention of God through Correctioun can this reversal of the natural order of things, with its attendant persecution of the virtues of Veritie and Chastitie, be overcome; as the orthodox Henryson understood very well, the slave of *temporalia* needs an external source of spiritual change:

> With proud plesour quha settis his traist thairin,
> But speciall grace lychtlie can not outwin.
> (*Morall Fabillis*, 2446–7)[40]

Lindsay's emphasis, as we have already noticed, is less upon grace than upon the corrective force which precedes it. Correctioun, as is clear from the later allusion to him as 'yon with the wingis' (4361), is God's avenging angel, sent to instigate reform at every level from the personal to the political and the ecclesiastical. Ultimately, of course, the two allegorical levels come together: as the reform of the court and the king's moral life are essential for the successful reform of the wider society, so too is moral change in each member of the audience. Lindsay's targets include every social group likely to be represented among the observers: grasping lairds; drunken, dishonest craftsmen; deficient clerics; and lascivious women. The coming of Correctioun, the play suggests, has implications for us all.

It is with the Interlude, ambiguously positioned between the two parts of the play proper, that the allegorical basis of the satire changes. The apparent placing of the Poor Man outside the dramatic action, calling forth from Diligence a threat to call off the performance, is a well-established theatrical device; but its purpose here is not diversion in any sense of the word. For the Poor Man is an inhabitant of the real world: he lives in the real Scotland, and his history of oppression and privation is quite different from the abstract abuses of Part One. The 'confusion' about his relation to the rest of the play reinforces the point, since he brings the actuality of the sufferings of ordinary people into the allegorical space of the play, and when his cause is taken up by John the Common-weill there can be no doubt that it is in the real world that reform must ultimately take place. It is hard to see how a modern production could recreate the frisson of alarm that the intervention of the Poor Man ought to generate, yet it is vital to the experience of the anger which fuels the debate and feeds its dramatic effectiveness. That the exchanges of charge and defence should be wordy is perhaps inevitable; what keeps them from becoming tedious is the sense of urgency, and sometimes of danger, which underlies the political rhetoric. Nor does the Interlude prepare us for the debate to follow solely by providing a sympathetic protagonist: in the huckstering of the Pardoner we see the Church at its least defensible, and the selling of the pardon for the Poor Man's last groat both implicitly exposes the theological weakness of the system of indulgences and enacts the rapacity of the clergy.

In many ways, the structure of Part Two is more straightforwad than that of Part One. It is built around several effective dramatic devices: the entrance of the Estates 'gangand bakwart'; the sudden appearance of John the Common-weill; the accusation of heresy against John and his recitation of the Creed; the despoiling of Flatterie, the Priores and the prelates, and the robing of the clerks and John the Common-weill; the hanging of Thift, Dissait and Falset; and the balanced sermons of the Doctour and Foly. Between these iconographic landmarks there is a steadily developing debate in which the misdeeds of the spiritual estate are documented, analysed and corrected. This narrowing of focus from the offences of all three Estates to those of the Spiritualitie is both a necessary tactic given Lindsay's priorities and a propaganda stroke in its own right, for the ready acceptance by lords and merchants of the criticisms of Gude Counsell and John the Common-weill (2521–2721) leaves the way clear for over a thousand lines in which the recalcitrance of the clergy is repeatedly underlined. The need for sweeping reform is thus 'justified' by the conduct of the clergy themselves, and the result is a powerful indictment of a Church which is seen to be willing to deny its spiritual duty in pursuit of its own secular power.

It is, then, not suprising that the decisions of the Parliament, gathered together in ll. 3823–3973, concentrate overwhelmingly on reform of the Church. We may well ask how radical a programme this would have appeared to Lindsay's original audience. In many respects, certainly, the proposals do not go far beyond the terms of the statutes of the 1549 Provincial Council: both the argument of the play and the acts of the Parliament lay great stress upon the need for preaching and for well-qualified clergy, and upon the undesirability of pluralism, and these points were common ground with reformers inside the Church.[41] But other parts of Lindsay's programme were much more controversial. He proposes the virtual abolition of death duties ('sa that our haly vickars be nocht wraith', which seems a ludicrous proviso!), and would repatriate to Scotland the provision of benefices. This last measure, together with the abolition of clerical celibacy, represents a direct attack upon the structure of the Catholic Church, and cannot leave any doubt about the extent of Lindsay's radicalism. With the skill of the consummate politician, Lindsay introduces another of his more controversial proposals incidentally: the dissolution of nunneries is not argued for as an end in itself, but merely as a way of funding improvements in the judicial system which would by common consent be regarded as desirable. With its emphasis on the reconstruction of the national Church and its relative lack of interest in theological questions, Lindsay's programme, like the preceding exposure of clerical abuse, is more reminiscent of the Henrician Reformation in England than it is of any Continental version of Reformed religion. But all in all, there can be no doubt: had such a programme actually been implemented, the Scottish Reformation, though different in form from that which actually took place under Knox's leadership in 1560, would unquestionably have arrived.

By l. 4301, the dramatic process of reformation is effectively complete. The Parliament has enacted its legislation, the Commonweill has been given a new, established place and the vices have been executed, only Flatterie escaping to impart his skills to 'the Hermeit of Lareit'. A precarious equilibrium has been achieved. And into this newly-ordered realm bursts Foly, echoing Falset's 'I wait not how to call my sell' and filling the stage with his nonsense. This final episode is puzzling, and it is perhaps not surprising that most modern productions have omitted it. Why did Lindsay apparently undermine the effectiveness of his reforms by allowing this reassertion of the forces of chaos? Is the Foly episode merely compensation for an audience which has put up with long debate, or does it fit in some serious way into the structure of Part Two? Foly's sermon is, as I suggested above, a counterbalance to that given by the Doctour: for all its absurdity, it observes the formal principles of medieval homily, its origins are, as we have already noted, in the *sermon joyeux* of the French *sotties*, and its text, *Stultorum numerus infinitus*, has a central place in the folly literature of the later Middle Ages. To appreciate the force of this, we must understand the medieval view of folly, which takes in both idiocy and *moral* blindness. Foly's distribution of 'folie hattis' asserts the power of sin rather than stupidity, and he covers many of the targets of the rest of the play: old men who marry young wives; ignorant and negligent prelates, and war-mongering princes. Does it follow from this, as Sandra Billington has recently suggested, that 'any claim to have set up a Reformation at all rebounds back on itself'?[42] There is no hint in Foly's comments that it is a Reformed society he is dealing with: the Pope, Emperor and King of France are all Catholic princes, it is the hierarchy of the Catholic Church that he attacks, and it is the friars who are singled out for a final, cutting crack. I would therefore see this subversive final episode more as a reminder of the pervasiveness of disorder than as a denial of what has gone before; it is, after all, only with God's direct help that change has been achieved in Humanitie or in his kingdom, and the capacity for sin always threatens whatever improvements may be achieved in human society. Foly's incursion perhaps serves to remind us that the outcome remains in doubt, and that in the real world beyond the play a start has yet to be made.

## Versification

One striking feature of the play is the way in which Lindsay varies the metrical structure according to the nature of the scene. This is a familiar pattern in Tudor moralities and interludes, but Lindsay develops the tradition so far that *The Thrie Estaitis* has been described as 'in many ways its apogee'.[43] Couplets, tail-rhyme stanzas and the eight-line 'Monk's Tale' stanza are the dominant forms, making up between them over 85% of the total, but within each Lindsay shifts from three-stress to four- and five-stress lines in order to modulate the pace of his dialogue. Compare, for example, the shift of tempo when the vices move from their conversation with one another to an approach to Spiritualitie:

> FALSET
>
> Bot wee sall ather gang or ryde
> To Lords of Spritualitie
> And gar them trow yon bag of pryde
> Hes spokin manifest heresie.
>
> FLATTERIE
>
> O reverent fatheris of the Sprituall stait,
> Wee counsall yow be wyse and vigilant:
> Dame Veritie hes lychtit now of lait,
> And in hir hand beirand the New Testament .....
>   (1093–1100)

The vices generally use tail-rhyme stanzas (rime couée), principally of eight four-stress lines rhyming *aaabcccb* but with a fairly frequent variant, six three-stress lines rhyming *aabccb*. These rather intricate forms are in turn mixed with couplets, often shared between two characters to give a sense of witty interplay, as in the opening exchange between Flatterie and Falset:

> FLATTERIE
>
> Quhy, Falset, brother, knawis thou not me?
> Am I nocht thy brother, Flattrie?
>
> FALSET
>
> Now welcome, be the Trinitie!
>   This meitting cums for gude.
> Now let me bresse the in my armis:
> Quhen freinds meits, harts warmis,
>   Quod Jok, that frely fud.
> How happinit yow into this place?

**FLATTERIE**

Now, be my saul, evin on a cace.
I come in sleipand at the port,
Or evir I wist, amang this sort.
Quhair is Dissait, that limmer loun?

**FALSET**

I left him drinkand in the toun;
He will be heir incontinent.

**FLATTERIE**

Now, by the haly Sacrament,
Thay tydingis comforts all my hart ..... (637–52)

This scene is an excellent example of Lindsay's skill in the manipulation of prosodic registers: Flatterie begins in his own distinctive variety of tail-rhyme stanza, rhyming *aabab*, but the bulk of the dialogue with Falset and Dissait is in rapid-fire four-stress couplets, often with two characters sharing them.

This form is retained when the King re-enters with his courtiers and the ladies (at l. 808), but the passage concludes with a more formal stanza of alternating rhyme, marking the transition back to the vices through its relative intricacy, but maintaining the pace in its use of four-stress lines:

**SOLACE**

Now schaw me, sir, I yow exhort,
How ar ye of your luif content?
Think ye not this ane mirrie sport?

**REX**

Yea, that I do in verament.
Quhat bairnis ar yon upon the bent?
I did nocht se them all this day.

**WANTONNES**

Thay will be heir incontinent:
Stand still and heir quhat thay will say.
(840–7)

The difference between such an exchange and the more elevated forms of ballad stanza is fairly obvious:

**CORRECTIOUN**

*Magister noster*, I ken how ye can teiche
Into the scuillis, and that richt ornatlie:
I pray yow now that ye wald please to preiche
In Inglis toung, land folk to edifie.

**DOCTOUR**

Soverane, I sall obey yow humbillie,
With ane schort sermon presentlie in this place,

xxxiii

And schaw the word of God unfeinyeitlie,
And sinceirlie, as God will give me grace.
    (3465–72)

This latter stanza is commonly used by Correctioun, Gude Counsall
and the other virtues, and sometimes by Humanitie as well; in
general, however, it is used as relief from the five-stress couplets
which predominate in the serious passages and which are therefore
typical of the parliamentary debates of Part Two. More formal
still is the alliterative stanza with which Diligence opens the
play; interestingly, Lindsay uses this again (ll. 214–26)
when Humanitie, who has previously spoken in three stanzas
in the 'Monk's Tale' form, first responds to the tail-rhymed
blandishments of his courtiers. These elevated beginnings are,
of course, not to be sustained: when the King next speaks, after
Wantonnes has sighted Sensualitie, he exchanges a couplet with
his minion (335–6) before falling into a four-stress octave
followed by the tail-rhyme appropriate to his about-to-be-fallen
condition. While Lindsay's verse is scarcely elegant and his poetic
range does not seem to have included any great lyrical heights, he is
able in *The Thrie Estaitis* to maintain dramatic momentum through
the deft manipulation of a variety of forms. There is little subtlety
in most of forms he employs, but the constant interplay between
them modulates the pace and tone more effectively than is perhaps
apparent in a casual reading of the text. It is, above all, verse to be
*performed*, and it is in performance that the full skill of Lindsay's
work as a dramatic poet manifests itself.

### The Cupar Proclamation

The short play which was used as a trailer for the 1552 performance
of *The Thrie Estaitis* has something in common with the burlesque
scenes of the longer play. As we noted above, both in its action and
its characters, it appears to owe much to the Continental tradition
of farce: its central motif, the duping of the Auld Man by his
wife and the Fuill, is a familiar piece of bawdy, and the antagonists
are in the same line of descent as the Pantalon and Zanni of the
*commedia del'arte*. Even more clearly recognisable, perhaps, is
Findlaw of the Fute Band, the *miles gloriosus* or *fanfaron* who is
omnipresent in low comedy from Plautus on. Lindsay's character
has a specifically Scottish reference: he was present (briefly)
at the disastrous battle of Pinkie (1547), and his name may
suggest that he is from the Gaidhealtachd, since 'Finlay' was a
much more common name on the west coast than elsewhere in
Scotland. His terror at the sight of a sheep's head wielded by

the Fuill is the comic climax of the play, but there may be a more serious purpose in his exchange with the Clerk, in which he asserts his determination to pray for war. He has no obvious analogue in *The Thrie Estaitis*, but he was no doubt portrayed by one of the actors who played the vices. The same may be true of the Fuill, while the 'presenter' Nuntius seems clearly equivalent to the role of Diligence in the play proper. As an advertisement for *The Thrie Estaitis*, the Proclamation is pretty misleading, although the exchanges between the Cotter and his wife have many echoes of the scenes involving the craftsmen and their spouses. The play's main purpose, no doubt, was to attract attention in and around the town, and Lindsay is at pains to specify the date, time and place of the performance in unambiguous terms; but as the sole Scottish representative of the medieval genre of farce it remains of more than passing interest in its own right.

# The Present Edition

Two texts of Lindsay's *Satyre of the Thrie Estaitis* are extant:

1. National Library of Scotland, Edinburgh: MS. Adv. 19.1.1 ('the Bannatyne manuscript'), ff. 164ʳ–210ʳ [*B*]

2. *Ane Satyre of the Thrie Estaits* (Robert Charteris: Edinburgh 1602) [*C*]. There are seven surviving copies of this edition, at least one and probably two of which were supplied with a new title page and published in London in 1604.[1] Of the remaining five copies, which show evidence of correction while the book was in type, the best is in the Bodleian Library, Oxford (Gough, Scotland, 221).[2] It is this copy which is here referred to as *C*: on the few occasions when the variants in other copied are noted, the following sigla are used:

Selden   Bodleian Library, 4° Z.3 Art. Seld.

NLS   National Library of Scotland, H 29 c. 24

1604   British Library, C. 122 e.7

George Bannatyne's manuscript copy of the play, although much earlier than the printed text, cannot be used as the basis for a critical edition, since it contains only certain sections of the play and amounts to only 3377 lines as against Charteris' 4630. Not only did Bannatyne cut substantial portions of Lindsay's text, but he rearranged the remaining material, changing the entire sequence of the work. His reasons for this editing the original are given at the outset:

> . . . quhilk I writtin bot schortly be interludis levand the grave mater thairof becaws the samyne abuse is weill reformit in Scotland, praysit be God, quhairthrow I omittit that principall mater and writtin only sertane mirry interludis thairof, verry plesand.[3]

Writing in the decade after the Reformation in Scotland, Bannatyne evidently considered that some of the play's politico-religious satire was now irrelevant: it should be noted, however, that he actually retains rather more of the 'grave mater' than he leads us to anticipate.[4]

Charteris' 1602 edition, by contrast, provides a full and continuous text of the play. An adequate critical text must therefore be based upon this version, although the alternative readings offered by Bannatyne, which provide an independent source much closer in date to the original composition of *The Thrie Estaitis*, cannot be excluded from consideration. The differences between the two texts include, apart from hundreds of minor verbal variations and the portions omitted by Bannatyne, a few passages which are found in *B* but not in *C*, all of which I have accepted as authentic and incorporated in my text. In preparing the present edition, I have used *C* as a basis, but all *B* variants have been considered on their merits, with due regard to Bannatyne's undoubted carelessness as a copyist. I have preferred *B* readings to those of *C* where:

1. the omission of whole lines from *C* can be rationally explained, e.g. ll. 827–8, 833–40, where the printer appears to have deleted certain passages because of their coarseness;

2. the *B* reading provides a smooth metrical version of a line metrically defective in *C*, e.g. l. 299, which is defective in *C* ('Sister, I was nocht sweir') and regular in *B* ('Sister, I was nevir sweir');

3. *B* provides a good version of a rhyme which has become defective in *C*, e.g. ll. 185 / 189, where the Scots rhyme *fuder / bruder* is printed by Charteris as *fidder / brother*;

4. the syntax or sense is impaired by a *C* reading which is apparently corrupt, e.g. l. 64, 'And' for 'Als'; l. 386, where 'riche', being more specific and reinforced by alliteration, seems stronger than *C*'s 'same';

5. the principle of *difficilior lectio* or some other test suggests that *B* provides an original reading obscured in *C* by the seventeenth-century printer's tendency to Anglicize his original;[5]

6. *C* contains an evident misprint. In all such cases, the accepted reading is printed in square brackets and the rejected one is noted in the Commentary. In the numerous examples of 'stage directions' given by *B* and not by *C*, I have printed the *B* text within square brackets without further comment; in other cases I have adopted the *C* version.

The problems presented by the texts of *The Thrie Estaitis* are considerable, and the practice of dealing with each variant independently necessarily introduces an element of personal judgment which is potentially controversial. My aim throughout has been to approximate as closely as possible Lindsay's own text, and although I have tended to assume the superiority of *C* in the absence of evidence to the contrary, I have been more liberal in adopting *B* readings than most of my predecessors. Even so, out of 209 variants in the first 500 lines, for example, excluding stage directions, I have preferred *B* in only 28 cases.

I have normalised the text in a number of ways. ' ſ ' is printed as 's', 'VV' as 'W', 'y' ( þ )\* as 'th', and 'z' ( ȝ )† as 'y'. Contractions have been silently expanded. Capitalizations and punctuation are editorial. One major problem is the tendency of Charteris to print the Scots '-is' ending in nouns and the third person singular of the present tense of verbs as '-s', which creates severe prosodic difficulties. In these cases I have added [i], but have not noted each emendation separately in the Commentary. In other respects, I have followed the originals as closely as possible.

The glossary at the foot of each page attempts to define any words likely to cause particular difficulty; each word is glossed only on its first appearance, except that a few words occurring at wide intervals, especially between Part One and Part Two, are glossed again when they reappear in the latter part of the play. Included at end of this introduction is a list of frequently-occurring words are not separately glossed.

Lindsay's numerous Latin phrases and quotations are included in the gloss. There is no direct evidence of which English version of the Bible he might have used; where he gives an English text himself, it does not correspond to those of the published English translations. I have generally quoted from the Matthew Bible, as printed by Nicholas Hyll in 1551. Based on Tyndale's translation, this text was widely used, and copies certainly found their way into Scotland. It may therefore be taken to give a reasonable sense of the vernacular Bible as Lindsay would have known it.

als, *as, also*
althocht *although*
awin *own*
ay *ever, always*
baith *both*
be *be, by*
beir *carry*
but *but, without*
eine *eyes*
fra *from*
gang *go*
gif, give *if*

haif *have*
intill *in, into*
lufe *love*
luik *look*
maist *most, greatest*
na *no, nor, than*
nane *none*
nocht *not*
nor *than*
or *or, before*
quha *who*
quhair *where*

quhen *when*
quhilk *which*
quhill *until*
sen *since*
sic, sik *such*
sould *should*
sune *soon*
syne *then*
thir *these*
till *to*
yit *yet*

\* The old English letter *thorn* often printed as y
† The middle English letter *yogh* often printed as z

## ACKNOWLEDGEMENTS

I am, like any editor, endebted to many colleagues who have, in one way or another, made this volume more satisfactory than it might otherwise have been. In particular, I record my thanks to Dr John Durkan (who once again asked more questions than I could answer in his comments on the Introduction and Commentary); and to Professor Bill Gordon, Dr Graham Runnalls, Professor Michael Samuels, Dr Angus Calder and Dr Sandra Billington, all of whom have provided information or clarified my thinking on specific points. Successive classes of students in the Department of Scottish Literature of the University of Glasgow have brought out issues quietly reflected in what appears here.

I am also grateful to Dr Roderick Watson, General Editor of the Canongate Classics series, and to Neville Moir, for their patience in dealing with an editor whose other duties too often stand in the way of scholarship to Dr Mark Partridge for his willing help with data-transfer; and to Letizia Pascalino for her careful proof-reading of the text. To Elizabeth and James, for their tolerance of an occasionally absent-minded (and sometimes simply absent) scholar, formal thanks are inadequate, but I nevertheless offer them wholeheartedly.

NOTES TO THE INTRODUCTION

1. *Statuta Ecclesiae Scoticana*, ed. Joseph Robertson (2 vols, Edinburgh 1866), II, 135–9.

2. *The Catechism of John Hamilton*, ed. T.G. Law (Oxford 1884), p. 140.

3. *APS*, II, 486–7.

4. *APC*, I, 114.

5. *ibid.*, I, 127–8.

6. See I.B. Cowan, *Regional Aspects of the Scottish Reformation* (London 1978), pp.10, 15–16.

7. See John Knox, *Historie of the Reformatioun, Works*, ed. David Laing (6 vols, Edinburgh 1846–55), I, 62–3.

8. John MacQueen, '*Ane Satyre of the Thrie Estaitis*', *SSL* 3 (1965–66), 129–43.

9. A.J. Mill, 'The Original Version of Lindsay's *Satyre of the Thrie Estaitis*', *SSL* 6 (1968–69), 67–75, at 70–1.

10. These documents were printed by Douglas Hamer in Sir David Lindsay, *Works* (4 vols, STS, Edinburgh 1931–36), II, 1–6. Hamer's view that they describe an early version of *The Thrie Estaitis* has been widely accepted, but cf. Joanne S. Kantrowitz, *Dramatic Allegory: Lindsay's Ane Satyre of the Thrie Estaitis* (Lincoln, Nebraska 1975), pp.12–23; and R.J. Lyall, 'The Linlithgow Interlude of 1540', in *Actes du 2e Colloque de Langue et de Littérature (Moyen Age et Renaissance)*, ed. Jean-Jacques Blanchot and Claude Graf (Strasbourg 1978), pp.409–21.

11. *Treasurer Accts*, VIII, 315 (the sum involved is £266.13.4).

12. John Row, *The History of the Kirk of Scotland*, ed. David Laing (Edinburgh 1842), pp. 6–8.

13. According to Row, the discovery that one of the pupils of the grammer school in Perth owned a copy of a work by Lindsay was made by Mr Andrew Simson, who did not matriculate at St Andrews until 1557.

14. But cf. the reference to the 'Schogait' (l. 4315); Dr John Durkan suggests to me that only Perth is known to have had a street of that name (although the existence of others is not improbable in itself).

15. Quoted by Hamer, *ed. cit.*, I, 398.

16. *ibid.*, VI, 139–43.

17. Hamer's case is most fully argued in 'The Bibliography of Sir David Lindsay (1490–1555)', *The Library* 10 (1929–30), 1–42, at 35–9; but his view was effectively rebutted by R.A. Houk, 'Versions of Lindsay's *Satire of the Three Estates*', *PMLA* 55 (1940), 396–405.

18. A.J. Mill, 'Representations of Lyndsay's *Satyre of the Thrie Estaitis*', *PMLA* 47 (1932), 636–51, at 640–1.

19. Kantrowitz, *op. cit.*, pp.17–22.

20. Hamer, *ed. cit.*, IV, 1.

21. *Protocol Book of John Foular*, I, 168 (no. 886).

22. *The Bannatyne Manuscript*, ed. W. Tod Ritchie (4 vols, STS, Edinburgh 1928–34), III, 13–14.

23. The story is reported by Lindsay's kinsman Robert Lindsay of Pitscottie, *Historie and Cronicles of Scotland*, ed. AE.J.G. Mackay (2 vols, STS, Edinburgh 1899), I, 379.

24. For a summary of the complex politics of this period, see Margaret H.B. Sanderson, *Cardinal of Scotland: David Beaton c.1494–1546* (Edinburgh 1986), pp.148–76.

25. Lindsay was commissioned to travel to the Imperial Court on 30 April 1544 (*Letters and Papers of Henry VIII*, XIX, i, 434); he was back in the country by 17 November 1544, when he attended Parliament (*APS*, II, 448).

26. See Knox, *Historie, Works*, I, 186–8. Lindsay was certainly commissioned by the Governor to speak to the insurgents in December 1546 (*State Papers*, V, 581–2); a messenger was sent to him 'in Fyf' in July 1547, presumably on State business (*Treasurer Accts*, IX, 96).

27. Pitscottie, *ed. cit.*, II, 141; for Hamer's suggestion, see *ed. cit.*, IV, 273.

28. Hamer, *ed. cit.*, I, 146–96. For a sensitive reading of this poem, see Felicity Riddy, 'Squyer Meldrum and the romance of chivalry', *YES* 4 (1974), 26–36.

29. Most of the documentary evidence is collected in A.J. Mill, *Medieval Plays in Scotland* (Edinburgh 1927).

30. See David Calderwood, *Historie of the Kirk of Scotland*, ed. T. Thomson (8 vols, Edinburgh 1842–49), I, 142.

31. A.J. Mill, 'The Influence of the Continental Drama on Lyndsay's *Satyre of the Thrie Estaitis*', *MLR* 25 (1930), 425–42, at 442.

32. Gari R. Muller, 'Theater of Folly: Allegory and Satire in the *Sottie*' (unpub. PhD. diss., Yale 1975), p.6. I am endebted to Dr Graham Runnalls for this reference.

33. On the *Sermon joyeux* and related forms, see Jean-Claude Aubailly, *Le Monologue, le Dialogue et la Sottie* (Paris 1976), pp.40–77.

34. Cf. Alan E. Knight, *Aspects of Genre in late Medieval French Drama* (Manchester 1983).

35. See the note to ll. 2105–6, p.194 below.

36. *Les trois estatz* is reprinted in the facsimile edition of *Le Receuil Trepperel*, ed. E. Droz (Geneva 1966), no. 20; for *L'Eglise, Noblesse et Povrete*, see *Receuil de farces, moralités et sermons joyeux*, ed. A. Leroux de Lincy and Françisque Michel (4 vols, Paris 1837), I, no. 23.

37. Cf. T.W. Craik, *The Tudor Interlude: Stage Costume and Acting* (Leicester 1967), pp.93–5.

38. William O. Harris, *Skelton's Magnyfycence and the Cardinall Virtue Tradition* (Chapel Hill, NC 1965), pp.12–45; but this view is countered in part by David M. Bevington, *Tudor Drama and Politics* (Cambridge, Mass. 1968), pp.56–63.

39. *An Enterlude called Lusty Juventus*, ed. Helen Scarborough Thomas (New York/London 1982), pp.xiii-xxxix.

40. Robert Henryson, *Works*, ed. Denton Fox (Oxford 1981), p.91.

41. Cf., for example, *Hamilton's Catechism*, ed. Law, p.60.

42. Sandra Billington, 'The Fool and the Moral in English and Scottish Morality Plays', in *Popular Drama in Northern Europe in the Later Middle Ages*, ed. Flemming G. Andersen *et al.* (Odense 1988), pp.113–33, at 127–33.

43. J.E. Bernard Jr, *The Prosody of the Tudor Interlude* (New Haven 1939), p.76; there is a valuable study of the prosody of the play, pp. 67–77.

1. Hamer, *ed. cit.*, IV, 70–73. A comparison of variants suggests that the Lincoln Cathedral Library copy (Rr.6.13[2]), usually described as a copy of 1602, is identical to the British Library copy of the 1604 reprint; the title-page of the Lincoln book is missing, and it is therefore not surprising that it has been assumed to be another example of the 1602 edition.

2. *ibid.*, IV, 71.

3. *Bannatyne Manuscript, ed. cit.*, III, 101.

4. So, for example, Bannatyne includes much of ll. 2556–2755, although this is largely concerned with secular reform, and may therefore have seemed still to be relevant.

5. There is an invaluable study of the variations between [B] and [C] in J. Derrick McClure, 'A Comparison of the Bannatyne MS and the Quarto Texts of Lyndsay's *Ane Satyre of the Thrie Estaitis*, in *Scottish Language and Literature, Medieval and Renaissance*, ed. Dietrich Strauss and Horst W. Drescher (Frankfurt 1986), pp.409–22. On Anglicization generally, see M.A. Bald, 'The Anglicisation of Scottish printing', *SHR* 23 (1926), 107–115

## Dramatis Personae
### in order of appearance

Diligence

Rex Humanitas

Wantonnes
Placebo
Solace
   *the King's courtiers*

Dame Sensualitie

Hamelines
Danger
Fund-Jonet
   *Sensualitie's ladies*

Gude Counsall

Flatterie
Falset
Dissait
  *the vices*

Veritie

Spiritualitie
Abbot
Persone
Priores
Abbasse

Temporalitie

Merchand

Chastitie

Sowtar

Taylour

Jennie, the Taylour's daughter

Taylour's Wyfe

Sowtar's Wyfe

Correctioun's Varlet

Divyne Correctioun

Pauper, the Pure Man

Pardoner

Wilkin Widdiefow, the Pardoner's boy

Johne the Common-weill

First Sergeant

Second Sergeant

Scrybe

Commoun Thift

Oppressioun

Doctour

First Licent

Second Licent

Foly

Glaiks, his daughter

Stult, his son

## Part One

DILIGENCE

The Father and founder of faith and felicitie,
That your fassioun formed to His similitude,
And His Sone our Saviour, scheild in necessitie,
That bocht yow from baillis, [ransonit on the Rude],
5    Repleadgeand His presonaris with His [pretious] blude,
The Halie Gaist, governour and grounder of grace,
Of wisdome and weilfair baith fontaine and flude,
[Save] yow all that I sie seasit in this place,
      And scheild yow from sinne,
10      And with His spreit yow inspyre
      Till I haue shawin my desyre.
      Silence, [soveranis], I requyre,
        For now I begin!

*Pausa*

Tak tent to me, my freinds, and hald yow coy!
15    For I am sent to yow as messingeir
From ane nobill and rycht redoubtit roy,
The quhilk hes bene absent this monie yeir:
Humanitie, give ye his name wald speir,
Quha bade me shaw to yow, but variance,
20    That he intendis amang yow to compeir
With ane [triumphant], awfull ordinance,
With crown and sword and scepter in his hand,
Temperit with mercie quhen penitence appeiris.
Howbeit that hee lang tyme hes bene sleipand,
25    Quhairthrow misreull hes rung thir monie yeiris,
[And] innocentis bene brocht [upoun] thair beiris
Be fals reporteris of this natioun;

---

baillis *harm*   seasit *seated*   tak tent *pay attention*   coy *quiet*
roy *king*   speir *ask*   but variance *without quarrelling*
compeir *appear*   rung *reigned*   beiris *biers*

Thocht young oppressouris at the elder[is] leiris,
Be now assurit of reformatioun.

30  Sie no misdoeris be sa bauld
As to remaine into this hauld:
For quhy, be Him that Judas sauld,
   Thay will be heich hangit.
Now faithfull folk for joy may sing;
35  For quhy, it is the just bidding
Of my soveraine lord the king
   That na man be wrangit.
Thocht he, ane quhyll into his flouris,
Be governit be vylde trompouris
40  And sumtyme lufe his paramouris,
   Hauld ye him excusit;
For quhen he meittis with Correctioun,
With Veritie and Discretioun,
Thay will be banisched aff the toun
45   Quhilk hes him abusit.

And heir be oppin proclamatioun
I wairne in name of his magnificence
The Thrie Estaitis of this natioun
That thay compeir with detfull diligence
50  And till his Grace mak thair obedience;
And first I wairne the Spritualitie,
And sie the burgessis spair not for expence,
Bot speid thame heir with Temporalitie.
Als I beseik yow famous auditouris,
55  Conveinit in this congregatioun,
To be patient the space of certaine houris
Till ye have hard our short narratioun.
And als we mak yow supplicatioun
That na man tak our wordis intill disdaine,
60  Althocht ye hear, be declamatioun,

---

leiris *learn*  hauld *place*  heich *high*  quhyll *while*
flouris *prime (see note)*  trompouris *deceivers*
paramouris *mistress*  detfull *dutiful*  conveinit *gathered*

The Commoun-weill richt pitiouslie complaine.

Rycht so the verteous ladie Veritie
Will mak ane pitious lamentatioun,
[And] for the treuth sho will impresonit be,
65 And banischit lang tyme out of the toun;
And Chastitie will mak narratioun
How sho can get na ludging in this land,
Till that the heavinlie king Correctioun
Meit with the king and commoun, hand for hand.

70 Prudent peopill, I pray yow all,
Tak na man greif in speciall,
For wee sall speik in generall,
    For pastyme and for play.
Thairfoir, till all our rymis be rung
75 And our mistoinit sangis be sung,
Let everie man keip weill ane toung,
    And everie woman tway!
    REX HUMANITAS
O Lord of Lords and King of kingis all,
Omnipotent of power, Prince but peir,
80 [Eterne] ringand in gloir celestiall,
[Unmaid makar quhilk], haifing na mateir,
Maid heavin and eird, fyre, air and watter cleir,
Send me Thy grace with peace perpetuall,
That I may rewll my realme to Thy pleaseir,
85 Syne bring my saull to joy angelicall.

Sen Thow hes givin mee dominatioun
And rewll of pepill subject to my cure,
Be I nocht rewlit be counsall and ressoun,
In dignitie I may nocht lang indure:
90 I grant my stait my self may nocht assure,
Nor yit conserve my lyfe in sickernes.
Have pitie, Lord, on mee Thy creature,

---

mistoinit *out of tune*   but peir *without equal*   ringand *reigning*
cure *care*   sickernes *security*

Supportand me in all my busines.

I Thee requeist, quha rent was on the Rude,
95 Me to defend from [deidis] of defame,
That my pepill report of me bot gude,
And be my saifgaird baith from sin and shame.
I knaw my dayis induris bot as ane dreame;
Thairfoir, O Lord, I hairtlie The exhort
100 To gif me grace to use my diadeame
To Thy pleasure and to my great comfort.

[*Heir sall the King pass to royall sait and sit with ane grave countenance till Wantones cum.*]

WANTONNES
My soveraine lord and prince but peir,
Quhat garris yow mak sic dreirie cheir?
Be blyth sa lang as ye ar heir
105     And pas tyme with pleasure,
For als lang leifis the mirrie man
As the sorie, for ocht he can:
His banis full sair, Sir, sall I ban
    That dois yow displeasure.
110 Sa lang as Placebo and I
Remaines into your company,
Your Grace sall leif richt mirrely—
    Of this haif ye na dout.
Sa lang as ye have us in cure,
115 Your Grace, Sir, sall want na pleasure:
War Solace heir, I yow assure
    He wald rejoice this rout!
PLACEBO
Gude brother myne, quhair is Solace,
The mirrour of all mirrines?
120 I have great mervell, be the Mes,
    He taries sa lang.

———

rent *torn*   garris *causes*   leifis *lives*
ocht he can *anything he can do*   ban *curse*   rout *crowd*

Byde he away wee ar bot shent:
I ferlie how he fra us went.
I trow he hes impediment
125     That lettis him [to] gang.

    WANTONNES

I left Solace, that same greit loun,
Drinkand into the burrows-toun:
It will cost him halfe of ane croun,
    Althocht [he] had na mair!
130 And als, he said hee wald gang see
Fair Ladie Sensualitie,
The [beriall] of all bewtie
    And portratour preclair.

    PLACEBO

Be God, I see him at the last,
135 As he war chaist, rynnand richt fast;
He glowris evin as he war agast,
    Or fleyit of ane gaist.
Na, he is wod drunkin, I trow!
Se ye not that he is wod fow?
140 I ken weill be his creischie mow
    He hes bene at ane feist.

    SOLACE

Now quha saw ever sic ane thrang?
Me thocht sum said I had gaine wrang.
Had I help I wald sing ane sang
145     With ane rycht mirrie noyse!
I have sic plesour at my hart
That garris me sing the [tribill] pairt;
Wald sum gude fallow fill the quart
    It wald my hairt rejoyce.
150 Howbeit my coat be short and nippit,
Thankis be to God I am weill hippit,
Thocht all my gold may [sone] be grippit

---

shent *ruined*    ferlie *wonder*    lettis *prevents*
beriall *beryl*    portratour *appearance*    preclair *fairest*
fleyit *frightened*    wod *mad*    fow *drunk*
creischie mow *greasy mouth*

Intill ane pennie pursse.
Thocht I ane servand lang haif bene,
155 My purchais is nocht worth ane preine :
I may sing 'Peblis on the Greine'
For ocht that I may tursse.
Quhat is my name? Can ye not gesse?
Sirs, ken ye nocht Sandie Solace?
160 Thay callit my mother Bonie Besse,
That dwelt betwene the Bowis.
Of twelf yeir auld sho learnit to swyfe,
Thankit be the great God on lyve !
Scho maid me fatheris four or fyve ;
165 But dout, this is na mowis.
Quhen ane was deid, sho gat ane uther—
Was never man had sic ane mother ;
Of fatheris sho maid me ane futher
Of lawit men and leirit.
170 Scho is baith wyse, worthie and wicht,
For scho spairis nouther kuik nor knycht :
Yea, four and twentie on ane nicht,
And ay thair eine scho bleirit.
And gif I lie, sirs, ye may speir !
175 Bot saw ye nocht the King cum heir?
I am ane sportour and playfeir
To that royall young king.
He said he wald, within schort space,
Cum pas his tyme into this place :
180 I pray the Lord to send him grace
That he lang tyme may ring.
PLACEBO
Solace, quhy taryit ye sa lang?
SOLACE
The feind a faster I micht gang !
I micht not thrist out throw the thrang

---

purchais *profit*   preine *pin*   tursse *carry away*
Bowis *archways of town gates ( see note )*   swyfe *fornicate*
mowis *joke*   futher *company*   lawit *common, ignorant*
wicht *strong*   playfeir *play-fellow*

185     Of wyfes fyftein [fuder].
       Then for to rin I tuik ane rink,
       Bot I felt never sik ane stink—
       For Our Lordis luif, gif me ane drink,
         Placebo, my deir [bruder]!

[*Heir sall Placebo gif Sollace ane drink.*]

      REX HUMANITAS
190  My servant Solace, quhat gart yow tarie?
      SOLACE
       I wait not, Sir, be sweit Saint Marie:
       I have bene in ane feirie farie,
         Or ellis intill ane trance.
       Sir, I have sene, I yow assure,
195  The fairest earthlie creature
       That ever was formit be Nature,
         And maist for to advance.
       To luik on her is great delyte,
       With lippis reid and cheikis quhyte:
200  I wald renunce all this warld quyte
         For till stand in hir grace.
       Scho is wantoun and scho is wyse,
       And cled scho is on the new gyse:
       It wald gar all your flesche up ryse
205      To luik upon hir face!
       War I ane king it sould be kend
       I sould not spair on hir to spend,
       And this same nicht for hir to send
         For my pleasure.
210  Quhat rak of your prosperitie
       Gif ye want Sensualitie?
       I wald nocht gif ane sillie flie
         For your treasure.
      REX
       Forsuith, my freinds, I think ye are not wyse
215  Till counsall me to break commandement

---

fuder *company*  rin *run*  rink *course*  feirie farie *great*
*confusion*  kend *known*  quhat rak of *what does it matter*

Directit be the Prince of Paradyce,
Considering ye knaw that my intent
Is for till be to God obedient,
Quhilk dois forbid men to be lecherous.
220 Do I nocht sa, perchance I will repent.
Thairfoir I think your counsall odious,
   The quhilk ye gaif mee till,
Becaus I have bene to this day
   *Tanquam tabula rasa* ;
225 That is als mekill as to say,
   Redie for gude and ill.
   PLACEBO
Beleive ye that we will begyll yow,
Or from your vertew we will wyle you,
Or with evill consall overseyll yow,
230    Both into gude and evill?
To tak your Graces part wee grant,
In all your deidis participant,
Sa that ye be nocht ane young sanct
   And syne ane auld devill.
   WANTONNES
235 Beleive ye, Sir, that lecherie be sin?
Na, trow nocht that ! This is my ressoun quhy :
First at the Romane [ court ] will ye begin,
Quhilk is the lemand lamp of lechery,
Quhair Cardinals and Bischops generally
240 To luif ladies thay think ane pleasand sport,
And out of Rome hes baneist Chastity,
Quha with our Prelats can get na resort.
   SOLACE
Sir, quhill ye get ane prudent Queine,
I think your Majestie serein
245 Sould have ane lustie concubein
   To play yow withall ;
For I knaw be your qualitie

---

*Tanquam tabula rasa*  *like a scraped writing-tablet ( of wax )*
*( see note )*  mekill *much*  wyle *beguile*  overseyll *deceive*
trow *believe*  lemand *shining*

Ye want the gift of chastitie.
Fall to *in nomine Domini*:
250     This is my counsall.
I speik, Sir, under protestatioun,
That nane at me haif indignatioun;
For all the Prelats of this natioun,
     For the maist part,
255 Thay think na schame to have ane huir,
And sum hes thrie under thair cuir:
This to be trew, Ile yow assuir,
     Ye sall heir eftirwart.
Sir, knew [ye] all the mater throch
260     To play ye wald begin:
Speir at the monks of Bamirrinoch
     Gif lecherie be sin!

PLACEBO

Sir, send ye for Sandie Solace,
Or ells your monyeoun Wantonnes,
265 And pray my Ladie Priores
     The suith till declair
Gif it be sin to tak [ane] Kaity,
Or to leif like ane bummillbaty:
The Buik sayis *Omnia probate*,
270     And nocht for to spair.

[*Heir sall entir Dame Sensualitie with hir madynnis
Hamelines and Denger.*]

SENSUALITIE

Luifers awalk! behald the fyrie spheir,
Behauld the naturall dochter of Venus;
Behauld, luifers, this lustie ladie cleir,
The fresche fonteine of knichtis amorous,
275 Repleit with joyis dulce and delicious.
Or quha wald mak to Venus observance
In my mirthfull chalmer melodious,

---

in nomine Domini  *in the name of the Lord* ( *see note* )   suith  *truth*
Bamirrinoch  *Balmerino* ( *see note* )   monyeoun  *minion*
bummillbaty  *idler*   Omnia probate  *'Examen all thynges'*
( *1 Thessal. 5:21* ) ( *see note* )   dulce  *sweet*

Thair sall thay find all pastyme and pleasance.
Behauld my heid, behauld my gay attyre,
280 Behauld my halse, lusum and lilie-quhite;
Behauld my visage, flammand as the fyre;
Behauld my papis of portratour perfyte.
To luke on mee luiffers hes greit delyte;
Rycht sa hes all the kinges of Christindome:
285 To thame I haif done pleasouris infinite,
And speciallie unto the Court of Rome.

Ane kis of me war worth in ane morning
A milyioun of gold to knicht or king.
And yit I am of nature sa towart
290 I lat no luiffer pas with ane sair hart.
Of my name wald ye wit the veritie,
Forsuith, thay call me Sensualitie.
I hauld it best, now or we farther gang,
To Dame Venus let us go sing ane sang.

HAMELINES
295 Madame, but tarying,
For to serve Venus deir,
We sall fall to and sing.
Sister Danger, cum neir!

DANGER
Sister, I was [nevir] sweir
300 To Venus observance!
Howbeit I mak dangeir,
Yit be continuance
Men may have thair pleasance.
Thairfoir let na man fray;
305 We will tak it, perchance,
Howbeit that wee say nay.

HAMELINES
Sister, cum on your way,
And let us nocht think lang:

———

halse *neck*   lusum *lovely*   towart *forward*
Danger *haughtiness (see note)*   sweir *unwilling*   fray *be afraid*

In all the haist wee may,
310 To sing Venus ane sang.
  DANGER
Sister, sing this sang I may not
Without the help of gude Fund-Jonet.
Fund-Jonet, hoaw, cum tak a part!
  FUND-JONET
That sall I do with all my hart.
315 Sister, howbeit that I am hais,
I am content to beir a bais.
Ye twa sould luif mee as your lyfe:
You knaw I [leird] yow baith to swyfe
In my chalmer, ye wait weill quhair;
320 Sensyne the feind ane man ye spair!
  HAMELINES
Fund-Jonet, fy! ye ar to blame!
To speik foull wordis think ye not schame?
  FUND-JONET
Thair is ane hundreth heir sitand by
That luifis geaping als weill as I,
325 Micht thay get it in privitie.
Bot quha begins the sang, let se.
  REX HUMANITAS
Up, Wantonnes! Thow sleipis to lang!
Me thocht I hard ane mirrie sang:
I the command in haist to gang
330 Se quhat yon mirth may meine.
  WANTONNES
I trow, Sir, be the Trinitie,
Yon same is Sensualitie.
Gif it be scho, sune sall I sie
  That [soverane] sereine.

[*Heir sall Wantonnes ga spy thame and cum agane
to the King.*]

————

hais *hoarse* leird *taught* wait *know* sensyne *then*
geaping *playing, sexual intercourse*

REX

335 Quhat war thay yon, to me declair.
    WANTONNES
    Dame Sensuall, baith gude and fair.
        PLACEBO
    Sir, scho is mekill to avance,
    For scho can baith play and dance,
    That perfyte patron of plesance,
340     Ane perle of pulchritude.
    Soft as the silk is hir quhyte lyre,
    Hir hair is like the goldin wyre;
    My hart burnis in ane flame of fyre,
        I sweir yow by the Rude.
345 I think scho is sa wonder fair
    That in the earth scho hes na compair.
    War ye weill leirnit at luifis lair
        And syne had hir anis sene,
    I wait, by Cokis passioun,
350 Ye wald mak supplicatioun,
    And spend on hir ane millioun
        Hir lufe for till obteine.
        SOLACE
    Quhat say ye, Sir? Ar ye content
    That scho cum heir incontinent?
355 Quhat vails your kingdome and your rent
        And all your great treasure
    Without ye haif ane mirrie lyfe
    And cast asyde all sturt and stryfe
    And sa lang as ye want ane wyfe
360     Fall to and tak your pleasure?
        REX
    Gif that be trew quhilk ye me tell,
        I will not langer tarie,
    Bot will gang preif that play my sell,
        Howbeit the warld me warie.
365 Als fast as ye may carie

---

lyre *complexion*   Cokis *Christ's (euphemism; see note)*
incontinent *immediately*   sturt *discord*   preif *test*
warie *troubles*

[ 12

Speid with all diligence;
Bring Sensualitie
   Fra-hand to my presence.
Forsuth, I wait not how it stands,
370 Bot sen I hard of your tythands
My bodie trimblis feit and hands
   And quhiles is hait as fyre.
I trow Cupido with his dart
Hes woundit me out-throw the hart;
375 My spreit will fra my bodie part
   Get I not my desyre.
Pas on away with diligence
And bring hir heir to my presence:
Spair not for travell nor expence—
380    I cair not for na cost.
Pas on your way schone, Wantonnes,
And tak with yow Sandie Solace,
And bring that ladie to this place,
   Or els I am bot lost!
385 Commend me to that sweitest thing,
And [hir present] with this [riche] ring,
And say I ly in languisching
   Except scho mak remeid.
With siching sair I am bot schent,
390 Without scho cum incontinent
My heavie langour to relent,
   And saif me now fra deid.
   WANTONNES
Or ye tuik skaith, be God[is croun],
I lever thair war not, up nor doun,
395 Ane tume cunt into this toun
   Nor twentie myle about.
Doubt ye nocht, Sir, bot wee will get hir;
Wee sall be feirie for till [fet] hir;

---

fra-hand *at once*  tythands *news*  quhiles *sometimes*
schone *soon*  skaith *harm*  lever *would prefer*
tume *empty*  feirie *eager*  fet *fetch*

Bot faith, wee wald speid all the better
400    Till gar our pursses rout.
   SOLACE
Sir, let na sorrow in yow sink,
Bot gif us ducats for till drink,
And wee sall never sleip ane wink
   Till it be back or eadge.
405 Ye ken weill, Sir, wee have no cunye.
   REX
Solace, sure that sall be no sunyie:
Beir ye that bag upon your lunyie.
   Now, sirs, win weill your wage—
I pray yow speid yow sone againe!
   WANTONNES
410 Ye, of this sang, Sir, wee ar faine.
Wee sall nether spair [for] wind nor raine
   Till our days wark be done.
Fairweill, for wee ar at the flicht!
Placebo, rewll our roy at richt.
415 We sall be heir, man, or midnicht,
   Thocht wee marche with the mone.

[*Heir sall thay depairt, singand mirrelly.*]

Pastyme with pleasance and greit prosperitie
Be to yow, Soveraine Sensualitie!
   SENSUALITIE
Sirs, ye ar welcum. Quhair go ye, eist or west?
   WANTONNES
420 In faith, I trow we be at the farrest.
   SENSUALITIE
Quhat is your name, I pray yow, Sir, declair?
   WANTONNES
Marie, Wantonnes, the King[i]s secretair.
   SENSUALITIE
Quhat king is that quhilk hes sa gay a boy?

---

rout  *cry out*   till it be back or eadge  *?come what may (see note)*
cunye  *money*   sunyie *cause for delay*  lunyie *back*

WANTONNES

Humanitie, that richt redoubtit roy,
425 [Quha] dois commend him to yow hartfullie,
And sends yow heir ane ring with ane rubie
In takin that abuife all creatour
He hes chosin yow to be his paramour:

He bade me say that he will be bot deid
430 Without that ye mak haistelie remeid.

SENSUALITIE

How can I help him, althocht he suld forfair?
Ye ken richt weill I am na medcinair.

SOLACE

Yes, lustie ladie, thocht he war never sa seik,
I wait ye beare his health into your breik:
435 Ane kis of your sweit mow, in ane morning,
Till his seiknes micht be greit comforting.
And als he maks yow supplicatioun
This nicht to mak with him collatioun.

SENSUALITIE

I thank His Grace of his benevolence;
440 Gude sirs, I sall be reddie evin fra-hand.
In me thair sall be fund na negligence,
Baith day and nicht, quhen His Grace will demand.
Pas ye befoir, and say I am cummand
And thinks richt lang to haif of him ane sicht,
445 And I to Venus [makis] ane faithfull band
That in his arms I think to ly all nicht.

WANTONNES

That sal be done; bot yit or I hame pas,
Heir I protest for Hamelynes, your las.

SENSUALITIE

Scho salbe at command, Sir, quhen ye will:
450 I traist scho sall find yow flinging your fill.

WANTONNES

Now hay! For joy and mirth I dance.
Tak thair ane gay gamond of France:

———

forfair *perish*   breik *buttocks*   collatioun *dinner*
band *promise*   flinging *capering*

Am I nocht worthie till avance,
   That am sa gude a page,
455 And that sa spedelie can rin
To tyst my maister unto sin?
The fiend a penny he will win

   Of this his mariage
I rew richt sair, be Sanct Michell,
460 Nor I had pearst hir, my awin sell,
For quhy, yon king, by Bryd[i]s bell,
   Kennis na mair of ane cunt
Nor dois the noveis of ane freir.
It war bot almis to pull my eir,
465 That wald not preif yon gallant geir.
   Fy, that I am sa blunt!
I think this day to win greit thank.
Hay, as ane brydlit cat I brank—
Alace, I have wreistit my schank,
470    Yit I gang, be Sanct Michaell!
Quhilk of my leggis, Sirs, as ye trow,
Was it that I did hurt evin now?
Bot quhairto sould I speir at yow?
   I think thay baith ar haill.

475 Good morrow, Maister, be the Mes!
   REX
Welcum, my minyeon Wantonnes.
How hes thow sped in thy travell?
   WANTONNES
Rycht weill, be Him that herryit Hell:
   Your erand is weill done.
   REX
480 Then, Wantonnes, how weill is me:
Thow hes deservit baith meit and fie,
   Be Him that maid the mone.
Thair is ane thing that I wald speir:

———

gamond *gambade, a lively dance ( see note )*  tyst *entice*
rew *regret*  brank *prance*  wrestit *twisted*

Quhat sall I do, quhen scho cums heir?
485 For I knaw nocht the craft perqueir
    Of luifers gyn;
Thairfoir at lenth ye mon me leir
    How to begin.
    WANTONNES
To kis hir and clap hir, Sir, be not affeard.
Scho will not schrink, thocht ye kis hir ane span
490                                within the baird!
Gif ye think that sho thinks shame, then hide
                                the bairns eine
With hir taill, and tent hir weill: ye wait quhat I meine.
Will ye leif me, Sir, first for to go to,
And I sall leirne yow all kewis how to do.
    REX
495 God forbid, Wantonnes, that I gif the leife!
Thou art over perillous ane page, sic practiks to preife.
    WANTONNES
Now, Sir, preife as ye pleis; I se hir cumand.
Use your self gravelie; wee sall by yow stand.
    SENSUALITIE
O Queene Venus, unto thy celsitude
500 I gif gloir, honour, laud and reverence,
Quha grantit me sic perfite pulchritude
That princes of my persone have pleasance.
I mak ane vow, with humbill observance,
Richt reverentlie thy tempill to visie,
505 With sacrifice unto thy [deitie].

Till everie stait I am so greabill
That few or nane refuses me at all:
Paipis, patriarks or prelats venerabill,
Common pepill and princes temporall
510 Ar subject all to me, Dame Sensuall.

---

perqueir *by heart*   gyn *skill*   mon *must*   clap *embrace*
baird *loose bodice*   tent *look after*   kewis *cues*
practiks *customs*   visie *visit*

Sa sall it be ay quhill the warld indures,
And speciallie quhair youthage hes the cures.
    Quha knawis the contrair?
I traist few in this companie,
515    Wald thay declair the veritie
How thay use Sensualitie,
    Bot with me makis repair.
And now my way I man avance
Unto ane prince of great puissance,
520    Quhom young men hes in governance,
    Rolland into his rage.
I am richt glaid, I yow assure,
That potent prince to get in cure,
Quhilk is of lustines the luir,
525    And greitest of curage.

[*Heir sall scho mak reverence and say* :]

O potent prince, of pulchritude preclair,
God Cupido preserve your celsitude,
And Dame Venus mot keip your court from cair,
As I wald sho suld keip my awin hart-blud.
    REX
530    Welcum to me, peirles in pulchritude ;
Welcum to me, thow sweiter nor the lamber,
Quhilk hes maid me of all dolour denude.
Solace, convoy this ladie to my chamber.

[*Heir sall scho pass to the chalmer and say* :]

    SENSUALITIE
I gang this gait with richt gude will.
535    Sir Wantonnes, tarie ye still,
And Hamelines, the cap yeis fill
    And beir him cumpanie.
[HAMELINES]
That sall I do, withoutin dout,

————

rolland *?roaring (see note)*   luir *lure*   lamber *amber*
gang this gait  *go this way*

And he and I sall play cap out.

WANTONNES

540 Now ladie, len me that batye tout:
    Fill in, for I am dry!
Your dame be this trewlie
    Hes gottin upon the gumis.
Quhat rak thocht ye and I
545     Go junne our justing lumis?

HAMELINES

Content I am, with [richt] gude will,
    Quhen ever ye ar reddie,
[All] your pleasure to fulfill.

WANTONNES

Now weill said, be our Ladie!
550 Ile bair my maister cumpanie
    Till that I may indure:
Gif [hee] be quisland wantounlie,
    We sall fling on the flure.

[Heir sall thay pass all to the chalmer and Gude Counsale
sall say:]

GUDE COUNSALL

Immortall God, maist of magnificence,
555 Quhais Majestie na clark can comprehend,
Must save yow all that givis sic audience
And grant yow grace Him never till offend,
Quhilk on the Croce did willinglie ascend
And sched His pretious blude on everie side;
560 Quhais pitious passioun from danger yow defend,
And be your gratious governour and gyde.
Now, my gude freinds, considder, I yow beseik,
The caus maist principall of my cumming:
Princis or potestatis ar nocht worth ane leik
565 Be thay not gydit be my gude governing.
Thair was never empriour, conquerour nor king

---

cap out  *empty the cup (a drinking game; see note)*
batye tout  *lusty*  drink (see note)  gumis  *gums*
justing lumis  *jousting weapons (see note)*  quisland  *whistling*
lair  *learning*

Without my wisdome that micht thair wil avance.
My name is Gude Counsall, without feinyeing;
Lords for lack of my lair ar brocht to mischance.

570 Finallie, for conclusioun,
Quha halds me at delusioun
Sall be brocht to confusioun,
    And this I understand;
For I have maid my residence
575 With hie princes of greit puissance,
In Ingland, Italie and France,
    And monie uther land.
Bot out of Scotland, wa alace!
I haif bene flemit lang tyme space,
580 That garris our gyders all want grace,
    And die befoir thair day:
Becaus thay lychtlyit Gude Counsall
Fortune turnit on thame hir saill,
Quhilk brocht this realme to meikill baill—
585    Quha can the contrair say?
My Lords, I came nocht heir to lie:
Wais me for King Humanitie,
Overset with Sensualitie
    In th'entrie of his ring
590 Throw vicious counsell insolent.
Sa thay may get riches or rent
To his weilfair thay tak na tent,
    Nor quhat sal be th'ending.

Yit in this realme I wald mak sum repair,
595 Gif I beleifit my name suld nocht forfair;
For, wald this king be gydit yit with ressoun,
And on misdoars mak punitioun,
Howbeit [that] I haif lang tyme bene exyllit
I traist in God my name sall yit be styllit.

———

flemit *expelled*  gyders *kings (see note)*  lychtlyit *scorned*
baill *harm*  ring *reign*  tak na tent *pay no attention*
forfair *perish*  styllit *honoured*

[ 20

600 Sa, till I se God send mair of His grace,
       I purpois til repois me in this place.

[*Heir entiris Flattery new landit owt of France and
stormested at the May*]

FLATTERIE

Mak roume, sirs, hoaw! that I may rin!
Lo, se quhair I am new cum [in],
    Begaryit all with sindrie hewis:
605 Let be your din till I begin,
    And I sall schaw yow of my newis.
Throuchout all Christindome I have past,
And am cum heir, now at the last,
    Tostit on sea, ay sen Yuill Day,
610 That wee war faine to hew our mast
    Nocht half ane myle beyond the May.
Bot now amang yow I will remaine:
I purpois never to sail againe,
    To put my lyfe in chance of watter.
615 Was never sene sic wind and raine,
    Nor of schipmen sic clitter-clatter!
Sum bade 'Haill!', and sum bade 'Standby!',
'On steirburd, hoaw!', 'Aluiff, fy, fy!',
    Quhill all the raipis beguith to rattil.
620 Was never roy sa fleyd as I
    Quhen all the sails playd brittill-brattill.
To se the waws it was ane wonder,
And wind that raif the sails in sunder:
    Bot I lay braikand like ane brok,
625 And shot sa fast, above and under,
    The Devill durst not cum neir my dok.
Now am I scapit fra that effray;
Quhat say ye, sirs, am I nocht gay?

—————

stormested *held up by bad weather*   the May *the isle of May*
(*see note*)   begaryit *wearing multi-coloured costume* (*see note*)
aluiff *steer close to the wind*   beguith *began*   roy *king*
fleit *frightened*   waws *waves*   braikand *breaking* (*wind*)
brok *badger*   shot *evacuated*   dok *buttocks*

          Se ye not Flatterie, your awin fuill,
630   That yeid to mak this new array?
          Was I not heir with yow at Yuill?
      Yes, by my faith, I think on weill!
      Quhair ar my fallowis, that wald [ I feill ] :
          We suld have cum heir for ane cast.
      Hoaw, Falset, hoaw!
          FALSET
635                           Wa [ serve ] the Divill!
      Quha is that that cryis for me sa fast?
          FLATTERIE
      Quhy, Falset, brother, knawis thou not me?
      Am I nocht thy brother, Flattrie?
          FALSET
      Now welcome, be the Trinitie!
640       This meitting cums for gude.
      Now let me bresse the in my armis :
      Quhen freinds meits, harts warmis,
          Quod Jok, that frely fud.
      How happinit yow into this place?
          FLATTERIE
645   Now, be my saul, evin on a cace.
      I come in sleipand at the port,
      Or evir I wist, amang this sort.
      Quhair is Dissait, that limmer loun?
          FALSET
      I left him drinkand in the toun ;
650   He will be heir incontinent.
          FLATTERIE
      Now, be the haly Sacrament,
      Thay tydingis comforts all my hart :
      I wait Dissait will tak my part.
      He is richt craftie, as ye ken,
655   And counsallour to the merchand-men.
      Let us ly doun heir baith, and spy

-------

      yeid *went*   Yuill *Christmas ( see note )*   feill *know*
      cast *game of dice ( or ploy )*   bresse *embrace*
      frelie fud *hearty fellow*   port *gate*   limmer *rascally*

Gif wee persave him cummand by.

DISSAIT

Stand by the gait, that I may steir!
I say, Koks bons, how cam I heir?
660 I can not mis to tak sum feir
        Into sa greit ane thrang.
Marie, heir ane cumlie congregatioun!
Quhat, ar ye, sirs, all of ane natioun?
Maisters, I speik be protestatioun,

665        In dreid ye tak me wrang.
Ken ye not, sirs, quhat is my name?
Gude faith, I dar not schaw it for schame:
Sen I was clekit of my dame
        Yit was I never leill,
670 For Katie Unsell was my mother,
And Common Theif my foster-brother;
Of sic freindship I had ane [futher],
        Howbeit I can not steill.
Bot yit I will borrow and len,
675 Als be my cleathing ye may ken
That I am cum of nobill men,
        And als I will debait
That querrell with my feit and hands—
And I dwell amang the merchands.
680 My name, gif onie man demands,
        Thay call me Dissait.
*Bon jour*, brother, with all my hart!
Heir am I cum to tak your part,
        Baith into gude and evill.
685 I met Gude Counsall be the way,
Quha pat me in a felloun fray,
        I gif him to the Devill!

FALSET

How chaipit ye, I pray yow tell?

———

Koks bons *Christ's bones ( see note )*   clekit *snatched*
futher *plenty*   pat *put*   felloun *great*   chaipit *escaped*

DISSAIT

I slipit [ in a fowll ] bordell
690 And hid me in a bawburds bed ;
Bot suddenlie hir schankis I sched,
With 'hoch !' hurland amang hir howis :
God wait gif wee maid monie mowis !
How came ye heir, I pray yow tell me?

FALSET

695 Marie, to seik King Humanitie.

DISSAIT

Now, be the gude ladie that me bair,
That samin hors is my awin mair !
Now with our purpois let us mell :
Quhat is your counsall, I pray yow tell?
700 Sen we thrie seiks yon nobill king,
Let us devyse sum subtill thing ;
And als, I pray yow as my brother
That we ilk ane be trew to uther.
I mak ane vow with all my hart
705 In gude and evill to tak your part :
I pray to God, nor I be hangit,
Bot I sall die or ye be wrangit !

FALSET

Quhat is thy counsall that wee do?

DISSAIT

Marie, sirs, this is my counsall, lo :
710 Till tak our tyme, quhill wee may get it,
For now thair is na man to let it.
Fra tyme the king begin to steir him,
Marie, Gude Counsall I dreid cum neir him ;
And we be knawin with Correctioun,
715 It will be our confusioun.
Thairfoir, my deir brother, devyse
To find sum toy of the new gyse.

FLATTERIE

Marie, I sall finde ane thousand wyles !

———

bordell *brothel*   bawburds *harlot's*   sched *parted*
mowis *tricks*   hurland ... howis *thrusting between her thighs*
( *see note* )   mell *deal*   let *prevent*

Wee man turne our claithis, and change our stiles,
720  And disagyse us, that na man ken us.
Hes na man clarkis cleathing to len us?

And let us keip grave countenance,
As wee war new cum out of France.
    DISSAIT
Now, be my saull, that is weill devysit!
725  Ye sall se me sone disagysit.
    FALSET
And sa sall I, man, be the Rude.
Now, sum gude fallow len me ane hude!

[*Heir sall Flattry help his twa marrowis*]

    DISSAIT
Now am I buskit, and quha can spy,
The Devill stik me, gif this be I?
730  If this be I or not I can not weill say—
Or hes the Feind or farie folk borne me away?
    FALSET
And gif my hair war up in ane how,
The feind a man wald ken me, I trow.
Quhat sayis thou of my gay garmoun?
    DISSAIT
735  I say thou luiks evin like ane loun!
Now, brother Flatterie, quhat do ye?
Quhat kynde of man schaip ye to be?
    FLATTERIE
Now, be my faith, my brother deir,
I will gang counterfit the freir.
    DISSAIT
740  A freir! Quhairto? Ye can not preiche!
    FLATTERIE
Quhat rak, man? I can richt weill fleich.
Perchance Ile cum [to] that honour
To be the Kings confessour.

———

stiles *names*  buskit *disguised*  how *coif, headdress*
fleich *flatter*

Pure freirs are free at any feast,
745 And marchellit ay amang the best.
Als God [hes lent to] them sic graces
That bischops put them in thair places,
Out-throw thair dioceis to preiche.
Bot ferlie nocht, howbeit thay fleich,
750 For schaw thay all the veritie,
Thaill want the bischops charitie.
And, thocht the corne war never sa skant,
The gudewyfis will not let freirs want;
For quhy, thay ar thair confessours,
755 Thair heavinlie prudent counsalours—
Thairfoir the wyfis plainlie taks thair parts,
And shawis the secreits of thair harts

To freirs, with better will, I trow,
Nor thay do to thair bed-fallow.
DISSAIT
760 And I reft anis ane freirs coull
Betwix Sanct-Johnestoun and Kinnoull:
I sall gang fetch it, gif ye will tarie.
FLATTERIE
Now play me of that companarie!
Ye saw him nocht this hundreth yeir
765 That better can counterfeit the freir.
DISSAIT
Heir is thy gaining, all and sum:
This is ane koull of Tullilum!
FLATTERIE
Quha hes ane [porteus] for to len me?
The feind ane saull, I trow, will ken me!
FALSET
770 Now gang thy way, quhair ever thow will—
Thow may be fallow to Freir Gill!
Bot with Correctioun gif wee be kend,
I dreid wee mak ane schamefull end.

———

Sanct-Johnestoun *Perth*   companarie *fellowship*
porteus *prayer book*

FLATTERIE

For that mater I dreid nathing:
775 Freiris ar exemptit fra the King,
And freiris will reddie entries get
Quhen lords ar haldin at the yet.

FALSET

Wee man do mair yit, be Sanct James,
For wee mon all thrie change our names.
780 Hayif me, and I sall baptize thee.

DISSAIT

Be God and thair-about may it be!
How will thou call me, I pray the tell?

FALSET

I wait not how to call my-sell!

DISSAIT

Bot yit anis name the bairn[i]s name.

FALSET

785 Discretioun, Discretioun, in Gods name!

DISSAIT

I neid nocht now to cair for thrift;
Bot quhat salbe my Godbairne gift?

FALSET

I gif yow all the devilis of hell!

DISSAIT

Na, brother, hauld that to thy sell!
790 Now sit doun, let me baptize the—
I wait not quhat thy name sould be.

FALSET

Bot yit anis name the bairn[i]s name.

DISSAIT

Sapience, in ane warld[i]s schame!

FLATTERIE

Brother Dissait, cum, baptize me.

DISSAIT

795 Then sit doun lawlie on thy kne.

FLATTERIE

Now, brother, name the bairn[i]s name.

---

yet *gate*   hayif *christen*

DISSAIT

Devotioun, [in] the Devillis name!

FLATTERIE

The Devill resave the, lurdoun loun!
Thou hes wet all my new-schawin croun.

DISSAIT

800 Devotioun, Sapience and Discretioun:
Wee thre may rewll this regioun.
Wee sall find monie craftie things
For to begyll ane hundreth kings;
For thow can richt weil crak and clatter,
805 And I sall feinye, and thow sall flatter.

FLATTERIE

Bot I wald have, or wee depairtit,
Ane drink to mak us better hartit.

[*Now the King sall cum fra his chamber.*]

DISSAIT

Weill said, be Him that herryit Hell!
I was evin thinkand that my-sell.
810 Now, till wee get the Kings presence,
Wee will sit doun and keip silence.
I se ane [yonder]: quhat ever [he] be,
Ile wod my lyfe, yon same is he.
Feir nocht, brother, bot hauld yow still
815 Till wee have heard quhat is his will.

REX

Now quhair is Placebo and Solace?
Quhair is my minyeoun, Wantonnes?
Wantonnes, hoaw! cum to me sone!

WANTONNES

Quhy cryit ye, sir, till I had done?

REX

820 Quhat was ye doand, tell me that!

WANTONNES

Mary, leirand how my father me gat.
I wait nocht how it stands, but doubt:
Me think the warld rinnis round about!

———

lurdoun *stupid*   crak *gossip*   wod *wager*   leirand *learning*

[ 28

### REX
And sa think I, man, be my thrift:
825 I see fy[f]teine mones in the lift.

### WANTONNES
Lat Hamelines, my lass, allane.
Scho bendit up ay twa for ane!
#### HAMELINES
Gat ye nocht that quhilk ye desyrit?
Sir, I beleif that ye ar tyrit!
#### DANGER
830 [And] as for Placebo and Solace,
I held them baith in mirrines.
Howbeid I maid it sumthing tewch,
I fand thame chalmer-glew annewch.
#### SOLACE
Mary, thow wald gar ane hundreth tyre:
835 Thow hes ane cunt lyke ane quaw-myre!
#### DANGER
Now fowll fall yow: it is na bourdis
Befoir ane king to speik fowll wourdis.
Or evir ye cum that gait agane,
To kiss my cloff ye salbe fane!
#### SOLACE
840 Now schaw me, sir, I yow exhort,
How ar ye of your luif content?
Think ye not this ane mirrie sport?
#### REX
Yea, that I do in verament.
Quhat bairnis ar yon upon the bent?
845 I did nocht se them all this day.
#### WANTONNES
Thay will be heir incontinent:
Stand still and heir quhat thay will say.

*Now the vycis cums and maks salutatioun, saying:*

---

bendit *cocked (of a gun)*   chalmer-glew *love-making*
tewch *tough*   annewch *enough*   quaw-myre *quagmire*
cloff *crotch*   in verament *truly*   bent *field*

DISSAIT

Laud, honor, gloir, triumph and victory
Be to your maist excellent Majestie!

REX

850 Ye ar welcum, gude freinds, be the Rude:
Appeirandlie ye seime sum men of gude.
Quhat ar your names, tell me without delay?

DISSAIT

Discretioun, sir; [that] is my name, perfay.

REX

Quhat is your name, sir, with the clipit croun?

FLATTERIE

855 But dout, my name is callit Devotioun.

REX

Welcum, Devotioun, be Sanct Jame:
Now, sirray, tell quhat is your name.

FALSET

Marie, sir, thay call me—quhat call thay me?
[I wat not weill, but gif I lie!]

REX

860 Can ye nocht tell quhat is your name?

FALSET

I kend it quhen I cam fra hame!

REX

Quhat gars ye can nocht schaw it now?

FALSET

Marie, thay call me Thin Drink, I trow.

REX

Thin Drink? Quhat kynde of name is that?

DISSAIT

865 Sapiens, thou servis to beir ane plat!
Me think thou schawis the not weill-wittit.

FALSET

Sypeins, sir, sypeins! Marie, now ye hit it!

FLATTERIE

Sir, gif ye pleis to let [me] say,
His name is Sapientia.

---

bot gif *unless*  beir ane plat *receive a blow*
sypeins *lees* (*see note to 863*)

FALSET

870 That same is it, be Sanct Michell!

REX

Quhy could thou not tell it thy sell?

FALSET

I pray your Grace appardoun me,
And I sall schaw the veritie:
I am sa full of Sapience

875 That sumtyme I will tak ane trance.
My spreit wes reft fra my bodie
Now, heich abone the Trinitie.

REX

Sapience suld be ane man of gude.

FALSET

Sir, ye may ken that be my hude.

REX

880 Now have I Sapience and Discretioun,
How can I faill to rewll this regioun?
And Devotioun to be my confessour!
Thir thrie came in ane happie hour.
Heir I mak the my secretar,

885 And thou salbe my thesaurar,
And thow salbe my counsallour
In sprituall things, and confessour.

FLATTERIE

I sweir to yow, sir, be Sanct An,
Ye met never with ane wyser man;

890 For monie a craft, sir, do I can,
    War thay weill knawin;
Sir, I have na feill of flattrie,
Bot fosterit with phil[o]sophie,
Ane strange man in astronomie,

895    Quhilk salbe schawin.

FALSET

And I have greit intelligence
In quelling of the quintessence.
Bot to preif my experience,

---

reft *seized*   feill *experience*   strange *extraordinary*
quelling *extracting*   quintessence *fifth element* (*see note*)

Sir, len me fourtie crownes
900 To mak multiplicatioun;
And tak my obligatioun,
Gif wee mak fals narratioun
    Hauld us for verie lownes!
        DISSAIT
Sir, I ken be your physnomie
905 Ye sall conqueis, or els I lie,
Danskin, Denmark and Almane,
Spittelfeild and the realme of Spane;
Ye sall have at your governaunce
Ranfrow and all the realme of France,
910 Yea, Rugland and the toun of Rome,
Castorphine and al Christindome!
Quhairto, sir, be the Trinitie,
Ye ar ane verie A-per-sie.
        FLATTERIE
Sir, quhen I dwelt in Italie
915 I leirit the craft of palmistrie.
Schaw me the lufe, sir, of your hand,
And I sall gar yow understand
Gif your Grace be infortunat,
Or gif ye be predestinat.
920 I see ye will have fyfteine queenes,
And fyfteine scoir of concubeines.
The Virgin Marie saife your Grace!
Saw ever man sa quhyte ane face,
Sa greit ane arme, sa fair ane hand?
925 Thairs nocht sic ane leg in al this land!
War ye in armis, I think na wounder
Howbeit ye dang doune fyfteine hunder.
        DISSAIT
Now, be my saull, thats trew thow sayis!
Wes never man set sa weill his clais:

———

Danskin *Danzig ( see note )*   Almane *Germany*
Rugland *Rutherglen*   A-per-sie *paragon*   leirit *learned*
lufe *palm*   dang *beat*   clais *clothes*

930　Thair is na man in Christintie
　　　Sa meit to be ane king as ye.
　　　　　FALSET
　　　Sir, thank the haly Trinitie,
　　　That send us to your cumpanie ;
　　　For God, nor I gaip in ane gallows,
935　Gif ever ye fand thrie better fallows.
　　　　　REX
　　　Ye ar richt welcum, be the Rude :
　　　Ye seime to be thrie men of gude.

*Heir sall Gude Counsell schaw himself in the feild.*

　　　Bot quha is yon that stands sa still?
　　　Ga spy and speir quhat is his will,
940　And gif he yearnis my presence
　　　Bring him to mee with diligence.
　　　　　DISSAIT
　　　That sall wee do, be Gods breid :
　　　We's bring him eather quick or deid.
　　　　　REX
　　　I will sit still heir and repois :
945　Speid yow agane to me, my Jois !
　　　　　FALSET
　　　Ye, hardlie, Sir, keip yow in clois
　　　And quyet till wee cum againe.
　　　Brother, I trow, be Coks toes,
　　　Yon bairdit bogill cums fra ane traine !
　　　　　DISSAIT
950　Gif he dois sa, he salbe slaine.
　　　I doubt him nocht, nor yit ane uther :
　　　Trowit I that he come for ane traine,
　　　Of my freindis I sould rais ane futher.
　　　　　FLATTERIE
　　　I doubt full sair, be God him sell,
955　That yon auld churle be Gude Counsell.

————————

　　　bogill *goblin*　traine *trick*

Gif he anis to the Kings presence,
We thrie will get na audience.

DISSAIT

That matter I sall tak on hand,
And say it is the Kings command
960 That he anone devoyd this place
And cum nocht neir the Kings grace,
And that under the paine of tressoun.

FLATTERIE

Brother, I hauld your counsell ressoun;
Now let us heir quhat he will say.
965 Auld lyart beard, gude day, gude day!

GUDE COUNSALL

Gude day againe, sirs, be the Rude;
The Lord mot mak yow men of gude!

DISSAIT

Pray nocht for us to lord nor ladie,
For we ar men of gude alreadie.
970 Sir, schaw to us quhat is your name.

GUDE COUNSALL

Gude Counsall thay call me at hame.

FALSET

Quhat says thow, carle, ar thow Gude Counsall?
Swyith, pak the sone, unhappie unsell!

GUDE COUNSALL

I pray yow, sirs, gif me licence
975 To cum anis to the Kings presence,
To speik bot twa words to his Grace.

FLATTERIE

Swyith, hursone carle, devoyd this place!

GUDE COUNSALL

Brother, I ken yow weill aneuch,
Howbeit ye mak it never sa teuch:
980 Flattrie, Dissait and Fals Report,
That will not suffer to resort

---

devoyd *quit*   lyart *grizzled*   mot *may*   swyith *quickly*
unsell *wicked person*   carle *villain*   hursone *whoresone*

Gude Counsall to the Kings presence.

DISSAIT

Suyith, hursun carle, gang, pak the hence!
Gif ever thou cum this gait agane,
985 I vow to God thou sall be slane.

*Heir sall thay hurle away Gude Counsall.*

[ GUDE COUNSELL ]
Sen at this tyme I can get na presence,
Is na remeid bot tak in patience.
Howbeit Gude Counsall haistelie be nocht hard,
With young princes yit sould thay noch[ t ] be skard;
990 Bot quhen youthheid hes blawin his wanton blast,
Then sall Gude Counsall rewll him at the last.

*Now the Vycis gangs to ane counsall.*

FLATTERIE

Now, quhill Gude Counsall is absent,
Brother, wee mon be diligent
And mak betwix us sikker bands,
995 Quhen vacands fallis in onie lands
That everie man help weill his fallow.

DISSAIT

I had, deir brother, be Alhallow,
Sa ye fische nocht within our bounds.

FLATTERIE

That sall I nocht, be Gods wounds!
1000 Bot I sall plainlie tak your partis.

FALSET

Sa sall we thyne, with all our hartis;
Bot haist us quhill the King is young.
Let everie man keip weill ane toung
And in ilk quarter have ane spy,
1005 Us till adverteis haistelly
Quhen ony casualities
Sall happin into our countries,

---

remeid *remedy*   skard *frightened off*   sikker *secure*
casualities *casual vacancies*

And let us mak provisioun
Or he cum to discretioun.
1010 Na mair he waits now nor ane sant
Quhat thing it is to haif or want.
Or he cum till his perfyte age
We sall be sikker of our wage,
And then let everie carle craif uther.

DISSAIT

1015 That mouth speik mair, my awin deir brother!
For God, nor I rax in ane raip,
Thow may gif counsall to the Paip.

*Now thay returne to the King.*

REX

Quhat gart you bid sa lang fra my presence?
I think it lang since ye depairtit thence.
1020 Quhat man was yon, with an greit bostous beird?
Me thocht he maid yow all thrie very feard.

DISSAIT

It was ane laidlie lurdan loun,
Cumde to break buithis into this toun:
Wee have gart bind him with ane poill,
1025 And send him to the theifis hoill.

REX

Let him sit thair with ane mischance,
And let us go to our pastance.

WANTONNES

Better go revell at the rackat,
Or ellis go to the hurlie hackat,
1030 Or than to schaw our curtlie corsses,
Ga se quha best can rin thair horsses.

SOLACE

Na, Soveraine, or wee farther gang,
Gar Sensualitie sing ane sang!

---

rax *stretch*  laidlie *loathsome*  lurdan *lazy*  loun *fellow*
break buithis *break into shops (see note)*  poill *pole*
pastance *pleasure*  hurlie hackat *sledging*  curtlie *courtly*
corsses *bodies*

*Heir sall the Ladies sing ane sang, the King sall ly*
*doun amang the Ladies, and then Veritie sall enter.*

VERITIE

*Diligite Justitiam qui judicatis terram.*

1035　Luif Justice, ye quha hes ane Judges cure
　　　In earth, and dreid the awfull judgement
　　　Of Him that sall cum judge baith rich and pure,
　　　Rycht terribilly with bludy wound[i]s rent:
　　　That dreidfull day into your harts imprent,
1040　Belevand weill how and quhat maner ye
　　　Use Justice heir till uthers, thair at lenth
　　　That day but doubt sa sall ye judgit be.
　　　Wo than and duill be to yow princes all,
　　　Sufferand the pure anes for till be opprest:
1045　In everlasting burnand fyre ye sall
　　　With Lucifer richt dulfullie be drest.
　　　Thairfoir in tyme, for till eschaip that nest,
　　　Feir God, do law and justice equally
　　　Till everie man: se that na puir opprest
1050　Up to the hevin on yow ane vengence cry.
　　　Be just judges, without favour or fead,
　　　And hauld the ballance evin till everie wicht;
　　　Let not the fault be left into the head,
　　　Then sall the members reulit be at richt.
1055　For quhy, subjects do follow day and nicht
　　　Thair governours in vertew and in vyce:
　　　Ye ar the lamps that sould schaw them the licht
　　　[To] leid them on this sliddrie rone of yce.
　　　*Mobile mutatur semper cum principe vulgus;*
1060　And gif ye wald your subjectis war weill gevin,
　　　Then verteouslie begin the dance your sell,
　　　Going befoir; then they anone, I wein,
　　　Sall follow yow, eyther till hevin or hell.

———

Diligite … terram *'Set your affeccion upon wysdom, ye that be*
*judges of the earth' (Wisdom 1:1; see note)*　fead *enmity*
wicht *person*　sliddrie *slippery*　rone *patch of ice*　cuir *care*
Mobile … vulgus *'The fickle crowd always changes with the prince*
*(see note)*　gevin *maintained*　wein *believe*

Kings sould of gude exempils be the well;
1065 Bot gif that your strands be intoxicate,
In steid of wyne thay drink the poyson fell:
Thus pepill follows ay thair principate.
*Sic luceat lux vestra coram hominibus ut videant opera vestra bona.*
And specially ye princes of the preists,
1070 That of the peopill hes spiritual cuir,
Dayly ye sould revolve into your breistis
How that thir haly words ar still maist sure:
In verteous lyfe gif that ye do indure,
The pepill wil tak mair tent to your deids
1075 Then to your words; and als baith rich and puir
Will follow yow baith in your warks and words.

*Heir sall Flattrie spy Veritie with ane dum countenance.*

Gif men of me wald have intelligence
Or knaw my name, thay call me Veritie.
Of Christis law I have experience,
1080 And hes oversaillit many stormie sey.
Now am I seikand King Humanitie,
For of his grace I have gude esperance:
Fra tyme that he acquaintit be with mee,
His honour and heich gloir I sall avance.

*Heir sall Veritie pas to hir sait.*

DISSAIT
1085 Gude day, father, quhair have ye bene?
Declair till us of your novels.
FLATTERIE
Thair is now lichtit on the grene
Dame Veritie, be buiks and bels!
Bot cum scho to the Kings presence,

---

Sic luceat … bona *'Let your lyght so shyne before men that they maye see your good woorckes'* (*Matthew 5:16*)   cuir   *care*
novels   *news*   be buiks and bels   *i.e. those used in the Mass*
(*see note*)

[ 38

1090     Thair is na buit for us to byde :
    Thairfoir I red us all go hence.

      FALSET

    That will we nocht yit, be Sanct Bride ;
    Bot wee sall ather gang or ryde
    To Lords of Spritualitie
1095     And gar them trow yon bag of pryde
    Hes spokin manifest heresie.

*Heir thay cum to the Spritualitie.*

      FLATTERIE

    O reverent fatheris of the Sprituall stait,
    Wee counsall yow be wyse and vigilant :
    Dame Veritie hes lychtit now of lait,
1100     And in hir hand beirand the New Testament.
    Be scho ressavit, but doubt wee ar bot schent :
    Let hir nocht ludge thairfoir into this land,
    And this wee reid yow do incontinent,
    Now, quhill the King is with his luif sleipand.

      SPIRITUALITIE

1105     Wee thank yow, freinds, of your benevolence :
    It sall be done evin as ye have devysit.
    Wee think ye serve ane gudlie recompence
    Defendand us, that wee be nocht supprysit.
    In this mater wee man be weill advysit,
1110     Now, quhill the King misknawis the veritie ;
    Be scho ressavit, then wee will be deprysit.
    Quhat is your counsell, brother, now let se ?

      ABBOT

    I hauld it best that wee incontinent
    Gar hauld hir fast into captivitie
1115     Unto the thrid day of the Parlament,
    And then accuse hir of hir herisie
    Or than banische hir out of this cuntrie ;
    For with the King gif Veritie be knawin
    Of our greit gloir wee will degradit be,

---

buit *remedy*   red *advise*   lychtit *arrived*   supprysit *oppressed*
deprysit *deprived*   thrid *third*

1120 And all our secreits to the commons schawin.

PERSONE

Ye se the King is yit effeminate
And gydit be Dame Sensualitie,
Rycht sa with young counsall intoxicate:
Swa at this tyme ye haif your libertie.

1125 To tak your tyme I hauld it best for me,
And go distroy all thir Lutherians,
In speciall yon Ladie Veritie.

SPIRITUALITIE

Schir Persone, ye sall be my commissair
To put this mater till executioun;

1130 And ye, Sir Freir, becaus ye can declair
The haill processe, pas with him in commissioun.
Pas all togidder with my braid bennisoun,
And gif scho speiks against our libertie
Then put hir in perpetuall presoun,

1135 That scho cum nocht to King Humanitie.

*Heir sall thay pass to Verity.*

PERSONE

Lustie Ladie, we wald faine understand
Quhat earand ye haif in this regioun:
To preich or teich quha gaif to yow command,
To counsall kingis how gat ye commissioun?

1140 I dreid without ye get ane remissioun
And syne renunce your new opiniones,
The sprituall stait sall put yow to perditioun,
And in the fyre will burne yow, flesche and bones.

VERITIE

I will recant nathing that I have schawin:

1145 I have said nathing bot the veritie.
Bot with the King, fra tyme that I be knawin,
I dreid ye spaiks of Spritualitie
Sall rew that ever I came in this cuntrie;
For gif the veritie plainlie war proclamit,

---

effeminate *addicted to women*   bennisoun *blessing*
remissioun *release from punishment* ( *see note* )
spaiks *spokes* ( *?or stakes* )

1150 And speciallie to the Kings Majestie,
For your traditions ye wilbe all defamit.
FLATTERIE
Quhat buik is that, harlot, into thy hand?
Out, walloway, this is the New Testament,
In Englisch toung, and prentit in England!
1155 Herisie, herisie! Fire, fire incontinent!
VERITIE
Forsuith, my freind, ye have ane wrang judgement,
For in this buik thair is na heresie,
Bot our Christs word, baith dulce and redolent,
Ane springing well of sinceir veritie.
DISSAIT
1160 Cum on your way, for all your yealow locks!
Your wanton words, but doubt, ye sall repent.
This nicht ye sall forfair ane pair of stocks,
And syne the morne be brocht to thoill judgment.
VERITIE
For our Christs saik, I am richt weill content
1165 To suffer all thing that sall pleis His grace;
Howbeit ye put ane thousand to torment,
Ten hundreth thowsand sall rise into thair place.

*Veritie sits doun on hir knies and sayis:*

Get up, thow sleipis all too lang, O Lord,
And mak sum ressonabill reformatioun
1170 On them that dois tramp doun Thy gracious word
And hes ane deidlie indignatioun
At them quha maks maist trew narratioun.
Suffer me not, Lord, mair to be molest,
Gude Lord, I mak The supplicatioun;
1175 With Thy unfreinds let me nocht be supprest.
Now, Lords, do as ye list:
I have na mair to say.
FLATTERIE
Sit doun and tak yow rest

———

forfair *endure*   thoill *suffer*

All nicht till it be day!

*Thay put Veritie in the stocks and returne to Spritualite.*

DISSAIT

1180 My Lord, wee have with diligence
Bucklit up weill yon bledrand baird.

SPRITUALITIE

I think ye serve gude recompence:
Tak thir ten crowns for your rewaird.

VERITIE

The prophesie of the Prophet Esay
1185 Is practickit, alace, on mee this day,
Quha said the veritie sould be trampit doun
Amid the streit, and put in strang presoun:
His fyve and fyftie chapter, quha list luik,
Sall find thir word[i]s writtin in his Buik.
1190 Richt sa Sanct Paull wrytis to Timothie
That men sall turne their earis from veritie.
Bot in my Lord God I have esperance;
He will provide for my deliverance.
Bot ye princes of Spritualitie,
1195 Quha sould defend the sinceir veritie,

I dreid the plagues of Johnes Revelatioun
Sal fal upon your generatioun:
I counsall yow this misse t'amend,
Sa that ye may eschaip that fatall end.

[*Heir sall entir Chaistetie and say*:]

CHASTITIE

1200 How lang sall this inconstant warld indure,
That I sould baneist be sa lang, alace?
Few creatures or nane takis on me cure,

———

bucklit *fastened*    bledrand baird *raving bard*
Esay *Isaiah* (*the reference is to Isaiah 59:14; see note*)
list *chooses to*    Timothie *i.e. 2 Timothy 4:4* (*see note*)
misse *offence*

Quhilk gars me monie nicht ly harbrieles.
Thocht I have past all yeir fra place to place,
1205 Amang the Temporal and Spirituall staits
Nor amang princes I can get na grace,
Bot boustuouslie am halden at the yetis.
DILIGENCE
Ladie, I pray yow, schaw [ to ] me your name:
It dois me noy, your lamentatioun.
CHASTITIE
1210 My freind, thairof I neid not [ think na ] schame:
Dame Chastitie, baneist from town to town.
DILIGENCE
Then pas to ladies of religioun,
[ Quha ] maks thair vow to observe Chastitie.
Lo, quhair thair sits ane priores of renown
1215 Amangs the rest of Spritualitie.
CHASTITIE
I grant yon ladie hes vowit chastitie,
For hir professioun thairto sould accord:
Scho maid that vow for ane abesie,
Bot nocht for Christ Jesus, our Lord.
1220 Fra tyme that thay get thair vows, I stand for'd,
Thay banische hir out of thair cumpanie:
With Chastitie thay can mak na concord,
Bot leids thair lyfis in sensualitie.
I sall observe your counsall gif I may:
1225 Cum on, and heir quhat yon ladie will say.

*Chastitie passis to the Ladie Priores and sayis*:

My prudent lustie Ladie Priores,
Remember how ye did vow chastitie:
Madame, I pray yow of your gentilnes
That ye wald pleis to haif of me pitie,
1230 And this ane nicht to gif me harberie:
For this I mak yow supplicatioun.

———

harbrieles *without shelter*    boustuouslie *roughly*    noy *annoy*
abesie abbey

Do ye nocht sa, Madame, I dreid, perdie,
It will be caus of depravatioun.

PRIORES

Pas hynd, Madame, be Christ, ye cum nocht heir!
1235 Ye ar contrair to my cumplexioun:
Gang seik ludging at sum auld monk or freir,
Perchance thay will be your protectioun.
Or to prelats mak your progressioun,
Quhilks ar obleist to yow als weill as I:
1240 Dame Sensuall hes gevin directioun
Yow till exclude out of my cumpany.

CHASTITIE

Gif ye wald wit mair of the veritie,
I sall schaw yow be sure experience
How that the lords of Sprituality
1245 Hes baneist me, alace, fra thair presence.

*Chastitie passes to the Lords of Spritualitie.*

My Lords, laud, gloir, triumph and reverence
Mot be unto your halie Sprituall stait!
I yow beseik of your benevolence
To harbry mee that am sa desolait.
1250 Lords, I have past throw mony uncouth schyre,
Bot in this land I can get na ludgeing.
Of my name gif ye wald haif knawledging,
Forsuith, my Lords, thay call me Chastitie.
I yow beseik, of your graces bening,
1255 Gif me ludging this nicht, for charitie.

SPRITUALITIE

Pas on, Madame, we knaw yow nocht;
Or be Him that the warld [hes] wrocht,
Your cumming sall be richt deir coft
Gif ye mak langer tarie.

———

perdie *by God*  depravatioun *deprivation (see note)*
hynd *hence*  wit *know*  uncouth *strange*  bening *gentle*
coft *bought*

[ 44

1260 But doubt wee will baith leif and die
　　　With our luif Sensualitie :
　　Wee will haif na mair deall with the
　　　Then with the Queene of Farie.

　　Pas hame amang the nunnis and dwell,
1265 　　Quhilks ar of chastitie the well ;
　　I traist thay will with buik and bell
　　　Ressave yow in thair closter.

　　Sir, quhen I was the nunnis amang
　　Out of thair dortour thay mee dang,
1270 And wald nocht let me bide sa lang
　　　To say my *Pater noster*.

　　I se na grace thairfoir to get :
　　I hauld it best, or it be lait,
　　For till go prove the Temporall stait,
1275 　　Gif thay will mee resaif.

　　Gud day, my Lord Temporalitie,
　　And yow, merchant of gravitie ;
　　Ful faine wald I have harberie,
　　　To ludge amang the laif.

1280 Forsuith, wee wald be weil content
　　To harbrie yow with gude intent,
　　War nocht we haif impediment :
　　　For quhy, we twa ar maryit.

　　Bot wist our wyfis that ye war heir,
1285 Thay wald mak all this town on steir :
　　Thairfoir we reid yow rin areir,
　　　In dreid ye be miscaryit.

　　Ye men of craft, of greit ingyne,
　　Gif me harbrie, for Christis pyne ;
1290 And win Gods bennesone and myne,

————

dortour *dormitory*　dang *drove*　on steir *astir*
rin areir *retreat*　miscaryit *harmed*　ingyne *skill, intelligence*
pyne *pain*

And help my hungrie hart!
SOWTAR
Welcum, be Him that maid the mone,
Till dwell with us till it be June:
We sall mend baith your hois and schone,
1295     And plainlie tak your part.
TAYLOUR
Is this fair Ladie Chastitie?
Now welcum, be the Trinitie:
I think it war ane great pitie
    That thou sould ly thairout.
1300 Your great displeasour I forthink:
Sit doun, Madame, and tak ane drink,
And let na sorrow in yow sink,
    Bot let us play cap out!
SOWTAR
Fill in and [drink about],
1305    For I am wonder dry:
The Devill snyp aff thair snout
    That haits this cumpany!

[*Heir sall thay gar Chestety sit down and drink.*]

JENNIE
Hoaw, Mynnie! Mynnie, Mynnie!
TAYLOURS WYFE
Quhat wald thow, my deir dochter Jennie?
1310 Jennie, my joy, quhair is thy dadie?
JENNIE
Mary, drinkand with ane lustie ladie,
Ane fair young mayden, cled in quhyte,
Of quhom my dadie taks delyte.
Scho hes the fairest forme of face,
1315 Furnischit with all kynd of grace:
I traist gif I can can reckon richt,
Sho schaips to ludge with him all nicht.
SOWTARS WYFE
Quhat dois the Sowtar, my gudman?

——————

forthink *regret*   Mynnie *Mummy*   schaips *intends*

JENNIE

Mary, fillis the cap and [tumes] the can :
1320 Or he cum hame, be God, I trow
He will be drunkin lyke ane sow.

TAYLOURS WYFE

This is ane greit dispyte, I think,
For to resave sic ane kow-clink.
Quhat is your counsell that wee do?

SOWTARS WYFE

1325 Cummer, this is my counsall, lo :
Ding ye the tane, and I the uther.

TAYLOURS WYFE

I am content, be God[i]s mother !
I think for me, thay huirsone smaiks
Thay serve richt weill to get thair paiks.
1330 Quhat maister feind neids all this haist,
For it is half ane yeir almaist
Sen ever that loun laborde my ledder.

SOWTARS WYFE

God, nor my trewker mence ane [tedder],
For it is mair nor fourtie dayis
1335 Sen ever he cleikit up my clayis,
And last quhen I gat chalmer-glew,
That foull Sowter began till spew.
And now thay will sit doun and drink
In company with ane kow-clink !
1340 Gif thay haif done us this dispyte,
Let us go ding them till thay dryte.

*Heir the wifis sall chase away Chastitie.*

TAYLOURS WYFE

Go hence, harlot ! How durst thow be sa bauld
To ludge with our gudemen but our licence?
I mak ane vow to Him that Judas sauld,

---

tumes *empties*   kow-clink *whore*   smaiks *wretched fellows*
get thair paiks *receive a thrashing*   loun *rogue*
laborde my ledder *made sexual advances to me*   trewker *deceiver*
mence ane tedder *adorned a gallows-rope*   clayis *clothes*
chalmer-glew *sexual intercourse*   dryte *defecate*

1345 This rock of myne sall be thy recompence.
Schaw me thy name, dudron, with diligence.

CHASTITIE

Marie, Chastitie is my name, be Sanct Blais.

TAYLOURS WYFE

I pray God nor He work on the vengence,
For I luifit never chastitie all my dayes!

SOWTARS WYFE

1350 Bot my gudeman, the treuth I sall the tell,
Gars mee keip chastitie, sair agains my will;
Becaus that monstour hes maid sic ane mint,
With my bedstaf that dastard beirs ane dint.
And als I vow, cum thow this gait againe,
1355 Thy buttoks salbe beltit, be Sanct Blaine!

*Heir sall thay speik to thair gudemen, and ding them.*

TAYLOURS WYFE

Fals hursoun carle, but dout thou sall forthink
That evar thow eat or drink with yon kow-clink!

SOWTARS WYFE

I mak ane vow to Sanct Crispine,
Ise be revengit on that graceles grume,
1360 And to begin the play, tak thair ane [platt]!

SOWTAR

The feind ressave the hands that gaif mee that!

SOWTARS WYFE

Quhat now, huirsun, begins thow for till ban?
Tak thair ane uther upon thy peild harne-pan!
Quhat now, cummer, will thow nocht tak my part?

TAYLOURS WYFE

1365 That sal I do, cummer, with all my hart!

*Heir sall thay ding thair gudemen with silence.*

TAYLOUR

Alace, gossop, alace! how stands with yow?

---

rock *distaff*  dudron *slut*  mint *attempt*  bedstaf *see note*
dastard *coward*  beirs ane dint *shall suffer a blow*
grume *fellow*  platt *blow*  peild harne-pan *bald skull*

[ 48

Yon cankart carling, alace, hes brokin my brow.
Now weils yow, preists, now weils yow all your lifes,
That ar nocht weddit with sic wickit wyfes!

SOWTAR

1370 Bischops ar blist, howbeit that thay be waryit,
For thay may fuck thair fill and be unmaryit!
Gossop alace, that blak band we may wary
That ordanit sic puir men as us to mary.
Quhat may be done bot tak in patience,

1375 And on all wyfis [to] cry ane loud vengeance?

*Heir sall the wyfis stand be the watter syde and say:*

SOWTARS WYFE
Sen of our cairls we have the victorie,
Quhat is your counsell, cummer, that be done?
TAYLOURS WYFE
Send for gude wine and hald our selfis merie:
I hauld this ay best, cummer, be Sanct Clone!
SOWTARS WYFE

1380 Cummer, will ye draw aff my hois and schone;
To fill the quart I sall rin to the toun.
TAYLOURS WYFE
That sal I do, be Him that made the mone,
With all my hart: thairfoir, cummer, sit doun.
Kilt up your claithis abone your waist,

1385 And speid yow hame againe in haist,
And I sall provyde for ane paist,
    Our corsses to comfort.
SOWTARS WYFE
Then help me for to kilt my clais.
Quhat gif the padoks nip my tais?

1390 I dreid to droun heir, be Sanct Blais,
    Without I get support.

———

cankart carling *ill-tempered witch*   weils *prosper*
howbeit *despite the fact*   waryit *cursed*   cairls *husbands*
paist *pastry*   padoks *toads*

[ 49

*Sho lifts up hir clais above hir waist and enters in the water.*

Cummer, I will nocht droun my-sell:
Go east about the nether mill.
    TAYLOURS WYFE
I am content, be Bryd[i]s bell,
1395   To gang with yow quhair ever ye will.

*Heir sall thay depairt and pas to the palyeoun.*

    DILIGENCE (to Chastitie)
Madame, quhat gars yow gang sa lait?
Tell me how ye have done debait
With the Temporall and Spirituall stait?
    Quha did yow maist kyndnes?
    CHASTITIE
1400  In faith, I fand bot ill and war:
Thay gart mee stand fra thame askar,
Evin lyk ane begger at the bar,
    And fleimit mair and lesse.
    DILIGENCE
I counsall yow, but tarying
1405  Gang tell Humanitie the King.
Perchance hee, of his grace bening,
    Will mak to yow support.
    CHASTITIE
Of your counsell I am content
To pas to him incontinent,
1410  And my service till him present,
    In hope of some comfort.

*Heir sall thay pas to the King.*

    DILIGENCE
Hoaw! Solace, gentil Solace, declair unto the King
How thair is heir ane ladie, fair of face,

———

the water *i.e. the stream which clearly bounded the playing-area*
(*see note*) palyeoun *pavilion* war *worse* askar *apart*
fleimit *driven away*

That in this cuntrie can get na ludging,
1415 Bot pitifullie flemit from place to place
Without the King, of his speciall grace,
As ane servand hir in his court resaif.
Brother Solace, tell the King all the cace,
That scho may be resavit amang the laif.

SOLACE

1420 Soverane, get up and se ane hevinlie sicht,
Ane fair ladie in quhyt abuilyement:
Scho may be peir unto ane king or knicht,
Most lyk ane angell, be my judg[e]ment.

REX

I sall gang se that sicht, incontinent.
1425 Madame, behauld gif ye have knawledging
Of yon ladie, or quhat is hir intent:
Thairefter wee sall turne but tarying.

SENSUALITIE

Sir, let me se quhat yon mater may meine,
Perchance that I may knaw hir be hir face.
1430 Bot doubt this is Dame Chastitie, I weine!
Sir, I and scho cannot byde in ane place:
But gif it be the pleasour of Your Grace
That I remaine into your company,
[Than] this woman richt haistelie gar chase,
1435 That scho na mair be sene in this cuntry.

REX

As evir ye pleis, sweit hart, sa sall it be.
Dispone hir as ye think expedient,
Evin as ye list, to let hir live or die:
I will refer that thing to your judgement.

SENSUALITIE

1440 I will that scho be flemit incontinent,
And never to cum againe in this cuntrie;
And gif scho dois, but doubt scho sall repent,
As als perchance a duilfull deid sall die.
Pas on, Sir Sapience and Discretioun,
1445 And banische hir out of the Kings presence.

---

abuilyement *clothing*   dispone *arrange, deal with*

That sall we do, Madame, be God[i]s passioun:
We sall do your command with diligence
And at your hand serve gudely recompence.
Dame Chastitie, cum on, be not agast:
1450 We sall rycht sone upon your awin expence
Into the stocks your bony fute mak fast!

*Heir sall thay harll Chastitie to the stoks and scho sall say:*

[ CHASTITIE ]
I pray yow, sirs, be patient,
For I sall be obedient
   Till do quhat ye command,
1455 Sen I se thair is na remeid,
Howbeit it war to suffer deid,
   Or flemit furth of the land.
I wyte the Empreour Constantine
That I am put to sic ruine
1460    And baneist from the Kirk,
For sen he maid the Paip ane king
In Rome I could get na ludging,
   Bot heidlangs in the mirk.
Bot Ladie Sensualitie
1465 Sensyne hes gydit this cuntrie,
   And monie of the rest;
And now scho reulis all this land,
And hes decryit at hir command
   That I suld be supprest.
1470 Bot all comes for the best
Til him that lovis the Lord:
Thocht I be now molest,
I traist to be restorde.

*Heir sall thay put hir in the stocks.*

Sister, alace, this is ane cairful cace,
1475 That we with princes sould be sa abhorde.

----

harll *drag*   remeid *remedy*   wyte *blame*

Be blyth, sister, I trust within schort space
That we sall be richt honorablie restorde,
And with the King we sall be at concorde,
For [I] heir tell Divyne Correctioun
1480 Is new landit, thankit be Christ our Lord:
I wait Hee will be our protectioun.

*Heir sall enter Corrections Varlet.*

VARLET

Sirs, stand abak and hauld yow coy!
I am the King Correctiouns boy
 Cum heir to dres his place.
1485 Se that ye mak obedience
Untill his nobill excellence
 Fra tyme ye se his face,
For he maks reformatiouns
Out-throw all Christin natiouns
1490  Quhair he finds great debaits;
And sa far as I understand,
He sall reforme into this land
 Evin all the Thrie Estaits.
God furth of Heavin hes him send
1495 To punische all that dois offend
 Against His majestie,
As lyks him best to tak vengence,
Sumtyme with sword and pestilence,
 With derth and povertie.
1500 Bot quhen thee peopill dois repent,
And beis to God obedient,
 Then will he gif them grace:
Bot thay that will nocht be correctit
Richt sudanlie will be dejectit,
1505  And fleimit from his face.
Sirs, thocht we speik in generall,
Let na man into speciall
 Tak our words at the warst:
Quhat ever wee do, quhat ever wee say,

---

dres *prepare* derth *famine* dejectit *cast down*

1510 I pray yow tak it all in play,
    And judg ay to the best.
For silence I protest,
    Baith of lord, laird and [leddy]:
Now will I rin but rest
1515     And tell that all is ready.

DISSAIT

Brother, heir ye yon proclamatioun?
I dreid full sair of reformatioun;
    Yon message maks me mangit.
Quhat is your counsell, to me tell?
1520 Remaine wee heir, be God Him-sell,
    Wee will be all thre hangit.

FLATTERIE

Ile gang to Spiritualitie,
And preich out-throw his dyosie,
    Quhair I will be unknawin;
1525 Or keip me closse into sum closter,
With mony piteous *Pater noster*,
    Till all thir blasts be blawin.

DISSAIT

Ile be weill treitit, as ye ken,
With my maisters, the merchand-men,
1530     Quhilk can mak small debait:
Ye ken richt few of them that thryfes,
Or can begyll the landwart wyfes,
    But me, thair man Dissait.
Now, Falset, quhat sall be thy schift?

FALSET

1535 Na, cuir thow nocht, man, for my thrift.
    Trows thou that I be daft?
Na, I will leif ane lustie lyfe
Withoutin ony sturt and stryfe,
    Amang the men of craft.

FLATTERIE

1540 I na mair will remaine besyd yow,

---

mangit *confused*   dyosie *diocese*   landwart *rustic*
schift *device*

Bot counsell yow rycht weill to gyde yow:
  Byde nocht on Correctioun.
Fair-weil, I will na langer tarie;
I pray the alrich Queene of Farie
1545    To be your protectioun.
  DISSAIT
Falset, I wald wee maid ane band,
Now, quhill the King is yit sleipand:
  Quhat rak to steill his box?
  FALSET
Now, weill said, be the Sacrament!
1550  I sall it steill incontinent,
  Thocht it had twentie lox.

*Heir sall Falset steill the Kings box with silence.*

Lo, heir the box: now let us ga;
This may suffice for our reward[s].
  DISSAIT
Yea, that it may, man, be this day:
1555  It may weill mak [us] landwart lairds.
Now let us cast away our clais,
In dreid sum follow on the chase.
  FALSET
Rycht weill devysit, man, be Sanct Blais!
Wald God wee war out of this place!

[*Heir sall thay cast away thair conterfit clais.*]

  DISSAIT
1560  Now, sen thair is na man to wrang us,
  I pray yow, brother, with my hart,
Let us ga part this pelf amang us:
  Syne haistely we sall depart.
  FALSET
Trows thou to get als mekill as I?
1565  That sall thou nocht! I staw the box:

———

thrift *success*   alrich *elfin*   pelf *money*   staw *stole*

Thou did nathing bot luikit by,
　Ay lurkand lyke ane wylie fox.
　DISSAIT
Thy heid sall beir ane cuppill of knox,
　Pellour, without I get my part.
1570　Swyith, huirsun smaik, ryfe up the lox,
　Or I sall stick the throuch the hart!

*Heir sall thay fecht with silence.*

[FALSET]
Alace for ever! My eye is out!
　Walloway, will na man red the men?
　DISSAIT
Upon thy craig tak thair ane clout!
1575　To be courtesse I sall the ken.

Fair-weill, for I am at the flicht;
　I will nocht byde on [na] demands.
And wee twa meit againe this nicht,
　Thy feit salbe [wirth] fourtie hands!

*Heir sall Dissait rin away with the box throuch the water.*

　DIVYNE CORRECTIOUN
1580　*Beati qui esuriunt et sitiunt Justitiam.*
Thir ar the words of the redoutit Roy,
The Prince of Peace, above all King[i]s King,
Quhilk hes me sent all cuntries to convoye,
And all misdoars dourlie to doun thring.
1585　I will do nocht without the conveining
Ane Parleament of the Estait[i]s all:
In thair presence I sall, but feinyeing,
Iniquitie under my sword doun thrall.

----

pellour *thief*　swyith *get away*　red *separate*　craig *neck*
ken *teach*　Beati … Justitiam *'Blessed are they whiche honger
and thruste [thirst] for righteousnes'* (Matthew 5:6)
convoye *lead*　dourlie *fiercely*　thring *thrust*
conveining *gathering*

Thair may no prince do act[i]s honorabill
Bot gif his Counsall thairto will assist:
How may he knaw the thing maist profitabil,
To follow vertew and vycis to resist,
Without he be instructit and solist?
And quhen the King stands at his Counsell sound,
Then welth sall wax and plentie, as he list,
And policie sall in his realme abound.
Gif ony list my name for till inquyre,
I am callit Divine Correc[t]ioun:
I fled throch mony uncouth land and schyre,
To the greit profit of ilk natioun.
Now am I cum into this regioun
To teill the ground that hes bene lang unsawin,
To punische tyrants for thair transgressioun,
And to caus leill men live upon thair awin.
Na realme nor land but my support may stand,
For I gar kings live into royaltie:
To rich and puir I beir ane equall band,
That thay may live into thair awin degrie.
Quhair I am nocht is no tranqu[i]llitie.
Be me tratours and tyrants ar put doun,
Quha thinks na schame of thair iniquitie
Till thay be punisched be mee, Correctioun.
Quhat is ane king? Nocht bot ane officiar,
To caus his leiges live in equitie,
And under God to be ane punischer
Of trespassours against his Majestie:
Bot quhen the king dois live in tyrannie,
Breakand justice for feare or affectioun,
Then is his realme in weir and povertie,
With schamefull slauchter but correctioun.
I am ane judge, richt potent and seveir,
Cum to do justice mony thowsand myle.
I am sa constant baith in peice and weir

---

solist *urged*  wax *grow*  policie *good government*
teill *till, cultivate*  band *covenant*  leiges *subjects*
potent *powerful*

Na bud nor favour may my sicht oversyle :
1625 Thair is, thairfoir, richt monie in this ile
Of my repair but doubt that dois repent,
Bot verteous men, I traist, sall on me smyle,
And of my cumming be richt weill content.

GUDE COUNSALL

Welcum, my Lord, welcum ten thousand tyms,
1630 Till all faithfull men of this regioun ;
Welcum for till correct all falts and cryms
Amang this cankerd congregatioun.
Louse Chastitie, I mak [ yow ] supplicatioun ;
Put till fredome fair Ladie Veritie ;
1635 Quha be unfaithfull folk of this natioun
Lyis bund full fast into captivitie.

CORRECTIOUN

I mervel, Gude Counsell, how that may be :
Ar ye nocht with the King familiar ?

GUDE COUNSALL

That am I nocht, my Lord, full wa is me,
1640 Bot lyke ane begger am halden at the bar ;
Thay play bo-keik evein as I war ane skar.
Thair came thrie knaves in cleithing counterfeit
And fra the King thay gart me stand afar,
Quhais names war Flattrie, Falset and Dissait ;
1645 Bot quhen thay knaves hard tell of your cumming,
Thay staw away, ilk ane ane sindrie gait,
And cuist fra them thair counterfit cleithing.
For thair leving full weill thay can debait :
The merchandmen, thay haif [ resset ] Dissait ;
1650 As for Falset, my Lord, full weill I ken
He will be richt weill treitit, air and lait,
Amang the maist part of the craft[ i ]smen.
Flattrie hes taine the habite of ane freir,
Thinkand to begyll Spiritualitie.

---

bud *bribe*   oversyle *seal up, blind*   louse *free*   skar *scarecrow*
cuist *cast*   resset *harboured ( see note )*   air and lait *early and late*
taine *taken*

#### CORRECTIOUN

1655 But dout, my freind, and I live half ane yeir,
I sall search out that great iniquitie.
Quhair lyis yon ladyes in captivitie?
How now, sisters? Quha hes yow sa disgysit?

#### VERITIE

Unfaithfull members of iniquitie
1660 Dispytfullie, my Lord, hes us supprysit.

#### CORRECTIOUN

Gang put yon ladyis to thair libertie
Incontinent, and break doun all the stocks!
But doubt thay ar full deir welcum to mee.
Mak diligence, me think ye do bot mocks;
1665 Speid hand, and spair nocht for to break the locks,
And tenderlie tak them up be the hand.
Had I them heir, thay knaves suld ken my knocks
That them opprest and baneist aff the land!

*Thay tak the ladyis furth of the stocks, and Veritie sall say:*

#### VERITIE

Wee thank you, Sir, of your benignitie,
1670 Bot I beseik your Majestie royall
That ye wald pas to King Humanitie
And fleime from him yon Ladie Sensuall,
And enter in his service Gude Counsell,
For ye will find him verie counsalabill.

#### CORRECTIOUN

1675 Cum on, sisters, as ye haif said, I sall,
And gar him stand with yow thrie, firme and stabill.

*Correctioun passis towards the King, with Veritie, Chastitie and Gude Counsell.*

#### WANTONNES

Solace, knawis thou not quhat I se?
Ane knicht or ellis ane king, thinks me,
With wantoun wings as he wald fle:
1680     Brother, quhat may this meine?
I understand nocht, be this day,

Quhidder he be freind or fay!
Stand still, and heare quhat he will say:
   Sic ane I haif nocht seine.

SOLACE

1685 Yon is ane stranger, I stand forde;
He semes to be ane lustie lord.
Be his heir-cumming for concorde
   And be kinde till our king,
He sall be welcome to this place
1690 And treatit with the Kingis grace;
Be it nocht sa, we sall him chace
   And to the Divell him ding.

PLACEBO

I reid us put upon the King
And walkin him of his sleiping.
1695 Sir, rise and se ane uncouth thing!
   Get up, ye ly too lang!

SENSUALITIE

Put on your hude, John Fule; ye raif!
How dar ye be so pert, Sir Knaif,
To tuich the King? Sa Christ me saif,
1700    Fals huirsone, thow sall hang!

CORRECTIOUN

Get up, Sir King! Ye haif sleipit aneuch
Into the armis of Ladie Sensual.
Be suir that mair belangis to the pleuch,
As efterward, perchance, rehears I sall.
1705 Remember how the King Sardanapall
Amang fair ladyes tuke his lust sa lang,
Sa that the maist part of his leiges al
Rebeld, and syne him duilfully doun thrang.

Remember how, into the tyme of Noy,
1710 For the foull stinck and sin of lechery
God be my wande did al the warld destroy:
Sodome and Gomore richt sa full rigorously
For that vyld sin war brunt maist cruelly.

---

fay *foe*   reid *counsel*   brunt *burned*

Thairfoir, I the command incontinent,
1715 Banische from the that huir Sensualitie,
Or els but doubt rudlie thow sall repent.

REX

Be quhom have ye sa greit authoritie?
Quha dois presume for til correct ane king?
Knaw ye nocht me, greit King Humanitie,
1720 That in my regioun royally dois ring?

CORRECTIOUN

I have power greit princes to doun thring,
That lives contrair the Majestie Divyne,
Against the treuth quhilk plainlie dois maling :
Repent they nocht, I put them to ruyne.

1725 I will begin at thee, quhilk is the head,
And mak on the first reformatioun :
Thy leiges than will follow the but pleid.
Swyith, harlot, hence without dilatioun !

SENSUALITIE

My Lord, I mak yow supplicatioun,
1730 Gif me licence to pas againe to Rome :
Amang the princes of that natioun
I lat yow wit my fresche beautie will blume.
Adew, Sir King, I may na langer tary !
I cair nocht that ; als gude luife cums as gais.
1735 I recommend yow to the Queene of Farie ;
I se ye will be gydit with my fais.
As for this king, I cure him nocht twa strais :
War I amang bischops and cardinals
I wald get gould, silver and precious clais.
1740 Na earthlie joy but my presence avails.

*Heir sall scho pas to Spiritualitie.*

My Lord[i]s of the Sprituall stait,
Venus preserve yow air and lait,

---

maling *malign*   but pleid *without argument*   dilatioun *delay*
clais *clothes*

For I can mak na mair debait :
    I am partit with your king,
1745 And am baneischt this regioun
Be counsell of Correctioun.
Be ye nocht my protectioun,
    I may seik my ludgeing.
    SPIRITUALITIE
Welcum, our dayis darling,
1750     Welcum with all our hart !
    Wee all, but feinyeing,
    Sall plainly tak your part.

*Heir sal the Bischops, Abbots and Persons kis the Ladies.*

    CORRECTIOUN
Sen ye ar quyte of Sensualitie,
Resave into your service Gude Counsall,
1755 And richt sa this fair Ladie Chastitie,
Till ye mary sum queene of blude royall :
Observe then chastitie matrimoniall.
Richt sa resave [ heir ] Veritie be the hand :
Use thair counsell, your fame sall never fall.
1760 With thame thairfoir mak ane perpetuall band.

*Heir sall the King resave [ Gude ] Counsell, Veritie and Chastitie.*

Now, Sir, tak tent quhat I will say :
Observe thir same baith nicht and day,
And let them never part yow fray ;
    Or els withoutin doubt,
1765 Turne ye to Sensualitie,
To vicious lyfe and rebaldrie,
Out of your realme richt schamefullie
    Ye sall be ruttit out,
As was Tarquine, the Romane king,
1770 Quha was for his vicious living
And for the schamefull ravisching
    Of the fair chaist Lucres,

He was [di]graidit of his croun
And baneist aff his regioun :
1775 I maid on him correctioun,
    As stories dois expres.

    REX

I am content your counsall [till] inclyne,
Ye beand of so gude conditioun.
At your command sall be all that is myne,
1780 And heir I gif yow full commissioun
To punische faults and gif remissioun.
To all vertew I salbe [consonable] :
With yow I sall confirme ane unioun,
And at your counsall stand ay firme and stabill.

*The King imbraces Correction with a humbil countenance.*

    CORRECTIOUN

1785 I counsall yow, incontinent
To gar proclame ane Parliament
    Of all the Thrie Estaits,
That thay be heir with diligence
To mak to yow obedience,
1790     And syne dres all debaits.

    REX

That salbe done but mair demand.
Hoaw! Diligence, cum heir fra hand,
    And tak your informatioun :
Gang warne the Spiritualitie,
1795 Richt sa the Temporalitie,
    Be oppin proclamatioun,
In gudlie haist for to compeir
In thair maist honorabill maneir,
    To gif us thair counsals.
1800 Quha that beis absent, to them schaw
That thay sall underly the law,
    And punischt be that fails.

---

digraidit *stripped*    consonable *harmonious*    underly *be subject to*

DILIGENCE

Sir, I sall baith in bruch and land
With diligence do your command,
1805  Upon my awin expens.
Sir, I have servit yow all this yeir,
Bot I gat never ane dinneir
  Yit for my recompence.

REX

Pas on, and thou salbe regairdit
1810 And for thy service weill rewairdit,
  For quhy, with my consent
Thou sall have yeirly for thy hyre
The teind mussellis of the [Fernie] myre,
  Confirmit in Parliament.

DILIGENCE

1815 I will get riches throw that rent
  Efter the day of Dume,
Quhen, in the colpots of Tranent,
  Butter will grow on brume!
All nicht I had sa meikill drouth
1820  I micht nocht sleip ane wink;
Or I proclame ocht with my mouth,
  But doubt I man haif drink.

CORRECTIOUN

Cum heir, Placebo and Solace,
With your companyeoun Wantonnes:
1825  I knaw weill your conditioun.
For tysting King Humanitie
To resave Sensualitie
  Ye man suffer punitioun.

WANTONNES

We grant, my lord, we have done ill;
1830 Thairfoir wee put us in your will—
  Bot wee haife bene abusit.
For in gude faith, Sir, wee beleifit
That lecherie had na man greifit,
  Becaus it is sa usit.

———

bruch *burgh*  teind *tithe (see note)*  colpots *coalpits*
drouth *thirst*

1835 Ye se how Sensualitie
With principals of ilk cuntrie
   Bene glaidlie lettin in,
And with our prelatis, mair and les.
Speir at my Ladie Priores
1840    Gif lecherie be sin!

SOLACE

Sir, wee sall mend our conditioun,
Sa ye give us remissioun;
   Bot give us live to sing,
To dance, to play at chesse and tabils,
1845 To reid stories and mirrie fabils,
   For pleasure of our king.

CORRECTIOUN

Sa that ye do na uther cryme
Ye sall be pardonit at this tyme,
   For quhy, as I suppois,
1850 Princes may sumtyme seik solace
With mirth and lawfull mirrines,
   Thair spirits to rejoyis;
And richt sa halking and hunting
Ar honest pastimes for ane king
1855    Into the tyme of peace,
And leirne to rin ane heavie spear,
That he into the tyme of wear
   May follow at the cheace.

REX

Quhair is Sapience and Discretioun?
1860 And quhy cums nocht Devotioun nar?

VERITIE

Sapience, Sir, was ane verie loun,
And [Devotioun was nyne tymes] war.
The suith, Sir, gif I wald report,
Thay did begyle your Excellence,
1865 And wald not suffer to resort
Ane of us thrie to your presence.

———

wear *war*

CHASTITIE

Thay thrie war Flattrie and Dissait,
And Falset, that unhappie loun,
Against us thrie quhilk maid debait
1870 And baneischt us from town to town.
Thay gart us twa fall into sowne
Quhen thay us lockit in the stocks:
That dastart knave, Discretioun,
Full thifteouslie did steill your box.

REX

1875 The Devill tak them, sen thay ar gane:
Me thocht them ay thrie verie smaiks.
I mak ane vow to Sanct Mavane,
Quhen I them finde, thays bear thair paiks:
I se thay have playit me the glaiks!
1880 Gude Counsall, now schaw me the best:
Quhen I fix on yow thrie my staiks,
How I sall keip my realme in rest.

GUDE COUNSELL

*Initium sapientie est timor Domini.*
Sir, gif your Hienes yearnis lang to ring,
1885 First dread your God abuif all uther thing;
For ye ar bot ane mortall instrument
To that great God and King Omnipotent,
Preordinat be His divine Majestie
To reull His peopill intill unitie.
1890 The principall point, Sir, of ane kings office
Is for to do to everilk man justice,
And for to mix his justice with mercie,
But rigour, favour or parcialitie.
Forsuith, it is na litill observance
1895 Great regions to have in governance:
Quha ever taks on him that kinglie cuir
To get ane of thir twa he suld be suir,
Great paine and labour, and that continuall,
Or ellis to have defame perpetuall.

———

sowne *swoon*  thifteouslie *thievingly*  glaiks *fool*
Initium ... Domini *'The feare of the Lord is the beginnynge of
wysdome' ( Vulgate Psalm 100:10 )*

1900 Quha guydis weill, they win immortall fame;
Quha the contrair, they get perpetuall schame,
Efter quhais death, but dout, ane thousand yeir
Thair life at lenth rehearst sall be perqueir.
The chroniklis to knaw I yow exhort:
1905 Thair sall ye finde baith gude and evill report,
For everie prince efter his qualitie,
Thocht he be deid, his deids sall never die.
Sir, gif ye please for to use my counsall,
Your fame and name sall be perpetuall.

*Heir sall the messinger Diligence returne and cry 'a Hoyzes, a
Hoyzes, a Hoyzes' and say:*

[DILIGENCE]
1910 At the command of King Humanitie
I wairne and charge all members of Parliament,
Baith sprituall stait and temporalite,
That till his Grace thay be obedient,
And speid them to the Court incontinent,
1915 In gude ordour arrayit royally:
Quha beis absent or inobedient,
The Kings displeasure thay sall underly.

And als I mak yow exhortatioun,
Sen ye haif heard the first pairt of our play,
1920 Go tak ane drink and mak collatioun;
Ilk man drink till his marrow, I yow pray.
Tarie nocht lang, it is lait in the day.
Let sum drink ayle, and sum drink claret wine;
Be great doctors of physick I heare say
1925 That michtie drink comforts the dull ingyne!

And ye ladies that list to pisch,
Lift up your taill, plat in ane disch;
And gif [your quhislecaw cry] quhisch,

---

a Hoyzes *'Oyez' (French: 'Hear ye'), introducing an official
proclamation* marrow *companion* plat *(?) splash*
quhislecaw *(?) anus*

        Stop in ane wusp of stray.
1930    Let nocht your bladder burst, I pray yow,
        For that war evin aneuch to slay yow;
        For yit thair is to cum, I say yow,
            The best pairt of our play.

*Now sall the peopill mak collatioun; then beginnis
    the Interlude, the Kings, Bischops and principall
    players being out of their seats.*

    ———

**wusp of stray**  *wisp of straw*

# Interlude

[*Heir sall entir the Peur Man*]

PAUPER, THE PURE MAN

Of your almis, gude folkis, for Gods luife of heavin,
1935 For I have motherles bairns, either sax or seavin;
Gif ye'ill gif me na gude, for the luife of Jesus,
Wische me the richt way till Sanct Androes!

DILIGENCE

Quhair have wee gotten this gudly companyeoun?
Swyith, out of the feild, fals raggit loun!
1940 God wait gif heir be ane weill keipit place,
Quhen sic ane wilde begger carle may get entres;
Fy on yow officiars, that mends nocht thir failyies!
I gif yow all till the Devill, baith Provost and Bailyies!
Without ye cum and chase this carle away,
1945 The Devill a word ye'is get mair of our play!
Fals huirsun raggit carle, quhat Devil is that thou rugs?

PAUPER

Quha Devill maid the ane gentill-man, that wald not
cut thy lugs?

DILIGENCE

Quhat now? Me thinks the carle begins to crack!
Swyith, carle, away, or be this day, Ise break thy back!

*Heir sall the Carle clim up and sit in the Kings tchyre.*

-------

wische *tell*  entres *entrance*  failyies *defects*  carle *peasant*
rugs *stir up*  cut thy lugs *amputate your ears* ( *a well-established
punishment* )  crack *chatter*

1950 Cum doun, or be Gods croun, fals loun, I sall slay the!
    PAUPER
    Now sweir be thy brunt schinis, the Devill ding
                                        them fra the!
    Quhat say ye till thir court dastards? Be thay
                                        get hail clais,
    Sa sune do thay leir to sweir and trip on thair tais!
    DILIGENCE
    Me thocht the carle callit me knave, evin in my face!
1955 Be Sanct Fillane, thou salbe slane, bot gif thou ask grace:
    Loup doun, or be the gude Lord, thow sall los thy heid!
    PAUPER
    I sal anis drink or I ga, thocht thou had sworne my deid!

*Heir Diligence castis away the ledder.*

    DILIGENCE
    Loup now gif thou list, for thou hes lost the ledder!
    PAUPER
    It is full weil thy kind to loup and licht in a [tedder];
1960 Thou sal be faine to fetch agane the ledder or I loup;
    I sall sit heir into this tcheir till I have tumde the stoup!

*Heir sall the Carle loup aff the scaffald.*

[DILIGENCE]
Swyith, begger bogill, haist the away!
Thow art over pert to spill our play.
    PAUPER
    I wil not gif for al your play worth an sowis fart,
1965 For thair is richt litill play at my hungrie hart.

———

tais *toes*  loup *jump*  tedder *gallows rope*
tumde *emptied*  bogill *goblin*  spill *ruin*

DILIGENCE

Quhat Devill ails this cruckit carle?

PAUPER

Marie, meikill sorrow;
I can not get, thocht I gasp, to beg nor to borrow.

DILIGENCE

Quhair, devill, is this thou dwels; or quhats thy intent?

PAUPER

I dwell into Lawthiane, ane myle fra Tranent.

DILIGENCE

1970 Quhair wald thou be, carle, the suth to me schaw?

PAUPER

Sir, evin to Sanct Androes, for to seik law.

DILIGENCE

For to seik law, in Edinburgh was the neirest way.

PAUPER

Sir, I socht law thair this monie deir day,
Bot I culd get nane at Sessioun nor Seinye:

1975 Thairfoir the mekill dum Devill droun all the meinye!

DILIGENCE

Shaw me thy mater, man, with al the circumstances,
How that thou hes happinit on thir unhappie chances.

PAUPER

Gude-man, will ye gif me your charitie,
And I sall declair yow the black veritie.

1980 My father was ane auld man and ane hoir,
And was of age fourscoir of yeirs and moir,
And Mald, my mother, was fourscoir and fyfteine;
And with my labour I did thame baith susteine.
Wee had ane meir that caryit salt and coill,

1985 And everie ilk yeir scho brocht us hame ane foill.
Wee had thrie ky that was baith fat and fair,
Nane tydier [hyne to] the toun of Air.

---

Sessioun *the Court of Session, the supreme secular court* ( *see note* )
Seinye *Consistory Court* ( *see note* )   meinye *company*
hoir *grey-haired*   ky *cattle*   tydier *rich in milk*   hyne *from here*

My father was sa waik of blude and bane
That he deit, quhairfoir my mother maid great maine;
1990 Then scho deit, within ane day or two,
And thair began my povertie and wo.
Our gude gray meir was baittand on the feild,
And our lands laird tuik hir for his hyreild.
The Vickar tuik the best cow be the head
1995 Incontinent, quhen my father was deid;
And quhen the Vickar hard tel how that my mother
Was dead, fra-hand he tuke to him ane uther.
Then Meg, my wife, did murne both evin and morow,
Till at the last scho deit for verie sorow;
2000 And quhen the Vickar hard tell my wyfe was dead,
The thrid cow he cleikit be the head.
Thair umest clayis, that was of rapploch gray,
The Vickar gart his clark bear them away.
Quhen all was gaine, I micht mak na debeat
2005 Bot with my bairns past for till beg my meat.
Now have I tald yow the blak veritie,
How I am brocht into this miserie.
    DILIGENCE
How did the person? Was he not thy gude freind?
    PAUPER
The Devil stick him, he curst me for my teind,
2010 And halds me yit under that same proces,
That gart me want the Sacrament at Pasche.
In gude faith, Sir, thocht [ye] wald cut my throt,
I have na geir except ane Inglis grot,
Quhilk I purpois to gif ane man of law.
    DILIGENCE
2015 Thou art the daftest fuill that ever I saw!
Trows thou, man, be the law to get remeid
Of men of kirk? Na, nocht till thou be deid!

---

baittand *grazing*   hyreild *heriot, the mortuary due owed to the*
*lord (see note)*   umest clayis *upper garments, along with the*
*corspresent or 'cow' mortuary dues owed to the vicar (see note)*
rapploch *homespun*   teind *tithe (see note)*   Pasche *Easter*
geir *property*   Inglis grot *an English coin, worth four pence*

PAUPER

Sir, be quhat law, tell me, quhairfoir or quhy
That ane Vickar sould tak fra me thrie ky?

DILIGENCE

2020 Thay have na law, exceptand consuetude,
Quhilk law to them is sufficient and gude.

PAUPER

Ane consuetude against the common weill
Sould be na law, I think, be sweit Sanct Geill!
Quhair will ye find that law, tell gif ye can,
2025 To tak thrie ky fra ane pure husband-man?
Ane for my father, and for my wyfe ane uther,
And the thrid cow he tuke [for] Mald my mother.

DILIGENCE

It is thair law, all that thay have in use,
Thocht it be cow, sow, ganer, gryse or guse.

PAUPER

2030 Sir, I wald speir at yow ane questioun:
Behauld sum prelats of this regioun,
Manifestlie during thair lustie lyfis
Thay swyfe ladies, madinis and uther men[ni]s wyfis,
And sa thair cunts thay have in consuetude!
2035 Quhidder say ye that law is evill or gude?

DILIGENCE

Hald thy toung, man, it seims that thou war mangit!
Speik thou of preists, but doubt thou will be hangit.

PAUPER

Be Him that bure the cruell croun of thorne,
I cair nocht to be hangit, evin the morne!

DILIGENCE

2040 Be sure of preistis thou will get na support.

PAUPER

Gif that be trew, the Feind resave the sort!
Sa, sen I se I get na uther grace,
I will ly doun and rest mee in this place.

*Pauper lyis doun in the feild. Pardoner enters.*

———

consuetude *custom*   ganer *gander*   gryse *suckling pig*

[ 73

**PARDONER**

*Bona dies, bona dies!*

2045   Devoit peopill, gude day I say yow.
      Now tarie ane lytill quhyll, I pray yow,
          Till I be with yow knawin:
      Wait ye weill how I am namit?—
      Ane nobill man and undefamit,
2050         Gif all the suith war schawin!
      I am Sir Robert Rome-raker,
      Ane perfite, publike pardoner,
         Admittit be the Paip.
      Sirs, I sall schaw yow for my wage
2055   My pardons and my [prevelage],
         Quhilk ye sall se and graip.
      I give to the Devill with gude intent
      This unsell wickit New Testament,
         With them that it translaitit:
2060   Sen layik men knew the veritie
      Pardoners gets no charitie,
         Without that thay debait it
      Amang the wives with wrinks and wyles,
      As all my marrowis men begyles
2065         With our fair fals flattrie.
      Yea, all the crafts I ken perqueir,
      As I was teichit be ane freir
         Callit Hypocrisie;
      Bot now, allace, our greit abusioun
2070   Is cleirlie knawin, till our confusioun,
         That we may sair repent.
      Of all credence now am I quyte,
      For ilk man halds me at dispyte
         That reids the New Testment.
2075   Duill fell the braine that hes it wrocht,
      Sa fall them that the Buik hame brocht;
         Als I pray to the Rude

---

Bona dies *Good day*   suith *truth*
Sir Robert Rome-raker *'Sir' is a courtesy-title for priests (see note)*
graip *hold*   unsell *unhallowed*   layik *lay*   wrinks *tricks*
quyte *deprived*   duill *sorrow*   fell *strike down*

That Martin Luther, that fals loun,
Black Bullinger, and Melancthoun,
2080    Had bene smorde in their cude!
Be Him that buir the crowne of thorne,
I wald Sanct Paull had never bene borne,
    And als I wald his buiks
War never red into the Kirk,
2085  Bot amangs freirs into the mirk,
    Or riven amang ruiks!

*Heir sall he lay doun his geir upon ane buird and say:*

My patent pardouns ye may se,
Cum fra the [Can] of Tartarie,
    Weill seald with oster-schellis;
2090  Thocht ye have na contritioun,
Ye sall have full remissioun,
    With help of buiks and bellis.
Heir is ane relict lang and braid,
Of Fine Macoull the richt chaft blaid,
2095    With teith and al togidder;
Of Collings cow heir is ane horne,
For eating of Makconnals corne
    Was slaine into Balquhidder;
Heir is ane coird baith great and lang
2100  Quhilk hangit [Jonnye] Armistrang,
    Of gude hemp soft and sound—
Gude halie peopill, I stand for'd,
Quha ever beis hangit with this cord
    Neids never to be dround!
2105  The culum of Sanct Bryd[i]s kow,
The gruntill of Sanct Antonis sow,
    Quhilk buir his haly bell—

---

Martin Luther (1483–1546), Bullinger (1504–75),
Melancthoun (1497–1560) *Protestant reformers (see note)*
smorde *smothered*  cude *crib*  buird *table*
Can *Khan (see note)*  Fine Macoull *legendary Irish hero
(see note)*  culum *anus*  gruntill *snout*

Quha ever he be heiris this bell clinck,
Gif me ane ducat for till drink,
2110   He sall never gang to Hell,
Without he be of Baliell borne.
Maisters, trow ye that this be scorne?
   Cum, win this pardoun, cum!
Quha luifis thair wyfis nocht with thair hart,
2115   I have power them for till part—
   Me think yow deif and dum!
Hes nane of yow curst wickit wyfis
That halds yow into sturt and stryfis?
   Cum, tak my dispensatioun;
2120   Of that cummer I sall mak yow quyte,
Howbeit your selfis be in the wyte
   And mak ane fals narratioun.
Cum, win the pardoun, now let se,
For meill, for malt, or for monie,
2125   For cok, hen, guse or gryse!
Of relicts heir I have ane hunder;
Quhy cum ye nocht? This is ane wonder:
   I trow ye be nocht wyse!
   SOWTAR
Welcum hame, Robert Rome-raker,
2130   Our halie patent pardoner!
   Gif ye have dispensatioun
To pairt me and my wickit wyfe
And me deliver from sturt and stryfe,
   I mak yow supplicatioun.
   PARDONER
2135   I sall yow pairt but mair demand,
Sa I get mony in my hand:
   Thairfoir let se sum cunye!
   SOWTAR
I have na silver, be my lyfe,
Bot fyve schillings and my schaipping knyfe:
2140   That sall ye have, but sunye.

———

wyte *wrong*   sunye *delay*

PARDONER

Quhat kynd of woman is thy wyfe?

SOWTAR

Ane quick Devill, Sir, ane storme of stryfe,
    Ane frog that fyles the winde,
Ane fistand flag, a flagartie fuffe;
2145  At ilk ane pant scho lets ane puffe,
    And hes na ho behind;
All the lang day scho me dispyts,
And all the nicht scho flings and flyts,
    Thus sleip I never ane wink.
2150  That cockatrice, that common huir,
The mekill Devill may nocht induir
    Hir stuburnnes and stink!

SOWTARS WYFE

Theif carle, thy words I hard rycht weill!
In faith, my freindschip ye sall feill
2155    And I the fang!

SOWTAR

Gif I said ocht, Dame, be the Rude,
Except ye war baith fair and gude,
    God nor I hang!

PARDONER

Fair dame, gif ye wald be ane wower,
2160  To part yow twa I have ane power.
    Tell on, ar ye content?

SOWTARS WIFE

Ye, that I am, with all my hart,
Fra that fals huirsone till depart,
    Gif this theif will consent.
2165  Causses to part I have anew,
Becaus I gat na chamber-glew,
    I tell yow verely.
I mervell nocht, sa mot I lyfe,
Howbeit that swingeour can not swyfe:
2170    He is baith cauld and dry.

---

fistand flag *belching slut*   flaggartie fuffe *sluttish stinker*
ho *pause*   flyts *scolds*   swingeour *scoundrel*
cauld and dry *of a melancholic temperament (see note)*

[ 77

PARDONER
Quhat will ye gif me for your part?
[SOWTARS WIFE]
Ane cuppill of sarks, with all my hart,
   The best claith in the land.
PARDONER
To part sen ye ar baith content,
2175 I sall yow part incontinent,
   Bot ye mon do command.
My will and finall sentence is:
Ilk ane of yow uthers arss[is] kis.
Slip doun your hois. Me thinkis the carle is glaikit!
2180 Set thou not be, howbeit scho kisse and slaik it!

*Heir sall scho kis his arsse with silence.*

Lift up hir clais; kis hir hoill with your hart.
   SOWTAR
I pray yow, Sir, forbid hir for to fart!

*Heir sall the Carle kis hir arsse with silence.*

   PARDONER
Dame, pas ye to the east end of the toun,
And pas ye west evin lyke ane cuckald loun;
2185 Go hence, ye baith, with Baliels braid blessing.
Schirs, saw ye evir mair sorrowles pairting?

*Heir sall the Boy cry aff the hill:*

   WILKIN
Hoaw, maister, hoaw! Quhair ar ye now?
   PARDONER
I am heir, Wilkin Widdiefow.
   WILKIN
Sir, I have done your bidding,
2190 For I have fund ane great hors-bane,
Ane fairer saw ye never nane,
   Upon Dame Fleschers midding.

---

glaikit *daft*   slaik *soak*   Baliel *Belial, the Devil* ( *see note* )

Sir, ye may gar the wyfis trow
It is ane bane of Sanct Bryds cow,
2195      Gude for the fever quartane :
Sir, will ye reull this relict weill,
All the wyfis will baith kis and kneill
      Betuixt this and Dumbartane.
PARDONER
Quhat say thay of me in the toun?
WILKIN
2200  Sum sayis ye ar ane verie loun ;
      Sum sayis, *Legatus natus* ;
Sum sayis y'ar ane fals Saracene ;
And sum sayis ye ar for certaine
      *Diabolus incarnatus.*
2205  Bot keip yow fra subjectioun
Of the curst King Correctioun,
      For be ye with him fangit,
Becaus ye ar ane Rome-raker,
Ane commoun publick cawsay-paker,
2210      But doubt ye will be hangit.
PARDONER
Quhair sall I ludge into the toun?
WILKIN
With gude kynde Christiane Anderson,
      Quhair ye will be weill treatit.
Gif ony limmer yow demands,
2215  Scho will defend yow with hir hands,
      And womanlie debait it.
Bawburdie says, be the Trinitie,
That scho sall beir yow cumpanie,
      Howbeit ye byde ane yeir.
PARDONER
2220  Thou hes done weill, be God[i]s mother !
Tak ye the taine and I the t'other :
      Sa sall we mak greit cheir.

---

fever quartan  *fever recurring every four days*
Legatus natus  *a bishop holding powers as a Papal Legate*
( *see note* )  Diabolus incarnatus  *the Devil incarnate*
cawsay-paker  *street-walker*  limmer  *villain*

WILKIN

I reid yow, speid yow heir,
And mak na langer tarie:
2225 Byde ye lang thair, but weir
I dreid your weird yow warie!

*Heir sall Pauper rise and rax him.*

PAUPER

Quhat thing was yon that I hard crak and cry?
I have bene dreamand and dreveland of my ky.
With my richt hand my haill bodie I saine:
2230 Sanct Bryd, Sanct Bryd, send me my ky againe!
I se standand yonder ane halie man;
To mak me help let me se gif he can.
Halie maister, God speid yow and gude morne!

PARDONER

Welcum to me, thocht thou war at the horne!
2235 Cum, win the pardoun, and syne I sall the saine.

PAUPER

Wil that pardoun get me my ky againe?

PARDONER

Carle, of thy ky I have nathing ado;
Cum, win my pardon, and kis my relicts to.

*Heir sall he saine him with his relictis.*

Now lows thy pursse and lay doun thy offrand,
2240 And thou sall have my pardon evin fra-hand.
With raipis and relicts I sall the saine againe;
Of gut or gravell thou sall never have paine.
Now win the pardon, limmer, or thou art lost!

PAUPER

My haly father, quhat wil that pardon cost?

PARDONER

2245 Let se quhat mony thou bearest in thy bag.

PAUPER

I have ane grot heir, bund into a rag.

————

weird *fate*   warie *curse*   rax *stretch*
dreveland *raving*   saine *bless, cross*   gravell *kidney stones*

PARDONER

Hes thou na uther silver bot ane groat?

PAUPER

Gif I have mair, sir, cum and rype my coat!

PARDONER

Gif me that grot, man, gif thou hest na mair.

PAUPER

2250 With all my heart, maister: lo, tak it thair.
Now let me se your pardon, with your leif.

PARDONER

Ane thousand yeir of pardons I the geif.

PAUPER

Ane thousand yeir? I will not live sa lang!
Delyver me it, maister, and let me gang.

PARDONER

2255 Ane thousand yeir I lay upon thy head,
With *totiens quotiens* now mak me na mair plead!
Thou hast resaifit thy pardon now already.

PAUPER

Bot I can se na thing, sir, be our [Leddy]!
Forsuith, maister, I trow I be not wyse
2260 To pay ere I have sene my marchandryse.
That ye have gottin my groat full sair I rew!
Sir, quhidder is your pardon black or blew?
Maister, sen ye have taine fra me my cunyie,
My marchandryse schaw me, withouttin sunyie,
2265 Or to the Bischop I sall pas and pleinyie
In Sanct Androis, and summond yow to the Seinyie.

PARDONER

Quhat craifis the, carle? Me thinks thou art not wise!

PAUPER

I craif my groat, or ellis my marchandrise.

PARDONER

I gaif the pardon for ane thowsand yeir.

PAUPER

2270 How shall I get that pardon, let me heir.

————

totiens quotiens  *'as often as … so often'* ( *see note* )

PARDONER

Stand still and I sall tell [the] the haill storie:
Quhen thow art deid and gais to Purgatorie,
Being condempit to paine a thowsand yeir,
Then sall thy pardoun the releif, but weir.
2275 Now be content. Ye ar ane mervalous man!

PAUPER

Sall I get nathing for my grot quhill than?

PARDONER

That sall thou not, I mak it to yow plaine.

PAUPER

Na? Than, gossop, gif me my grot againe!
Quhat say ye, maisters? Call ye this gude resoun,
2280 That he sould promeis me ane gay pardoun
And he resave my money in [this] stead,
Syne mak me na payment till I be dead?
Quhen I am dead, I wait full sikkerlie,
My sillie saull will pas to Purgatorie:
2285 Declair me this, now God nor Baliell bind the,
Quhen I am thair, curst carle, quhair sall I find the?
Not into Heavin, bot rather into Hell:
Quhen thou are thair, thou can not help thy sel!
Quhen will thou cum my dolours till abait?
2290 Or I the find, my hippis will get ane hait.
Trowis thou, butcheour, that I will by blind lambis?
Gif me my grot, the Devill dryte [on] thy gambis!

PARDONER

Swyith, stand aback, I trow this man be mangit!
Thou gets not this, carle, thocht thou suld be hangit.

PAUPER

2295 Gif me my grot, weill bund into ane clout,
Or, be Gods breid, Robin sall beir ane rout!

*Heir sall thay fecht with silence, and Pauper sall*

———

stead *place*   hait *heat*   gambis *tricks*

*cast doun the buird and cast the relicts in the water.*

DILIGENCE
Quhat kind of daffing is this al day?
Swyith, smaiks, out of the feild, away !
Into ane presoun put them sone,
2300   Syne hang them quhen the play is done !

———

buird *table*    daffing *fooling*

# Part Two

*Heir sall Diligence mak his proclamatioun.*

DILIGENCE
Famous peopill, tak tent and ye sall se
The Thrie Estait[ i ]s of this natioun
Cum to the Court with ane strange gravitie;
Thairfoir I mak yow supplication,
2305 Till ye have heard our haill narratioun
To keip silence and be patient, I pray yow:
Howbeit we speik be adulatioun,
We sall say nathing bot the suith, I say yow.
Gude verteous men, that luifis the veritie,
2310 I wait thay will excuse our negligence;
Bot vicious men, denude of charitie,
As feinyeit fals flattrand Saracens,
Howbeit thay cry on us ane loud vengence
And of our pastyme mak ane fals report,
2315 Quhat may wee do bot tak in patience,
And us refer unto the faithfull sort?

Our Lord Jesus, Peter nor Paull,
Culd nocht compleis the peopill all,
    Bot sum war miscontent:
2320 Howbeit thay schew the veritie,
Sum said that it war heresie,
    Be thair maist fals judgement.

*Heir sall the Thrie Estaits cum fra the palyeoun gangand*
*backwart, led be thair vyces.*

WANTONNES
Now braid benedicite!
Quhat thing is yon that I se?
2325    Luke, Solace, my hart!

———

be adulatioun *( ? ) in pretence*    suith *truth*    denude *stripped*
compleis *satisfy*

SOLACE

Brother Wantonnes, quhat thinks thow?
Yon ar the Thrie Estaits, I trow,
   Gangand backwart.

WANTONNES

Backwart? Backwart? Out, wallaway!
2330 It is greit schame for them, I say,
   Backwart to gang.
I trow the King Correctioun
Man mak ane reformatioun,
   Or it be lang.
2335 Now let us go and tell the King.

*Pausa*

Sir, wee have seen ane mervelous thing,
   Be our judgement:
The Thrie Estaits of this regioun
Ar cummand backwart throw this toun,
2340    To the Parlament!

REX

Backwart? Backwart? How may that be?
Gar speid them haistelie to me,
   In dreid that thay ga wrang.

PLACEBO

Sir, I se them yonder cummand:
2345 Thay will be heir evin fra-hand,
   Als fast as thay may gang.

GUDE COUNSELL

Sir, hald you still, and skar them nocht
Till ye persave quhat be thair thocht,
   And se quhat men them leids;
2350 And let the King Correctioun
Mak ane scharp inquisitioun,
   And mark them be the heids.
Quhen ye ken the occasioun
That maks them sic persuasioun,
2355    Ye mak expell the caus,

———

skar *frighten*   be the heids *by the leaders*

Syne them reforme as ye think best,
Sua that the realme may live in rest,
   According to Gods lawis.

*Heir sall the Thrie Estaits cum and turne thair faces
to the King.*

SPIRITUALITIE

Gloir, honour, laud, triumph and victorie
2360 Be to your michtie, prudent excellence!
Heir ar we cum, all the Estait[i]s Thrie,
Readie to mak our dew obedience
At your command, with humbill observance,
As may pertene to Spiritualitie,
2365 With counsell of the Temporalitie.

TEMPORALITIE

Sir, we with michtie curage at command
Of your superexcellent Majestie
Sall mak service baith with our hart and hand,
And sall not dreid in thy defence to die.
2370 Wee ar content, but doubt, that wee may se
That nobill heavinlie King Correctioun,
Sa he with mercie mak punitioun.

MERCHAND

Sir, we ar heir, your burgessis and merchands:
Thanks be to God that we may se your face,
2375 Traistand wee may now into divers lands
Convoy our geir with support of your Grace,
For now I traist wee sall get rest and peace.
Quhen misdoars ar with your sword overthrawin,
Then may leil merchands live upon thair awin.

REX

2380 Welcum to me, my prudent Lord[i]s all:
Yee ar my members, suppois I be your head.
Sit doun, that we may with your just counsall
Aganis misdoars find soveraine remeid.
Wee sall nocht spair, for favour nor for feid,
2385 With your avice, to mak punitioun,

———

convoy *transport*   geir *goods*

And put my sword to executioun.

CORRECTIOUN

My tender freinds, I pray yow with my hart,
Declair to me the thing that I wald speir :
Quhat is the caus that ye gang all backwart?
2390 The veritie thairof faine wald I heir.

SPIRITUALITIE

Soveraine, we have gaine sa this mony a yeir.
Howbeit ye think we go undecently,
We think wee gang richt wonder pleasantly.

DILIGENCE

Sit doun, my Lords, into your proper places ;
2395 Syne let the King consider all sic caces.
Sit doun, Sir Scribe, and sit doun Dampster, to,
And fence the court as ye war wont to do.

*Thay ar set doun, and Gud Counsell sal pas to his seat.*

REX

My prudent Lord[i]s of the Thrie Estaits,
It is our will abuife all uther thing
2400 For to reforme all them that maks debaits
Contrair the richt, quhilk daylie dois maling,
And thay that dois the Common-weil doun thring.
With help and counsell of King Correctioun,
It is our will for to mak punisching,
2405 And plaine oppressours put to subjectioun.

SPIRITUALITIE

Quhat thing is this, Sir, that ye have devysit?
Schirs, ye have neid for till be weill advysit :
Be nocht haistie into your executioun,
And be nocht our extreime in your punitioun !
2410 And gif ye please to do, Sir, as wee say,
Postpone this Parlament till ane uther day.
For quhy, the peopill of this regioun
May nocht indure extreme correctioun.

―――――――

Dampster *dempster, a court official responsible for announcing the sentence (see note)* maling *wickedly*

CORRECTIOUN

Is this the part, my Lords, that ye will tak
2415  To mak us supportatioun to correct?
It dois appeir that ye ar culpabill,
That ar nocht to Correctioun applyabill.
Swyith, Diligence, ga schaw it is our will
That everilk man opprest geif in his bill.

DILIGENCE

2420  All maneir of men I wairne that be opprest,
Cum and complaine, and thay salbe redrest;
For quhy, it is the nobill Princes will
That ilk compleiner sall gif in his bill.

JOHNE THE COMMON-WEILL

Out of my gait! For Gods saik, let me ga!
2425  Tell me againe, gude maister, quhat ye say.

DILIGENCE

I warne al that be wrangouslie offendit,
Cum and complaine, and thay sall be amendit.

JOHN

Thankit be Christ that buir the croun of thorne,
For I was never sa blyth sen I was borne!

DILIGENCE

2430  Quhat is thy name, fallow? That wald I feil.

JOHN

Forsuith, thay call me Johne the Common-weil.
Gude maister, I wald speir at you ane thing:
Quhair traist ye I sall find yon new-[maid] king?

DILIGENCE

Cum over, and I sall schaw the to His Grace.

JOHN

2435  Gods bennesone licht on that luckie face!
Stand by the gait; let se gif I can loup.
I man rin fast, in cace I get ane coup!

*Heir sall Johne loup the stank, or els fall in it.*

---

supportatioun *help*   applyabill *amenable*   bill *statement*
feil *know*   bennesone *blessing*   coup *fall*   stank *ditch*

DILIGENCE

Speid the away; thou taryis all to lang!

JOHN

Now, be this day, I may na faster gang.

(*To the King*:) Gude day, gud day, grit God saif
2440                                   baith your Graces.
Wallie, wallie, fall thay twa weill-fairde faces!

REX

Schaw me thy name, gude man, I the command.

JOHN

Marie, Johne the Common-weil of fair Scotland.

REX

The Common-weil hes bene amang his fais!

JOHN

2445 Ye, Sir, that gars the Common-weil want clais.

REX

Quhat is the caus the Common-weil is crukit?

JOHN

Becaus the Common-weill hes bene overlukit.

REX

Quhat gars the luke sa with ane dreirie hart?

JOHN

Becaus the Thrie Estaits gangs all backwart.

REX

2450 Sir Common-weill, knaw ye the limmers that them leids?

JOHN

Thair canker cullours, I ken them be the heads:
As for our reverent fathers of Spiritualitie,
Thay ar led be Covetice and cairles Sensualitie;
And as ye se, Temporalitie hes neid of correctioun,
2455 Quhilk hes lang tyme bene led be publick oppressioun.
Loe, quhair the loun lyis lurkand at his back—
Get up, I think to se thy craig gar ane raip crak!
Loe, heir is Falset and Dissait, weill I ken,
Leiders of the merchants and sillie craft[i]s-men.
2460 Quhat mervell thocht the Thrie Estaits backwart gang

---

limmers *scoundrels*    cullours *specious arguments*

Quhen sic an vyle cumpanie dwels them amang,
Quhilk hes reulit this rout monie deir dayis,
Quhilk gars John the Commoun-weil want his clais?
Sir, call them befoir yow and put them in ordour,
2465 Or els John the Common-weil man beg on the bordour.
Thou feinyeit Flattrie, the Feind fart in thy face:
Quhen ye was guyder of the Court we gat litill grace!
Ryse up, Falset and Dissait, without ony sunye:
I pray God nor the Devils dame dryte on thy grunye.
2470 Behauld as the loun lukis evin lyke a thief:
Monie wicht warkman thou brocht to mischief!
My soveraine Lord Correctioun, I mak yow supplicatioun,
Put thir tryit truikers from Christis congregatioun!

CORRECTIOUN

As ye have devysit, but doubt it salbe done.
2475 Cum heir, my Sergeants, and do your debt sone:
Put thir thrie pellours into pressoun strang—
Howbeit ye sould hang them, ye do them na wrang!

FIRST SERGEANT

Soverane [Lord], wee sall obey your commands.
Brother, upon thir limmers lay on thy hands.
2480 Ryse up sone, loun, thou luiks evin lyke ane lurden;
Your mouth war meit to drink an wesche jurden!

SECOND SERGEANT

Cum heir, gossop, cum heir, cum heir!
Your rackles lyfe ye sall repent.
Quhen was ye wont to be sa sweir?
2485 Stand still, and be obedient!

FIRST SERGEANT

Thair is nocht in all this toun—
Bot I wald nocht this taill war tald—
Bot I wald hang him for his goun,
Quhidder that it war laird or [lawid].
2490 I trow this pylour be [spurgawd]!
Put in thy hand into this cord:

———

sunye *delay*   dryte on thy grunye *crap on your snout*
truikers *rogues*   pellours *thieves*   lurden *idler*
jurden *chamber-pot*   sweir *idle*   lawid *common person*
spurgawd *driven mad by spurs (see note)*

Howbeit I se thy skap skyre [skawd],
Thou art ane stewat, I stand foird!

*Heir sall the Vycis be led to the stocks.*

SECOND SERGEANT

Put in your leggis into the stocks,
2495  For ye had never ane meiter hois.
Thir stewats stinks as thay war broks!
Now ar ye sikker, I suppois.

*Pausa.*

My Lords, wee have done your commands;
Sall wee put Covetice in captivitie?
CORRECTIOUN
2500  Ye, hardlie lay on them your hands;
Rycht sa upon Sensualitie.
SPIRITUALITIE
Thir is my grainter and my chalmerlaine,
And hes my gould and geir under hir cuiris.
I mak ane vow to God I sall complaine
2505  Unto the Paip how ye do me injuris.
COVETICE
My reverent fathers, tak in patience:
I sall nocht lang remaine from your p[r]esence.
Thocht for ane quhyll I man from yow depairt,
I wait my spreit sall remaine in your hart;
2510  And quhen this King Correctioun beis absent,
Then sall we twa returne incontinent.
Thairfoir adew!
SPIRITUALITIE
           Adew, be Sanct Mavene!
Pas quhair ye wil, we ar twa naturall men.
SENSUALITIE
Adew, my Lord.

———

skap skyre skawd   *scalp scarred by a cancer (see note)*
stewat  *stinker*   grainter  *keeper of the granary*

Adew, my awin sweit hart.

2515 Now duill fell me, that wee twa man depart!

SENSUALITIE

My Lord, howbeit this parting dois me paine,
I traist in God we sal meit sone agane.

SPIRITUALITIE

To cum againe I pray yow do your cure:
Want I yow twa, I may nocht lang indure.

*Heir sall the Sergeants chase them away, and thay sal gang to
the seat of Sensualitie.*

TEMPORALITIE

2520 My Lords, ye knaw the Thrie Estaits
For Common-weill suld mak debaits:
Let now amang us be devysit
Sic actis that with gude men be [prysit],
Conforming to the Common Law,
2525 For of na man we sould stand aw;
And, for till saif us fra murmell,
Schone Diligence fetch us Gude Counsell,
For quhy, he is ane man that knawis
Baith the Cannon and Civill Lawis.

DILIGENCE

2530 Father, ye man incontinent
Passe to the Lords of Parliament,
For quhy, thay ar determinat all
To do na thing [bot] by your counsall.

GUDE COUNSALL

That sal I do within schort space,
2535 Praying the Lord to send us grace
For till conclude or wee depart
That thay may profeit efterwart
Baith to the Kirk and to the King;
I sall desyre na uther thing.

*Pausa.*

———

duill fell *may sorrow befall*   murmell *rumour*

2540 My Lords, God glaid the cumpanie!
     Quhat is the caus ye send for me?

     Sit doun and gif us your counsell,
     How we sall slaik the greit murmell
     Of pure peopill, that is weill knawin
2545 And as the Common-weill hes schawin;
     And als wee knaw it is the Kings will
     That gude remeid be put thairtill.
     Sir Common-weill, keip ye the bar:
     Let nane except your-self cum nar!

2550 That sall I do as I best can:
     I sall hauld out baith wyfe and man.
     Ye man let this puir creature
     Support me for till keip the dure;
     I knaw his name full sickerly—
2555 He will complaine als weill as I.

     My worthy Lords, sen ye have taine on hand
     Sum reformatioun to mak into this land,
     And als ye knaw it is the King[i]s mynd,
     Quha till the Common-weill hes ay bene kynd,
2560 Thocht reif and thift wer stanchit weill aneuch,
     Yit sumthing mair belangis to the pleuch—
     Now, into peace, ye sould provyde for weirs,
     And be sure of how mony thowsand speirs
     The King may be, quhen he hes ocht ado;
2565 For quhy, my Lords, this is my ressoun, [lo]:
     The husband-men and commons, that war wont
     Go in the battell formest in the front,
     Bot I have tint all my experience
     Without ye mak sum better diligence:
2570 The Common-weill mon uther wayis be styllit,
     Or, be my faith, the King wilbe begyllit.
     Thir pure commouns daylie, as ye may se,

---

slaik *allay*   reif *robbery*   belangis to the pleuch *is appropriate
to the farming community (see note)*   tint *lost*

Declynis doun till extreme povertie,
For sum ar hichtit sa into thair maill,
2575 Thair winning will nocht find them water-kaill.
How prelats heichts thair teinds, it is well knawin,
That husband-men may not weill hald thair awin.
And now begins ane plague amang them new :
That gentill-men thair steadings taks in few ;
2580 Thus man thay pay great ferme, or lay thair steid,
And sum ar plainlie harlit out be the heid
And ar distroyit without God on them rew.

PAUPER

Sir, be Gods breid that taill is verie trew !
It is weill kend I had baith nolt and hors ;
2585 Now all my geir ye se upon my cors.

CORRECTIOUN

Or I depart, I think to mak [gud] ordour.

JOHN

I pray yow, Sir, begin first at [the] Bordour,
For how can we fend us aganis Ingland
Quhen we can nocht within our native land
2590 Destroy our awin Scots common trator theifis,
Quha to leill laborers daylie dois mischeifis?
War I ane King, my Lord, be God[i]s wounds,
Quha ever held common theifis within thair bounds
Quhairthrow that dayly leilmen micht be wrangit,
2595 Without remeid thair chiftanis suld be hangit :
Quhidder he war ane knicht, ane lord or laird,
The Devill draw me to Hell and he war spaird !

TEMPORALITIE

Quhat uther enemie hes thou, let us ken?

JOHN

Sir, I compleine upon the idill men.
2600 For quhy, Sir, it is Gods awin bidding
All Christian men to wirk for thair living.

———

hichtit *raised*  maill *rent*  water-kaill *cabbage water*
heichts *raise*  teinds *tithes*  steadings *farmsteads*
in few *in feu*  great ferme *annual rent*  lay *dispose of (?)*
harlit *dragged*  nolt *cattle*

Sanct Paull, that pillar of the Kirk,
Sayis to the wretchis that will not wirk,
And bene to vertews [labour] laith:
2605 *Qui non laborat non manducet.*
This is in Inglische toung or leit:
Quha labouris nocht, he sall not eit.
This bene against the strang beggers,
Fidlers, pypers and pardoners;
2610 Thir jugglars, jestars and idill cuitchours;
Thir carriers and thir quintacensours;
Thir babil-beirers and thir bairds;
Thir sweir swyngeours with lords and lairds
Ma then thair rent[i]s may susteine,
2615 Or to thair profeit neidfull bene,
Quhilk bene ay blythest of discords
And deidly feid amang thar lords;
For then they sleutchers man be treatit
Or els thair querrels undebaitit;
2620 This bene against thir great fat freiris,
Augustenes, Carmleits and Cordeleirs,
And all uthers that in cowls bene cled,
Quhilk labours nocht and bene weill fed—
I mein nocht laborand spirituallie,
2625 Nor for thair living corporallie,
Lyand in dennis lyke idill doggis,
I them compair to weil-fed hoggis.
I think they do them-selfis abuse,
Seing that thay the warld refuse,
2630 Haifing profest sic povertie,
Syne fleis fast fra necessitie.
Quhat gif thay povertie wald professe
And do as did Diogenes,
That great famous philosophour,
2635 Seing in earth bot vaine labour,

---

leit *language*  cuitchours *gamblers*
quintacensours *alchemists (cf. l. 897)*  babil-beirers *fools*
bairds *bards*  sweir *bold*  swyngeours *scoundrels*
sleutchers *idlers*

Alutterlie the warld refusit,
And in ane tumbe him-self inclusit,
And leifit on herbs and water cauld—
Of corporall fude na mair he wald.
2640 He trottit nocht from toun to toun,
Beggand to feid his carioun :
Fra tyme that lyfe hee did profes,
The wa[r]ld of him was cummerles.
Rycht sa of Marie Magdalene,
2645 And of Mary th'Egyptiane,
And of auld Paull, the first hermeit :
All thir had povertie compleit.
Ane hundreth ma I micht declair,
Bot to my purpois I will fair,
2650 Concluding sleuthfull idilnes
Against the Common-weill expresse.

CORRECTIOUN

Quhom upon ma will ye compleine?

JOHNE

Marie, on ma and ma againe,
For the pure peopill cryis with cairis
2655 The infetching of the Justice Airis,
Exercit mair for covetice
Then for the punisching of vyce.
Ane peggrell theif that steillis ane kow
Is hangit, bot he that steillis ane bow
2660 With als meikill geir as he may turs,
That theif is hangit be the purs.
Sic pykand peggrall theifis ar hangit,
Bot he that all the warld hes wrangit,
Ane cruell tyrane, ane strang transgressour,
2665 Ane common publick plaine oppressour,
By buds may he obteine favours
Of tresurers and compositours ;
Thocht he serve greit punitioun,

———

alluterlie *entirely*   cummerles *unencumbered*   ma *more*
infetching *demands, exactions (see note)*   peggrell *paltry*
bow *herd*   turs *carry off*   buds *bribes*

Gets easie compositioun,
2670 And throch lawis consistoriall,
Prolixt, corrupt and [pertiall],
The common peopill ar put sa under,
Thocht thay be puir, it is na wonder.

CORRECTIOUN

Gude Johne, I grant all that is trew:
2675 Your infortoun full sair I rew.
Or I pairt aff this natioun
I sall mak reformatioun.
And als, my Lord Temporalitie,
I yow command in tyme that ye
2680 Expell oppressioun aff your lands;
And als I say to yow merchands,
Gif ever I find be land or sie
Dissait be in your cumpanie,
Quhilk ar to Common-weill contrair,
2685 I vow to God I sall not spair
To put my sword to executioun,
And mak on yow extreme punitioun.
Mairover, my Lord [Temporalitie],
In gudlie haist I will that ye
2690 Set into few your temporall lands
To men that labours with thair hands,
Bot nocht to ane [jynkine] gentill-man,
That nether will he wirk, nor can;
Quhair-throch the policy may incresse.

TEMPORALITIE

2695 I am content, Sir, be the Messe,
Swa that the Spiritualitie
Sets thairs in few als weill as wee.

CORRECTIOUN

My Spirituall Lords, ar ye content?

SPIRITUALITIE

Na, na, wee man tak advysement;
2700 In sic maters for to conclude
Ovir haistelie, wee think nocht gude.

---

pertiall *partial, biased*   jynkine *dodging*

CORRECTIOUN

Conclude ye nocht with the Common-weil,
Ye salbe punischit, be Sanct Geill!

*Heir sall the Bischops cum with the Freir.*

SPIRITUALITIE

Schir, we can schaw exemptioun
2705 Fra your temporall punitioun,
The quhilk wee purpois till debait.

CORRECTIOUN

Wa than, ye think to stryve for stait.
My Lords, quhat say ye to this play?

TEMPORALITIE

My soverane Lords, we will obay
2710 And tak your part with hart and hand;
Quhat-ever ye pleis us to command.

*Heir sall the Temporal stait sit doun on thair knies and say:*

Bot wee beseik yow, Soveraine,
Of all our cryms that ar bygaine
To gif us ane remissioun,
2715 And heir wee mak to yow conditioun
The Common-weill for till defend
From hence-forth till our lives end.

CORRECTIOUN

On that conditioun I am content
Till pardon yow, sen ye repent.
2720 The Common-weill tak be the hand,
And mak with him perpetuall band.

*Heir sall the Temporal staits, to wit, the Lords and Merchands, imbreasse Johne the Common-weill.*

Johne, have ye ony ma debaits
Against the Lords of Spirituall staits?

JOHNE

Na, Sir, I dar nocht speik ane word.

To plaint on preists, it is na bourd!

   CORRECTIOUN
Flyt on thy fow fill, I desyre the,
Swa that thou schaw bot the veritie.

   JOHNE
Grandmerces, then I sall nocht spair
First to compleine on the Vickair:
2730 The pure cottar being lyke to die,
Haifand young infants twa or thrie,
And hes twa ky, but ony ma,
The Vickar most haif ane of thay
With the gray frugge that covers the bed,
2735 Howbeit the wyfe be purelie cled;
And gif the wyfe die on the morne,
Thocht all the bairns sould be forlorne,
The uther kow he cleiks away
With the pure cot of raploch gray.
2740 Wald God this custome war put doun,
Quhilk never was foundit be ressoun!

   TEMPORALITIE
Ar all thay tails trew that thou telles?

   PAUPER
Trew, sir, the Divill stick me elles.
For be the Halie Trinitie,
2745 That same was practeisit on me;
For our Vickar, God give him pyne,
Hes yit thrie tydie kye of myne,
Ane for my father, and for my wyfe ane uther,
And the thrid cow he tuke for Mald, my mother.

   JOHNE
2750 Our Persone heir, he takis na uther pyne,
Bot to ressave his teinds and spend them syne;
Howbeit he be obleist by gude ressoun
To preich the Evangell to his parochoun,
Howbeit thay suld want preiching sevintin yeir,

---

bourd *joke*   fow *full*   frugge *quilt*   cleiks *snatches*
cot *coat*   raploch *coarse material*   parochoun *parishioners*

2755 Our Person will not want ane scheif of beir.
           PAUPER
       Our bishops with thair lustie rokats quhyte,
       Thay flow in riches, [royaltie] and delyte;
       Lyke Paradice bene thair palices and places,
       And wants na pleasour of the fairest faces.
2760 Al thir prelates hes great prerogatyves,
       For quhy, thay may depairt ay with thair wyves
       Without ony correctioun or damnage,
       Syne tak ane uther wantoner, but mariage.
       But doubt I wald think it ane pleasant lyfe,
2765 Ay on quhen I list to part with my wyfe,
       Syne tak ane uther of far greiter bewtie!
       Bot ever alace, my Lords, that may not be,
       For I am bund, alace, in mariage;
       Bot thay lyke rams rudlie in thair rage
2770 Unpysalt rinnis amang the sillie yowis,
       Sa lang as kynde of Nature in them growis.
           PERSOUN
       Thou lies, fals huirsun raggit loun!
       Thair is na priests in all this toun
       That ever usit sic vicious crafts.
           JOHNE
2775 The Feind ressave thay flattrand chafts!
       Sir Domine, I trowit ye had be dum.
       Quhair Devil gat we this ill-fairde blaitie-bum?
           PERSOUN
       To speik of preists, be sure it is na bourds:
       Thay will burne men now for rakles words,
2780 And all thay words ar herisie in deid.
           JOHNE
       The mekill Feind resave the saul that leid!
       All that I say is trew, thocht thou be greifit,
       And that I offer on thy pallet to preif it.

_____

beir _bere_   rokats _rochets, white surplices worn by bishops and_
_abbots_   unpysalt _with an erection_   chafts _jaws_
blaitie-bum _idler_   rakles _careless_   pallet _head_

My Lords, quhy do ye thoil that lurdan loun
2785 Of kirk-men to speik sic detractioun?
I let yow wit, my Lords, it is na bourds
Of prelats for till speik sic wantoun words.

*Heir Spiritualitie fames and rages.*

Yon villaine puttis me out of charitie!
TEMPORALITIE
Quhy, my Lord, sayis he ocht bot verity?
2790 Ye can nocht stop ane pure man for till pleinye:
Gif he hes faltit, summond him to your seinye.
SPIRITUALITIE
Yea, that I sall. I mak greit God a vow
He sall repent that he spak of the kow.
I will not suffer sic words of yon villaine.
PAUPER
2795 Then gar gif me my thrie fat ky againe!
SPIRITUALITIE
Fals carle, to speik to me stands thou not aw?
PAUPER
The Feind resave them that first devysit that law!
Within an houre efter my Dade was deid
The Vickar had my kow hard by the heid.
PERSOUN
2800 Fals huirsun carle, I say that law is gude,
Becaus it hes bene lang our consuetude.
PAUPER
Quhen I am Paip, that law I sal put doun;
It is ane sair law for the pure commoun.
SPIRITUALITIE
I mak an vow, thay words thou sal repent!
GUDE COUNSALL
2805 I yow requyre, my Lords, be patient.
Wee came nocht heir for disputatiouns;
Wee came to make gude reformatiouns:
Heirfoir of this your propositioun

---

seinye  *consistory court*

Conclude, and put to executioun.
          MERCHAND
2810  My Lords, conclud that al the temporal lands
      Be set in few to laboreris with thair hands
      With sic restrictiouns as sall be devysit,
      That thay may live and nocht to be supprysit,
      With ane ressonabill augmentatioun,
2815  And quhen thay heir ane proclamatioun
      That the Kings Grace dois mak him for the weir,
      That thay be reddie with harneis, bow and speir.
      As for myself, my Lord, this I conclude.
          GUDE COUNSALL
      Sa say we all, your ressoun be sa gude:
2820  To mak ane Act on this we ar content.
          JOHNE
      On that, Sir Scribe, I tak ane instrument.
      Quhat do ye of the corspresent and kow?
          GUDE COUNSALL
      I wil conclude nathing of that as now,
      Without my Lord of Spiritualitie
2825  Thairto consent, with all this haill cleargie.
      My Lord Bischop, will ye thairto consent?
          SPIRITUALITIE
      Na, na, never till the Day of Judgement:
      Wee will want nathing that wee have in use,
      Kirtill nor kow, teind lambe, teind gryse nor guse.
          TEMPORALITIE
2830  Forsuith, my Lord, I think we suld conclude:
      Seing this kow ye have in consuetude,
      Wee will decerne heir that the King[i]s Grace
      Sall wryte unto the Paipis Holines;
      With his consent be proclamatioun,
2835  Baith corspresent and cow wee sall cry doun.
          SPIRITUALITIE
      To that, my Lords, wee plainlie disassent.
      Noter, thairof I tak ane instrument.

      ———

      augmentatioun  *promotion in dignity*   corspresent  *death duty*
      kirtill  *gown*   gryse  *sucking pig*   decerne  *decree*
      noter  *notary public ( see note )*

#### TEMPORALITIE

My Lord, be Him that al the warld hes wrocht,
Wee set nocht by quhider ye consent or nocht:
2840  Ye ar bot ane Estait, and we ar twa,
*Et ubi major pars ibi tota*!

#### JOHNE

My Lords, ye haif richt prudentlie concludit.
Tak tent now how the land is clein denudit
Of gould and silver, quhilk daylie gais to Rome
2845  For buds, mair then the rest of Christindome.
War I ane king, Sir, be Coks Passioun,
I sould gar mak ane proclamatioun
That never ane penny sould go to Rome at all,
Na mair then did to Peter nor to Paull.
2850  Do ye nocht sa, heir for conclusioun
I gif yow all my braid black malesoun.

#### MERCHAND

It is of treuth, sirs, by my Christindome,
That mekil of our money gais to Rome.
For we merchants, I wait, within our bounds,
2855  Hes furneist preists ten hundreth thowsand punds
For thair finnance; nane knawis sa weill as wee.
Thairfoir, my Lords, devyse sum remedie,
For throw thir playis and thir promotioun,
Mair for denners nor for devotioun,
2860  Sir Symonie hes maid with them ane band,
The gould of weicht thay leid out of the land.
The Commoun-weil thair throch bein sair opprest,
Thairfoir devyse remeid as ye think best.

#### GUDE COUNSALL

It is schort tyme sen ony benefice
2865  Was sped in Rome, except greit bischopries;
Bot now for ane unworthie vickarage
Ane preist will rin to Rome in pilgramage.
Ane cavell quhilk was never at the scule

---

Et ubi … ibi tota 'And where the greater part is, there is the whole'
(*see note*)   malesoun *curse*   playis *pleas*   cavell *wretch*

Will rin to Rome and keip ane bischops mule,
2870 Ane syne cum hame with mony colorit crack,
With ane buirdin of benefices on his back;
Quhilk bene against the law, ane man alane
For till posses ma benefices nor ane.
Thir greit commands, I say withoutin faill,
2875 Sould nocht be given bot to the blude royall:
Sa I conclude, my Lords, and sayis for me,
Ye sould annull all this pluralitie.

SPIRITUALITIE

The Paip hes given us dispensatiouns!

GUDE COUNSALL

Yea, that is be your fals narratiouns,
2880 Thocht the Paip for your pleasour will dispence,
I trow that can nocht cleir your conscience.
Advyse, my Lords, quhat ye think to conclude.

TEMPORALITIE

Sir, be my faith, I think it verie gude
That fra hence furth na preistis sall pas to Rome,
2885 Becaus our substance thay do still consume;
For pleyis and for thair profeit singulair
Thay haif of money maid this realme bair.
And als I think it best, be my advyse,
That ilk preist sall haif bot ane benefice;
2890 And gif thay keip nocht that fundatioun
It sall be caus of deprivatioun.

MERCHAND

As ye haif said, my Lord, we wil consent:
Scribe, mak ane act on this, incontinent.

GUDE COUNSALL

My Lords, thair is ane thing yit unproponit:
2895 How prelatis and preists aucht to be disponit.
This beand done, we have the les ado.
Quhat say ye, sirs? This is my counsall, lo:
That or wee end this present parliament
Of this mater to tak rype advysement.

---

colorit *inflated*   commands *offices in commendam* ( *see note* )
unproponit *undeclared*

[ 104

2900 Mark weill, my Lords, thair is na benefice
Given to ane man, bot for ane gude office :
Quha taks office and syne thay can nocht us it,
Giver and taker, I say, ar baith abusit.
Ane bischops office is for to be ane preichour,
2905 And of the Law of God ane publick teachour ;
Richt sa the persone unto his parochoun
Of the Evangell sould leir them ane lessoun.
Thair sould na man desyre sic dignities
Without he be abill for that office,
2910 And for that caus, I say without leising,
Thay have thair teinds, and for na uther thing.

SPIRITUALITIE

Freind, quhair find ye that we suld prechours be?

GUDE COUNSALL

Luik quhat Sanct Paul wryts unto Timothie.
Tak thair the Buik ; let se gif ye can spell !

SPIRITUALITIE

2915 I never red that ; thairfoir reid it your sell !

*Gude Counsall sall read thir wordis on ane buik :*

[GUDE COUNSALL]
*Fidelis sermo, si quis Episcopatum desiderat, bonum
opus desiderat. Oportet [ ergo ], eum irreprehensibilem
esse, unius uxoris virum, sobrium, prudentem, ornatum,
pudicum, hospitalem, doctorem non vinolentum, non
2920 percussorem sed modestum.*
That is : 'This is a true saying, If any man desire
the office of a Bishop, he desireth a worthie worke :
A Bishop therefore must be unreproveable, the husband
of one wife, etc.

SPIRITUALITIE

2925 Ye temporall men, be Him that heryit Hell,
Ye are ovir peart with sik maters to mell.

TEMPORALITIE

Sit still, my Lord, ye neid not for til braull :
Thir ar the verie words of th'Apostill Paull.

---

leir *teach*   peart *bold*

**SPIRITUALITIE**

Sum sayis, be Him that woare the croun of thorne,
It had been gude that Paull had neir bene borne.

**GUDE COUNSALL**

Bot ye may knaw, my Lord, Sanct Pauls intent.
Schir, red ye never the Newtestament?

**SPIRITUALITIE**

Na, sir, be him that our Lord Jesus sauld,
I red never the New Testament nor Auld,
Nor ever thinks to do, sir, be the Rude:
I heir freiris say that reiding dois na gude.

**GUDE COUNSALL**

Till yow to reid them, I think it is na lack,
For anis I saw them baith bund on your back,
That samin day that ye was consecrat.
Sir, quhat meinis that?

**SPIRITUALITIE**

The Feind stick them that wat!

**MERCHAND**

Then befoir God how can ye be excusit,
To haif ane office, and waits not how to us it?
Quhairfoir war gifin yow all the temporal lands,
And all thir teinds ye haif amang your hands?
Thay war givin yow for uther causses, I weine,
Nor mummil matins and hald your clayis cleine.
Ye say to the Appostils that ye succeid,
Bot ye schaw nocht that into word nor deid.
The law is plaine: our teinds suld furnisch teichours.

**GUDE COUNSALL**

Yea, that it sould, or susteine prudent preichours.

**PAUPER**

Sir, God nor I be stickit with ane knyfe
Gif ever our persoun preichit in all his lyfe!

**PERSOUN**

Quhat devil raks the of our preiching, undocht?

**PAUPER**

Think ye that ye suld have the teinds for nocht?

————

wat *know*    undocht *wretch*

PERSOUN

2955 Trowis thou to get remeid, carle, of that thing?

PAUPER

Yea, be Gods breid ; richt sone, war I ane king.

PERSOUN

Wald thou of prelats mak deprivatioun?

PAUPER

Na, I suld gar them keip thair fundatioun.
Quhat devill is this? Quhom of sould kings stand aw
2960 To do the thing that thay sould be the law?
War I ane king, be Coks deir passioun,
I sould richt sone mak reformatioun !
Failyeand thairof, your Grace sould richt sone finde
That preists sall leid yow lyke ane bellie blinde.

JOHNE

2965 Quhat gif King David war leivand in thir dayis,
The quhilk did found sa mony gay abayis?
Or out of Heavin quhat gif he luikit doun
And saw the great abominatioun
Amang thir abesses and thir nunries,
2970 Thair publick huirdomes and thair harlotries?
He wald repent he narrowit sa his bounds,
Of yeirlie rent thriescoir of thowsand pounds.
His successours maks litill ruisse, I ges,
Of his devotioun, or of his holines.

ABBASSE

2975 How dar thou, carle, presume for to declair,
Or for to mell the with sa heich a mater?
For in Scotland thair did yit never ring,
I let the wit, ane mair excellent king :
Of holines he was the verie plant,
2980 And now in Heavin he is ane michtfull Sanct
Becaus that fyftein abbasies he did found,
Quhair-throw great riches hes ay done abound
Into our Kirk, and daylie yit abunds.
Bot kings now, I trow, few abbasies founds !
2985 I dar weill say thou art condempnit in Hel,

---

bellie blinde *blindfolded player in Blind Man's Buff* ruisse *boast*

That dois presume with sic maters to mell.
Fals huirsun carle, thou art ovir arrogant,
To judge the deids of sic ane halie sanct!

JOHNE

King James the First, roy of this regioun,
2990 Said that he was ane sair sanct to the croun;
I heir men say that he was sumthing blind,
That gave away mair nor he left behind.
His successours that halines did repent
Quhilk gart them do great inconvenient.

ABBASSE

2995 My Lord Bischop, I mervel how that ye
Suffer this carle for to speik heresie,
For be my faith, my Lord, will ye tak tent,
He servis for to be brunt incontinent.
Ye can nocht say bot it is heresie,
3000 To speik against our law and libertie.

SPIRITUALITIE

Sancte pater, I mak yow supplicatioun:
Exame yon carle, syne mak his dilatioun.
I mak ane vow to God omnipotent,
That bystour salbe brunt incontinent!

[FLATTERIE]

3005 Venerabill father, I sall do your command;
Gif he servis deid, I sall sune understand.

Pausa

Fals huirsun carle, schaw furth thy faith.

JOHNE

Me think ye speik as ye war wraith!
To yow I will nathing declair,
3010 For ye ar nocht my ordinair.

FLATTERIE

Quhom in trowis thou, fals monster mangit?

---

mell *meddle*   brunt *burnt*   exame *examine*
dilatioun *delay*   bystour *railer*   ordinair *bishop or other*
*Church dignitary with legal jurisdiction over an area*   mangit *mad*

JOHNE

I trow to God to se the hangit!
War I ane king, be Coks passioun,
I sould gar mak ane congregatioun
3015 Of all the freirs of the four ordouris,
And mak yow vagers on the bordours.
Schir, will ye give me audience,
And I sall schaw your Excellence,
Sa that your Grace will give me leife,
3020 How into God that I beleife.

CORRECTIOUN

Schaw furth your faith, and feinye nocht.

JOHNE

I beleife in God, that all hes wrocht
And creat everie thing of nocht,
And in His Son, our Lord Jesu,
3025 Incarnat of the Virgin trew;
Quha under Pilat tholit passioun,
And deit for our salvatioun,
And on the thrid day rais againe,
As Halie Scriptour schawis plane;
3030 And als, my Lord, it is weill kend
How He did to the Heavin ascend,
And set Him doun at the richt hand
Of God the Father, I understand,
And sall cum judge on Dumisday.
3035 Quhat will ye mair, Sir, that I say?

CORRECTIOUN

Schaw furth the rest; this is na game.

JOHNE

I trow *Sanctam Ecclesiam*—
Bot nocht in thir bischops nor thir freirs,
Quhilk will for purging of thir neirs
3040 Sard up the ta raw and doun the uther.
The mekill Devill resave the fidder!

CORRECTIOUN

Say quhat ye will, sirs, be Sanct Tan,

---

vagers *vagrants*   tholit *suffered*   neirs *kidneys*
sard *copulate*   ta *one*   raw *row*

Me think Johne ane gude Christian man.

**TEMPORALITIE**

My lords, let be your disputatioun :
3045 Conclude with firm deliberatioun
How prelats fra thyne sall be disponit.

**MERCHAND**

I think for me evin as ye first proponit :
That the Kings Grace sall gif na benefice
Bot till ane p[r]eichour that can use that office.
3050 The sillie saul[i]s that bene Christis scheip
Sould nocht be givin to gormand wolfis to keip.
Quhat bene the caus of all the heresies
But the abusioun of the prelacies?
Thay will correct, and will nocht be correctit,
3055 Thinkand to na prince thay wil be subjectit ;
Quhairfoir I can find na better remeid
Bot that thir kings man take it in thair heid
That thair be given to na man bischopries
Except thay preich out throch thair diosies,
3060 And ilk persone preich in his parochon ;
And this I say for finall conclusioun.

**TEMPORALITIE**

Wee think your counsall is verie gude :
As ye have said, wee all conclude.
Of this conclusioun, noter, wee mak ane act.

**SCRYBE**

3065 I wryte all day, bot gets never ane plack !

**PAUPER**

Och, my Lords, for the Halie Trinitie,
Remember to reforme the consistorie !
It hes mair neid of reformatioun
Nor Ploutois court, Sir, be Coks passioun.

**PERSOUN**

3070 Quhat caus hes thou, fals pellour, for to pleinye?
Quhair was ye ever summond to thair seinye?

**PAUPER**

Marie, I lent my gossop my mear to fetch hame coills,

———

plack *fourpenny piece*   pellour *thief*   gossop *neighbour*

And he hir drounit into the querrell hollis;
And I ran to the consistorie for to pleinye,
3075 And thair I happinit amang ane greidie meinye.
Thay gave me first ane thing thay call *citandum*;
Within aucht dayis I gat bot *lybellandum*;
Within ane moneth I gat *ad opponendum*;
In half ane yeir I gat *interloquendum*;
3080 And syne I gat, how call ye it?—*ad replicandum*;
Bot I could never ane word yit understand him.
And than thay gart me cast out mony plackis,
And gart me pay for four and twentie actis.
Bot or thay came half gait to *concludendum*,
3085 The feind a plack was left for to defend him!
Thus thay postponit me twa yeir with thair traine,
Syne *hodie ad octo* bad me cum againe.
And than thir ruiks, thay roupit wonder fast:
For sentence-silver thay cryit at the last.
3090 Of *pronunciandum* thay maid me wonder faine,
Bot I gat never my gude gray meir againe.

   TEMPORALITIE
My Lords, we mon reforme thir consistory lawis,
Quhais great defame above the heavins blawis:
I wist ane man, in persewing of ane kow,
3095 Or he had done he spendit half ane bow.
Sa that the kings honour wee may avance
Wee will conclude as thay have done in France:
Let sprituall maters pas to Spritualitie,
And temporall maters to Temporalitie.
3100 Quha failyeis of this sall cost them of thair gude.
Scribe, mak ane act, for sa wee will conclude.

   SPIRITUALITIE
That act, my Lords, plainlie I will declair,
It is againis our profeit singulair.
Wee will nocht want our profeit, be Sanct Geill!

---

querrell *quarry*   citandum *the first of a series of legal terms
from the Consistory courts ( see note )*   half gait *halfway*
roupit *croaked*   bow *herd*

3105   Your profeit is against the Common-weil.
      It salbe done, my Lords, as ye have wrocht :
      We cure nocht quhidder ye consent or nocht.
      Quhairfoir servis then all thir temporall judges
      Gif temporall maters sould seik at yow refuges?
3110   My Lord, ye say that ye ar sprituall :
      Quhairfoir mell ye then with things temporall?
      As we have done conclude, sa sall it stand.
      Scribe, put our acts in ordour, evin fra-hand !

     SPIRITUALITIE

      Till all your acts plainlie I disassent.
3115   Notar, thairof I tak ane instrument !

*Heir sall Veritie and Chastitie mak thair plaint at the bar.*

     VERITIE

      My soverane, I beseik your Excellence,
      Use justice on Spritualitie,
      The quhilk to us hes done great violence :
      Becaus we did rehers the veritie
3120   Thay put us close into captivitie,
      And sa remanit into subjectioun,
      Into great langour and calamitie,
      Till we war fred be King Correctioun.

     CHASTITIE

      My Lord, I haif great caus for to complaine :
3125   I could get na ludging intill this land,
      The Sprituall stait had me sa at disdane.
      With Dame Sensuall thay have maid sic ane band
      Amang them all na freindschip, sirs, I fand ;
      And quhen I came the nobill [ nunnis ] amang,
3130   My lustie Ladie Priores fra-hand
      Out of hir dortour durlie scho me dang.

     VERITIE

      With the advyse, Sir, of the Parliament,
      Hairtlie we mak yow supplicatioun :
      Cause King Correctioun tak, incontinent,

---

cure *care*    dortour *dormitory*    durlie *roughly*

3135     Of all this sort examinatioun
        Gif thay be digne of deprivatioun.
        Ye have power for to correct sic cases :
        Chease the maist cunning clerks of this natioun
        And put mair prudent pastours in thair places.
3140     My prudent lords, I say that pure craftsmen
        Abufe sum prelats ar mair for to commend :
        Gar exame them, and sa ye sall sune ken
        How thay in vertew bischops dois transcend.

    SCRIBE
        Thy life and craft mak to thir king[i]s kend :
3145     Quhat craft hes thow, declair that to me plaine.

    TAILYEOUR
        Ane tailyour, Sir, that can baith mak and mend,
        I wait nane better into Dumbartane.

    SCRIBE
        Quahirfoir of tailyeours beir[i]s thou the styl?

    TAILYEOUR
        Becaus I wait is nane within ane myll
3150     Can better use that craft, as I suppois,
        For I can mak baith doublit, coat and hois.

    SCRIBE
        How cal thay you, sir, with the schaiping knife?

    SOWTAR
        Ane sowtar, Sir ; nane better into Fyfe.

    SCRIBE
        Tel me quhairfoir ane sowtar ye ar namit?

    SOWTAR
3155     Of that surname I neid nocht be aschamit,
        For I can mak schone, brotekins and buittis :
        Gif mee the coppie of the King[i]s cuittis
        And ye sall se richt sune quhat I can do.
        Heir is my lasts, and weill-wrocht ledder [to] !

    GUDE COUNSALL
3160     O Lord my God, this is an mervelous thing,
        How sic misordour in this realme sould ring !

---

digne *worthy*    chease *choose*    brotekins *half-boots*
cuittis *ankles*

Sowtars and tailyeours, thay ar far mair expert
In thair pure craft and in thair handie art
Nor ar our prelatis in thair vocatioun.
3165 I pray yow, sirs: mak reformatioun.

VERITIE

Alace, alace ! quhat gars thir temporal kings
Into the Kirk of Christ admit sic doings?
My Lords, for lufe of Christ[i]s passioun,
Of thir ignorants mak deprivatioun,
3170 Quhilk in the court can do bot flatter and fleich,
And put into thair places that can preich ;
Send furth and seik sum devoit cunning clarks
That can steir up the peopill to gude warks.

CORRECTIOUN

As ye have done, Madame, I am content.
3175 Hoaw, Diligence, pas hynd incontinent
And seik out throw all town[i]s and cities,
And visie all the universities ;
Bring us sum doctours of divinitie,
With licents in the law and theologie,
3180 With the maist cunning clarks in all this land.
Speid sune your way, and bring them heir fra-hand.

DILIGENCE

Quhat gif I find sume halie provinciall
Or minister of the Gray Freiris all,
Or ony freir that can preich prudentlie?
3185 Sall I bring them with me in cumpanie?

CORRECTIOUN

Cair thou nocht quhat estait sa ever he be,
Sa thay can teich and preich the veritie.
Maist cunning clarks with us is best beluifit ;
To dignitie thay salbe first promuifit.
3190 Quhidder thay be munk, channon, preist or freir,
Sa thay can preich, faill nocht to bring them heir.

DILIGENCE

Than fair-weill, Sir, for I am at the flicht.
I pray the Lord to send yow all gude-nicht.

*Heir sall Diligence pas to the palyeoun.*

Sir, we beseik your soverane Celsitude
3195 Of our dochtours to have compassioun,
Quhom wee may na way marie, be the Rude,
Without wee mak sum alienatioun
Of our land for thair supportatioun.
For quhy? The markit raisit bene sa hie,
3200 That prelats dochtours of this natioun
Ar maryit with sic superfluitie,
Thay will nocht spair to gif twa thowsand pound
With thair dochtours to ane nobill man,
In riches sa thay do superabound.
3205 Bot we may nocht do sa, be Sanct Allane;
Thir proud prelats our dochtours sair may ban,
That thay remaine at hame sa lang unmaryit.
Schir, let your barrouns do the best thay can,
Sum of our dochtours, I dreid, salbe miscaryit.

CORRECTIOUN
3210 My Lord, your complaint is richt ressonabill,
And richt sa to our dochtours profitabill.
I think, or I pas aff this natioun,
Of this mater till mak reformatioun.

*Heir sall enter Common Thift.*

THIFT
Ga be the gait, man, let me gang!
3215 How, Devill, came I into this thrang?
With sorrow I may sing my sang,
    And I be taine.
For I have run baith nicht and day;
Throw speid of fut I gat away.
3220 Gif I be kend heir, wallaway!
    I will be slaine.
PAUPER
Quhat is thy name, man, be thy thrift?
THIFT
Huirsun, thay call me Common Thrift,
For quhy, I had na uther schift
3225 Sen I was borne.

In Eusdaill was my dwelling place;
Mony ane wyfe gart I cry 'alace'.
At my hand thay gat never grace,
    Bot ay forlorne.
3230 Sum sayis ane king is cum amang us
That purposis to head and hang us;
Thair is na grace gif he way fang us
    Bot on an pin.
Ring he, we theifis will get na gude:
3235 I pray God and the Halie Rude
He had bene smoird into his cude,
    And all his kin.
Get this curst king me in his grippis,
My craig will wit quhat weyis my hippis!
3240 The Devill I gif his toung and lippis
    That of me tellis!
Adew, I dar na langer tarie,
For, be I kend, thay will me carie
And put me in ane fierie farie:
3245     I se nocht ellis.
I raife—be Him that herryit Hell,
I had almaist foryet my-sell.
Will na gude fallow to me tell
    Quhair I may finde
3250 The Earle of Rothus best haiknay?
That was my earand heir away—
He is richt starck, as I heir say,
    And swift as winde.
Heir is my brydill and my spurris
3255 To gar him race ovir [feild] and furris;
Micht I him get to Ewis durris
    I tak na cuir.
Of that hors micht I get ane sicht,
I haife na doubt yit or midnicht

---

Eusdaill *Ewesdale, Dumfriesshire (see note)*  fang *seize*
ring *reign*  weyis *weighs*  farie *confusion*
haiknay *a horse suitable for long journeys*  starck *strong*
furris *furrows*

3260 That he and I sould tak the flicht
    Throch Dysert mure.
That he and I sould tak the flicht
Of cumpanarie tell me, brother,
Quhilk is the richt way to the Strother?
I wald be welcum to my mother
3265     Gif I micht speid.
I wald gif baith my coat and bonet
To get my Lord Lindesayis broun jonet:
War he beyond the watter of Annet
    We sould nocht dreid.
3270 Quhat now, Oppressioun, my maister deir,
Quhat mekill Devill hes brocht yow heir?
Maister, tell me the caus perqueir,
    Quhat is that ye have done?

OPPRESSIOUN

Forsuith, the King[i]s majestie
3275 Hes set me heir, as ye may se.
Micht I speik [with] Temporalitie,
    He wald me releife sone.
I beseik yow, my brother deir,
Bot halfe ane houre for to sit heir:
3280 Ye knaw that I was never sweir
    Yow to defend.
Put in your leg into my place,
And heir I sweir, be God[di]s grace,
Yow to releife within schort space,
3285     Syne let yow wend.

THIFT

Than, maister deir, gif me your hand,
And mak to me ane faithfull band
That ye sall cum agane fra-hand,
    Withoutin faill.

OPPRESSIOUN

3290 Tak thair my hand richt faithfullie;
Als I promit the verelie

---

Strother *Struthers Castle, Fife (see note)*   jonet *jennet, a small Spanish horse*   Annet *Annat Water, Perthshire (see note)* sweir *idle*   wend *go*

To gif to the ane cuppill of kye
In Liddisdaill.

*Heir sall Commoun Thift put his feit in the stokkis, and
Oppressioun sall steill away and betra him.*

Bruder, tak patience in thy pane,
3295 For I sweir the, be Sanct Fillane,
We twa sall nevir meit agane
In land nor toun.
THIFT
Maister, will ye not keip conditioun,
And put me forth of this suspitioun?
OPPRESSIOUN
3300 Na, nevir quhill I get remissioun!
A-dew to my companyeoun:
I sall commend the to thy dame.
THIFT
Adew than, in the Divillis name:
For to be fals thinkis thow na schame
3305 To leif me in this pane?
Thow art ane loun, and that ane liddir!
OPPRESSIOUN
Bo, man! I will go to Balquhiddir.
It sall be Pasche, be Goddis moder,
Or evir we meit agane.]
3310 Haif I nocht maid ane honest schift,
That hes betrasit Common Thift?
For thair is nocht under the lift
Ane curster cors;
I am richt sure that he and I
3315 Within this hal[f] yeir craftely
Hes stolne ane thowsand scheip and ky,
By meiris and hors.
Wald God I war baith sound and haill
Now liftit into Liddisdaill;
3320 The Mers sould find me beif and kaill—

———

liddir *lazy one* lift *heavens* by *not counting*

Quhat rak of bread?
War I thair liftit with my life,
The Devill sould stick me with ane knyfe
And ever I come againe to Fyfe
3325    Quhill I war dead!
Adew, I leife the Devill amang yow,
That in his fingers he may fang yow,
With all leill men that dois belang yow;
    For I may rew
3330  That ever I came into this land,
For quhy, ye may weill understand:
I gat na geir to turne my hand.
    Yit anis, adew!

*Heir sall Diligence convoy the thrie clarks.*

DILIGENCE
Sir, I have brocht unto your Excellence
3335  Thir famous clarks, of greit intelligence,
For to the common peopill thay can preich,
And in the scuilis in Latine toung can teich.
This is ane Doctour of Divinitie,
And thir twa licents-men of gravitie.
3340  I heare men say thair conversatioun
Is maist in divine contemplatioun.
DOCTOUR
Grace, peace and rest from the hie Trinitie
Mot rest amang this godlie cumpanie!
Heir ar we cumde as your obedients,
3345  For to fulfil your just commandements.
Quhat-evir it please your Grace us to command,
Sir, it sall be obeyit evin fra-hand.
REX
Gud freinds, ye ar richt welcome to us all.
Sit doun all thrie, and geif us your counsall.
CORRECTIOUN
3350  Sir, I give yow baith counsal and command:
In your office use exercitioun,

--------

exercitioun *industry*

First that ye gar search out throch all your land
Quha can nocht put to executioun
Thair office efter the institutioun
3355 Of godlie lawis, conforme to thair vocatioun;
Put in thair places men of gude conditioun,
And this ye do without dilatioun.
Ye ar the head, Sir, of this congregatioun,
Preordinat be God omnipotent,
3360 Quhilk hes me send to mak yow supportatioun,
Into the quhilk I salbe diligent.
And quha-saever beis inobedient
And will nocht suffer for to be correctit,
Thay salbe all deposit incontinent,
3365 And from your presence thay sall be dejectit.

    GUDE COUNSALL
Begin first at the spritualitie,
And tak of them examinatioun
Gif thay can use their divyne dewetie;
And als I mak yow supplicatioun,
3370 All thay that hes thair offices misusit,
Of them make haistie deprivatioun,
Sa that the peopill be na mair abusit.

    CORRECTIOUN
Ye ar ane prince of spritualitie:
How have ye usit your office, now let se.

    SPIRITUALITIE
3375 My Lords, quhen was thair ony prelats wont
Of thair office till ony king mak count?
Bot of my office gif ye wald have the feill,
I let yow wit I have it usit weill;
For I tak in my count twyse in the yeir,
3380 Wanting nocht of my teind ane boll of beir.
I gat gude payment of my temporall lands,
My buttock-maill, my coattis and my offrands,
With all that dois perteine my benefice.
Consider now, my Lord, gif I be wyse.

———

dejectit *thrown out*   boll *measure of grain*
buttock-maill *fine for fornication*

3385 I dar nocht marie contrair the common law:
Ane thing thair is, my Lord, that ye may knaw—
Howbeit I dar nocht plainlie spouse ane wyfe,
Yit concubeins I have had four or fyfe,
And to my sons I have givin rich rewairds,
3390 And all my dochters maryit upon lairds.
I let yow wit, my Lord, I am na fuill,
For quhy, I ryde upon ane amland muill.
Thair is na temporall lord in all this land
That maks sic cheir, I let yow understand;
3395 And als, my Lord, I gif with gude intentioun
To divers temporall lords ane yeirlie pensioun,
To that intent that thay with all thair hart
In richt and wrang sal plainlie tak my part.
Now have I tauld yow, Sir, on my best ways,
3400 How that I have exercit my office.

    CORRECTIOUN

I weind your office had bene for til preich,
And Gods law to the peopill [for til] teich.
Quhairfoir weir ye that mytour, ye me tell?

    SPIRITUALITIE

I wat nocht, man, be Him that herryit Hel.

    CORRECTIOUN

3405 That dois betakin that ye with gude intent
Sould teich and preich the Auld and Newtestament.

    SPIRITUALITIE

I have ane freir to preiche into my place:
Of my office ye heare na mair quhill Pasche!

    CHASTITIE

My Lords, this Abbot and this Priores,
3410 Thay scorne thair gods. This is my reason quhy:
Thay beare an habite of feinyeit halines,
And in thair deid thay do the contrary.
For to live chaist thay vow solemnitly,
Bot fra that thay be sikker of thair bowis
3415 Thay live in huirdome and in harlotry.

———

amland *ambling*   weind *believed*   sikker *sure*
bowis   *papal Bulls, here giving formal confirmation of
the Abbot's election*

Examine them, Sir, how thay observe thair vowis.

CORRECTIOUN

Sir scribe, ye sall at Chasties requeist
Pas and exame yon thrie in gudlie haist.

SCRIBE

Father Abbott, this counsall bids me speir,
3420 How ye have usit your abbay thay wald heir;
And als thir kings hes givin to me commissioun
Of your office for to mak inquisitioun.

ABBOT

Tuiching my office, I say to yow plainlie
My monks and I, we leif richt easilie.
3425 Thair is na monks from Carrick to Carraill
That fairs better, and drinks mair helsum aill.
My prior is ane man of great devotioun;
Thairfoir daylie he gets ane double portioun.

SCRIBE

My Lords, how have ye keip[i]t your thrie vows?

ABBOT

3430 Indeid, richt weill till I gat hame my bows.
In my abbay quhen I was sure professour,
Then did I leife as did my predecessour:
My paramours is baith als fat and fair
As ony wench into the toun of Air.
3435 I send my sons to Pareis to the scullis;
I traist in God that thay salbe na fuillis.
And all my douchters I have weill providit;
Now judge ye gif my office be weill gydit.

SCRIBE

Maister persoun, schaw us gif ye can preich.

PERSOUN

3440 Thocht I preich not, I can play at the caiche.
I wait thair is nocht ane amang yow all
Mair ferilie can play at the fut-ball;
And for the carts, the tabils and the dyse,
Abone all persouns I may beir the pryse.

———

helsum *beneficial*   caiche *hand tennis*   ferilie *nimbly*
carts *playing cards*   tabils *backgammon*

3445 Our round bonats we mak them now four- nuickit,
Of richt fyne stuiff, gif yow list cum and luik it.
Of my office I have declarit to the:
Speir quhat ye pleis, ye get na mair of me.

SCRIBE
Quhat say ye now, my lady priores?
3450 How have ye usit your office, can ye ges?
Quhat was the caus ye refusit harbrie
To this young lustie ladie, Chastitie?

PRIORES
I wald have harborit hir with gude intent,
Bot my complexioun thairto wald not assent.
3455 I do my office efter auld use and wount:
To your Parliament I will mak na mair count.

VERITIE
Now caus sum of your cunning clarks
Quhilk ar expert in heavinlie warks,
And men fulfillit with charitie
3460 That can weill preich the veritie,
And gif to sum of them command
Ane sermon for to mak fra-hand.

CORRECTIOUN
As ye have said, I am content
To gar sum preich incontinent.

*Pausa*

3465 *Magister noster*, I ken how ye can teiche
Into the scuillis, and that richt ornatlie:
I pray yow now that ye wald please to preiche
In Inglisch toung, land folk to edifie.

DOCTOUR
Soverane, I sall obey yow humbillie,
3470 With ane schort sermon presentlie in this place,
And schaw the word of God unfeinyeitlie,
And sinceirlie, as God will give me grace.

---

four-nuikit *four-cornered ( see note )*   complexioun *temperament*
Inglisch *Lowland Scots ( see note )*   land folk *country people*

*Heir sall the Doctor pas to the pulpit and say:*

*Si vis ad vitam ingredi, serva mandata.*
Devoit peopill, Sanct Paull the preichour sayis
3475 The fervent luife and fatherlie pitie
Quhilk God Almichtie hes schawin mony wayis
To man in his corrupt fragilitie
Exceids all luife in earth, sa far that we
May never to God mak recompence conding;
3480 As quha-sa lists to reid the veritie,
In Halie Scripture he may find this thing:
*Sic Deus dilexit mundum.*
Tuiching nathing the great prerogative
Quhilk God to man in his creatioun lent,
3485 How man of nocht creat superlative
Was to the image of God Omnipotent,
Let us consider that speciall luife ingent
God had to man quhen our foir-father fell,
Drawing us all in his loynis immanent,
3490 Captive from gloir in thirlage to the Hel:
Quhen angels fell, thair miserabill ruyne
Was never restorit, bot for our miserie
The Son of God, secund persone divyne,
In ane pure virgin tuke humanitie;
3495 Syne for our saik great harmis suffered He
In fasting, walking, in preiching, cauld and heit,
And at the last ane schamefull death deit He—
Betwix twa theifis in Croce He yeild the spreit,
And quhair an drop of His maist precious blude
3500 Was recompence sufficient and conding
Ane thowsand warlds to ransoun from that wod
Infernall Feind, Sathan, notwithstanding
He luifit us sa that for our ransoning

---

Si vis ... mandata *'But if thou wilte entre into lyfe, kepe the
commaundements' (Matt. 19:17)* devoit *devout*
conding *suitable* Sic Deus dilexit mundum *'For God so loveth
the worlde ...' (John 3:16)* ingent *innate* thirlage *bondage*
wod *mad*

[ 124

He sched furth all the blude of His bodie,
3505 Riven, rent and sair wondit quhair He did hing,
Naild on the Croce on the Mont Calvary.

*Et copiosa apud eum redemptio.*
O cruell death, be the the venemous
Dragon, the Devill infernall, lost his pray;
3510 Be the the stinkand, mirk, contageous,
Deip pit of Hell mankynd escaipit fray;
Be the the port of Paradice alsway
Was patent maid unto the Heavin sa hie,
Opinnit to man and maid ane reddie way
3515 To gloir eternall with th'Haly Trinitie.
And yit for all this luife incomparabill
God askis na rewaird fra us againe
Bot luife for luife; in His command but fabill
Conteinit ar all haill the Lawis ten,
3520 Baith ald and new, commandements ilk ane.
Luife bene the ledder quhilk hes bot steppis twa,
Be quhilk we may clim up to lyfe againe,
Out of this vaill of miserie and wa.

*Diliges Dominum Deum tuum ex toto corde tuo, et*
3525 *proximum tuum sicut teipsum: in his duobus*
*mandatis etc.*

The first step suithlie of this ledder is
To luife thy God as the fontaine and well
Of luife and grace; and the secund, I wis,
3530 To luife thy nichtbour as thou luifis thy sell.
Quha tynis ane stop of thir twa gais to Hel
Bot he repent and turne to Christ anone:
Hauld this na fabill, the Halie Evangell

---

Et copiosa ... redemptio '*For with [Him] there is ... plenteous*
*redempcion*' (*Vulgate Psalm 129:7*)   patent *open*   but fabill *truly*
Diliges ... datis '*Love the Lorde thy God with al thyne*
*hearte ... [Love] thyne neyghboure as thy selfe. In these two*
*commaundementes [ hang all the lawe and the Prophetes' ]*
(*Matt. 22:37–40; see note*)   tynis *loses*   stop *step*

Bears in effect thir word[i]s everie one.

3535   *Si vis ad vitam ingredi, serva mandata Dei.*
       Thay tyne thir steps all thay quha evir did sin,
       In pryde, invy, in ire and lecherie,
       In covetice or ony extreme win,
       Into sweirnes or into gluttonie,
3540   Or quha dois nocht the deid[i]s of mercie,
       Gif hungrie meit and gif the naikit clayis.
           PERSOUN
       Now, walloway! Thinks thow na schame to lie?
       I trow the Devill a word is trew thow sayis!
       Thow sayis thair is not twa steppis to the Heavin;
3545   Quha failyeis them man backwarts fall in Hell.
       I wait it is ten thowsand mylis and sevin
       Gif it be na mair, I do it upon thy sell.
       Schort-leggit men, I se be Bryd[i]s bell,
       Will nevir cum thair, thay steppis bene sa wyde:
3550   Gif thay be the words of the Evangell,
       The sprituall men hes mister of ane gyde!
           ABBOT
       And I beleif that cruikit men and blinde
       Sall never get up upon sa hich ane ledder:
       By my gude faith, I dreid to ly behinde,
3555   Without God draw me up into ane tedder!
       Quhat and I fal? Than I will break my bledder!
       And I cum thair this day, the Devill speid me,
       Except God make me lichter nor ane fedder,
       Or send me doun gude widcok wingis to flie.
           PERSONE
3560   Cum doun, dastart, and gang sell draiff!
       I understand nocht quhat thow said—
       Thy words war nather corne nor caiff.
       I walde thy toung againe war laide!
       Quhair thou sayis pryde is deidlie sin,

-------

win *profit*   sweirnes *idleness*   mister *need*
hich *high*    widcok *woodcock*     draiff *draff, hogswill*
caiff *chaff*  laide *quietened*

3565     I say pryde is bot honestie,
      And covetice of warldlie win
      Is bot wisdome, I say for me.
      Ire, hardines and gluttonie
      Is nathing ellis but lyfis fude ;
3570     The naturall sin of lecherie
      Is bot trew luife: all thir ar gude.
        DOCTOUR
      God and the Kirk hes givin command
      That all gude Christian men refuse them.
        PERSONE
      Bot war thay sin, I understand,
3575     We men of kirk wald never use them !
        DOCTOUR
      Brother, I pray the Trinitie
      Your faith and charitie to support,
      Causand yow knaw the veritie,
      That ye your subjects may confort.
3580     To your prayers, peopill, I recommend
      The rewlars of this nobill regioun,
      That our Lord God His grace mot to them send,
      On trespassours to mak punitioun ;
      Prayand to God from feind[ i ]s yow defend,
3585     And of your sins to gif yow full remissioun.
      I say na mair ; to God I yow commend.

*Heir Diligence spyis the Freir roundand to the Prelate.*

      DILIGENCE
      My Lords, I persave that the Sprituall stait
      Be way of deid purpois to mak debait,
      For be the counsall of yon flattrand freir
3590     Thay purpois to mak all this toun on steir.
      FIRST LICENT
      Traist ye that thay wilbe inobedient
      To that quhilk is decreitit in Parliament?

---

roundand *whispering*   on steir *astir*

DILIGENCE

Thay se the Paip with awfull ordinance
Makis weir against the michtie King of France;
3595 Richt sa thay think that prelats suld nocht sunyie
Be way of deid defend thair patrimonie.

FIRST LICENT

I pray the, brother, gar me understand
Quhair ever Christ possessit ane fut of land.

DILIGENCE

Yea, that He did, Father, withoutin fail,
3600 For Christ Jesus was King of Israell.

FIRST LICENT

I grant that Christ was King abufe al kings;
Bot He mellit never with temporall things,
As He hes plainlie done declair Him-sell,
As thou may reid in His halie Evangell.
3605 Birds hes thair nests and todis hes thair den,
Bot Christ Jesus, the Saviour of men,
In all this warld hes nocht ane penny braid
Quhair-on He may repois His heavinlie heid.

DILIGENCE

And is that trew?

[FIRST LICENT]

Yes, brother, be Alhallows!
3610 Christ Jesus had na propertie bot the gallows,
And left not, quhen He yeildit up the Spreit,
To by Himself ane simpill winding-scheit.

DILIGENCE

Christs successours, I understand,
Thinks na schame to have temporall land;
3615 Father, thay have na will, I yow assure,
In this warld to be indigent and pure.
Bot, Sir, sen ye ar callit sapient,
Declair to me the caus with trew intent
Quhy that my lustie Lady Veritie
3620 Hes nocht bene weill treatit in this cuntrie?

BATCHELER

Forsuith, quhair prelats uses the counsall

---

sunyie *hesitation*   mellit *meddled*   todis *foxes*

Of beggand freirs in monie regioun,
And thay prelats with princes principall,
The veritie but doubt is trampit doun
3625 And Common-weill put to confusioun:
Gif this be trew to yow I me report.
Thairfoir, my Lords, mak reformatioun
Or ye depart, hairtlie I yow exhort.
Sirs, freirs wald never, I yow assure,
3630 That ony prelats usit preiching;
And prelats tuke on them that cure,
Freirs wald get nathing for thair fleiching:
Thairfoir I counsall yow fra-hand,
Banische yon freir out of this land,
3635     And that incontinent.
Do ye nocht sa, withoutin weir,
He will mak all this toun on steir—
    I knaw his fals intent.
Yon Priores, withoutin fabill,
3640 I think scho is nocht profitabill
    For Christis regioun.
To begin reformatioun
Mak of them deprivatioun:
    This is my opinioun.
FIRST SERGEANT
3645 Sir, pleis ye that we twa invaid them,
And ye sall se us sone degraid them
    Of cowll and chaplarie.
CORRECTIOUN
Pas on; I am richt weill content:
Syne banische them incontinent
3650     Out of this cuntrie.
FIRST SERGEANT
Cum on, Sir Freir, and be nocht fleyit:
The King our maister mon be obeyit,
    Bot ye sall have na harme—
Gif ye wald travell fra toun to toun,
3655 I think this hude and heavie goun

_____

chaplarie *scapular ( see note )*   fleyit *frightened*

Will hald your wambe ovir warme!

FLATTERIE

Now, quhat is this that thir monster meins?
I am exemptit fra kings and queens,
    And fra all humane law.

SECUND SERGEANT

3660 Tak ye the hude and I the gown:
This limmer luiks als lyke ane lown
    As any that ever I saw!

FIRST SERGEANT

Thir freirs to chaip punitioun
Haulds them at their exemptioun,
3665     And na man will obey;
Thay ar exempt, I yow assure,
Baith fra Paip, kyng and Empreour,
    And that maks all the pley.

SECUND SERGEANT

On Dumisday, quhen Christ sall say
3670     *Venite benedicti*,
The freirs will say without delay
    *Non sumus exempti*.

*Heir sall thay spuilye Flattrie of the freirs habite.*

GUDE COUNSALL

Sir, be the Halie Trinitie,
This same is feinyeit Flatt[e]rie:
3675     I ken him be his face.
Beleivand for to get promotioun,
He said that his name was Devotioun,
    And sa begylit your Grace.

FIRST SERGEANT

Cum on, my Ladie Priores,
3680     We sall leir yow to dance,
And that within ane lytill space,
    Ane new pavin of France.

———

wambe *belly*    Venite benedicti *'Come, ye blessed'* (*Matt.* 25:34)
Non sumus exempti *'We are not exempt'*
pavin *pavane, a stately dance*

*Heir sall thay spuilye the Priores and scho sall have ane kirtill of silk under hir habite.*

Now brother, be the Masse!
  Be my judgement I think
3685 This halie Priores
  Is turnit in ane cowclink!
  PRIORES
I gif my freinds my malisoun
That me compellit to be ane nun,
  And wald nocht let me marie:
3690 It was my freind[i]s greadines
That gart me be ane Priores—
  Now hartlie them I warie!
Howbeit that nunnis sing nichts and dayis,
Thair hart waitis nocht quhat thair mouth sayis:
3695   The suith I yow declair,
Makand yow intimatioun
To Christis congregatioun
  Nunnis ar nocht necessair.
Bot I sall do the best I can,
3700 And marie sum gude honest man,
  And brew gude aill and tun;
Mariage, be my opinioun,
It is better religioun
  As to be freir or nun.
  FLATTERIE
3705 My Lords, for Gods saik let not hang me,
Howbeit that widdiefows wald wrang me!
  I can mak na debait
To win my meit at pleuch nor harrowis,
Bot I sall help to hang my marrowis,
3710   Baith Falset and Dissait.
  CORRECTIOUN
Than pas thy way and greath the gallous;

---

kirtill *gown*  cowclink *whore*  malisoun *curse*
tun *put into a tun or cask*  widdiefows *gallows-birds*
marrowis *companions*  greath *prepare*

Syne help for to hang up thy [fallowis]—
    Thou gets na uther grace.

[FLATTERIE]
Of that office I am content,
3715  Bot our prelates I dread repent,
    Be I fleimde from thair face.

*Heir sall Flattrie sit besyde his marrowis.*

DISSAIT
Now Flattrie, my auld companyeoun,
Quhat dois yon King Correctioun?
    Knawis thou nocht his intent?
3720  Declair to us of thy novellis.
[FLATTERIE]
Ye'ill all be hangit, I se nocht ellis,
    And that incontinent.
DISSAIT
Now, walloway! Will [he] gar hang us?
The Devill brocht yon curst king amang us,
3725    For mekill sturt and stryfe!
FLATTERIE
I had bene put to deid amang yow
War nocht I tuke on hand till hang yow,
    And sa I saifit my lyfe.
I heir them say thay will cry doun
3730  All freirs and nunnis in this regioun,
    Sa far as I can feill,
Becaus thay ar nocht necessair,
And als thay think thay ar contrair
    To Johne the Commoun-weill.

*Heir sal the Kings and the Temporal Stait round togider.*

CORRECTIOUN
3735  With the advice of King Humanitie,
Heir I determine with rype advysement
That all thir prelats sall deprivit be,

———

fleimde *banished, driven*   novellis *news*   sturt *discord*

And be decreit of this present Parliament
That thir thrie cunning clark[i]s sapient
3740 Immediatlie thair places sall posses,
Becaus that thay have bene sa negligent,
Suffring the Word of God for till decres.

REX HUMANITAS
As ye have said, but dout it salbe done:
Pas to and mak this interchainging sone.

*The Kings servants lay hands on the thrie prelats and says:*

WANTONNES
3745 My Lords, we pray yow to be patient,
For we will do the Kings commandement.

SPIRITUALITIE
I mak ane vow to God, and ye us handill
Ye salbe curst and gragit with buik and candill;
Syne sall we pas unto the Paip and pleinyie,
3750 And to the Devill of Hell condemne this meinye.
For quhy, sic reformatioun as I weine,
Into Scotland was never hard nor seine!

*Heir sall thay spuilye them with silence, and put thair habite
on the thrie clarks.*

MERCHANT
We mervell of yow paintit sepulturis,
That was sa bauld for to accept sic cuiris,
3755 With glorious habite rydand upon your muillis:
Now men may se ye ar bot verie fuillis.

SPIRITUALITIE
We say the kings war greiter fuillis nor we,
That us promovit to sa greit dignitie.

ABBOT
Thair is ane thowsand in the Kirk, but doubt,
3760 Sic fuillis as we, gif thay war weill socht out!
Now brother, sen it may na better be,
Let us ga soup with Sensualitie.

---

gragit *excommunicated*   sepulturis *tombs*

*Heir sall thay pas to Sensualitie.*

SPIRITUALITIE

Madame, I pray yow mak us thrie gude cheir;
We cure nocht to remaine with yow all yeir.

SENSUALITIE

3765 Pas fra us, fuillis, be Him that hes us wrocht:
Ye ludge nocht heir, becaus I knaw yow nocht!

SPIRITUALITIE

Sir Covetice, will ye also misken me?
I wait richt weill ye will baith gif and len me:
Speid hand, my freind, spair nocht to break the lockis:
3770 Gif me ane thowsand crouns out of my box.

COVETICE

Quhairfoir, sir fuil, gif yow ane thowsand crowns?
Ga hence! Ye seime to be thrie verie lowns.

SPIRITUALITIE

I se nocht els, brother, withoutin faill,
Bot this fals warld is turnit top ovir taill;
3775 Sen all is vaine that is under the lift,
To win our meat we man mak uther schift.
With our labour except we mak debait,
I dreid full sair we want baith drink and meat.

PERSONE

Gif with our labour we man us defend,
3780 Then let us gang quhair we war never kend.

SPIRITUALITIE

I wyte thir freirs that I am thus abusit,
For by thair counsall I have bene confusit.
Thay gart me trow it suffysit, allace,
To gar them plainlie preich into my place.

ABBOT

3785 Allace, this reformatioun I may warie,
For I have yit twa dochters for to marie,
And thay ar baith contractit, be the Rude,
And waits nocht how to pay thair tocher-gude.

PERSONE

The Devill mak cair for this unhappie chance,

---

lift *sky, heaven*   wyte *blame*   tocher-gude *dowry*

3790 For I am young, and thinks to pas to France
And tak wages amang the men of weir,
And win my living with my sword and speir.

*The Bischop, Abbot, persone and Priores depairts altogidder.*

GUDE COUNSALL

Or ye depairt, Sir, aff this regioun,
Gif Johne the Common-weill ane gay garmoun ;
3795 Becaus the Common-weill hes bene overluikit,
That is the caus that Common-weill is cruikit.
With singular profeit he hes bene sa supprysit,
That he is baith cauld, naikit and disgysit.

CORRECTIOUN

As ye have said, Father, I am content :
3800 Sergeants, gif Johne ane new abuilyement,
Of sating, damais or of the velvot fyne,
And gif him place in our Parliament syne.

*Heir sal thay claith Johne the Common-weil gorgeouslie and*
*set him doun amang them in the Parliament.*

All verteous peopil now may be rejoisit,
Sen Common-weill hes gottin ane gay garmoun ;
3805 And, ignorants out of the Kirk deposit,
Devoit Doctours and clark[ i ]s of renoun
Now in the Kirk sall have dominioun ;
And Gude Counsall with Ladie Veritie
Ar profest with our King[ i ]s Majestie.
3810 Blist is that realme that hes ane prudent king
Quhilk dois delyte to heir the veritie,
Punisching thame that plainlie dois maling
Contrair the Common-weill and equitie :
Thair may na peopill have prosperitie,
3815 Quhair ignorance hes the dominioun,
And Common-weil be tirants trampit doun.

———

abuilyement *apparel*   sating *satin*   damais *damask*

Now, maisters, ye sall heir incontinent,
At great leysour in your presence proclamit
The nobill Act[i]s of our Parliament,
3820 Of quhilks we neid nocht for to be aschamit.
Cum heir, Trumpet, and sound your warning tone,
That every man may knaw quhat we have done.

*Heir sall Diligence with the Scribe and the Trumpet pas to the*
*pulpit and proclame the Actis.*

[DILIGENCE]
The First Act
It is devysit be thir prudent kings,
Correctioun and King Humanitie,
3825 That thair leigis, induring all thair ringis,
With the avyce of the Estait[i]s Thrie,
Sall manfullie defend and fortifie
The Kirk of Christ and His religioun,
Without dissimulance or hypocrisie,
3830 Under the paine of thair punitioun.
   2. Als thay will that the Act[i]s honorabill
Maid be our Prince in the last Parliament,
Becaus thay ar baith gude and profitabill,
Thay will that everie man be diligent
3835 Them till observe with unfeinyeit intent;
Quha disobeyis inobedientlie,
Be thir lawis, but doubt, thay sall repent,
And painis conteinit thairin sall underly.
   3. And als, the Common-weil for til advance,
3840 It is statute that all the temporall lands
Be set in few, efter the forme of France,
Till verteous men that labours with thair hands,
Reasonabillie restrictit with sic bands
That thay do service nevertheles,
3845 And to be subject ay under the wands,
That riches may with policie incres.

———

induring *throughout*   ringis *reigns*   bands *bonds, obligations*

4. Item, this prudent Parliament hes devysit,
Gif lords halds under thair dominioun
Theifis, quhair-throch puir peopil bein supprisit,
3850 For them thay sall make answeir to the Croun
And to the puir mak restitutioun;
Without thay put them in the judges hands
For thair default to suffer punitioun,
Sa that na theifis remaine within thair lands.

3855 5. To that intent that justice sould incres,
It is concludit in this Parliament
That into Elgin or into Innernesse
Sall be ane sute of clark[i]s sapient,
Togidder with ane prudent Precident,
3860 To do justice in all the norther airtis
Sa equallie, without impediment,
That thay neid nocht seik justice in thir pairts.

6. With licence of the Kirk[i]s halines,
That justice may be done continuallie,
3865 All the maters of Scotland, mair and les,
To thir twa famous saits perpetuallie
Salbe directit; becaus men seis plainlie
Thir wantoun nunnis ar na way necessair
Till Commoun-weill, nor yit to the glorie
3870 Of Christ[i]s Kirk, thocht thay be fat and fair,
And als that fragill ordour feminine
Will nocht be missit in Christs religioun,
Thair rent[i]s usit till ane better fyne,
For Common-weill of all this regioun:
3875 Ilk Senature for that erectioun,
For the uphalding of thair gravitie,
Sall have fyve hundreth mark of pensioun.
And also bot twa sall thair nummer be:
Into the north saxteine sall thair remaine,
3880 Saxtein rycht sa in our maist famous toun
Of Edinburgh, to serve our Soveraine,
Chosin without partiall affectioun
Of the maist cunning clarks of this regioun;

---

sute *company*   airtis *districts*   fyne *end, purpose*

Thair Chancellar chosen of ane famous clark,
3885 Ane cunning man of great perfectioun,
And for his pensioun have ane thowsand mark.

7. It is devysit in this Parliament
From this day furth na mater temporall
(Our new prelats thairto hes done consent)
3890 Cum befoir judges consistoriall,
Quhilk hes bene sa prolixt and partiall,
To the great hurt of the communitie:
Let temporall men seik judges temporall,
And sprituall men to spritualitie.

3895 8. Na benefice beis giffin in tyme cumming
Bot to men of gude eruditioun,
Expert in the Halie Scripture and cunning,
And that they be of gude conditioun,
Of publick vices but suspitioun,
3900 And qualefiet richt prudentlie to preich
To thair awin folk, baith into land and toun,
Or ellis in famous scullis for to teich.

9. Als, becaus of the great pluralitie
Of ignorant preists, ma then ane legioun,
3905 Quhair-throch of teicheouris the heich dignitie
Is vilipendit in ilk regioun,
Thairfoir our Court hes maid provisioun
That na B[i]schops mak teichours in tyme cumming
Except men of gude eruditioun,
3910 And for preistheid qualefeit and cunning;
Siclyke, as ye se in the borrows-toun
Ane tailyeour is nocht sufferit to remaine
Without he can mak doublet, coat and gown,
He man gang till his prentischip againe,
3915 Bischops sould nocht ressave, me think certaine,
Into the Kirk except ane cunning clark:
Ane ideot preist Esay compaireth plaine
Till ane dum dogge that can nocht byte nor bark.

10. From this day furth se na prelats pretend,

---

prolixt *long-winded*  vilipendit *condemned, despised*
Esay *Isaiah (56:10: 'They are all domme dogges, not being able to barcke')*

[ 138

3920 Under the paine of inobedience,
At prince or Paip to purchase ane command
Againe the kow, becaus it dois offence;
Till ony preist we think sufficience
Ane benefice, for to serve God withall:
3925 Twa prelacies sall na man have from thence,
Without that he be of the blude royall.

11. Item, this prudent counsall hes concludit,
Sa that our haly vickars be nocht wraith,
From this day furth, thay salbe cleane denudit
3930 Baith of corspresent, cow and umest claith,
To the pure commons becaus it hath done skaith;
And, mairover, we think it lytill force,
Howbeit the barrouns thairto will be laith,
From thine-furth thay sall want thair hyrald hors.

3935 12. It is decreit that in this Parliament
Ilk bischop, minister, priour and persoun,
To the effect thay may tak better tent
To saulis under thair dominioun,
Efter the forme of thair fundatioun
3940 Ilk bischop in his diosie sall remaine,
And everilk persone in his parachoun,
Teiching thair folk from vices to refraine.

13. Becaus that clarks our substance dois consume
For bils and proces of thair prelacies,
3945 Thairfoir thair sall na money ga to Rome,
From this day furth, [f]or any benefice,
Bot gif it be for greit Archbischopries;
As for the rest, na money gais at all
For the incressing of thair dignities,
3950 Na mair nor did to Peter nor to Paull.

14. Considering that our preists for the maist part
Thay want the gift of chastitie, we se,
Cupido hes sa perst them throch the hart,
We grant them licence and frie libertie
3955 That thay may have fair virgins to thair wyfis,

---

agane the kow *in expectation of future income from death duties*
corspresent *see l. 1993 and note*   laith *reluctant*

And sa keip matrimoniall chastitie,
And nocht in huirdome for to leid thair lyfis.
    15. This Parliament richt sa hes done conclude,
From this day furth our barrouns temporall
3960   Sall na mair mix thair nobil ancient blude
With bastard bairns of Stait Spirituall.
Ilk stait amang thair awin selfis marie sall ;
Gif nobils marie with the spritualitie,
From thyne subject thay salbe, and all
3965   Sal be degraithit of thair nobilitie,
And from amang the nobils cancellit
Unto the tyme thay by thair libertie,
Rehabilit be the civill magistrate.
And sa sall marie the spiritualitie :
3970   Bischops with bischops [ sall ma ]k affinitie,
Abbots and priors with the priores,
As Bischop Annas, in Scripture we may se,
Maryit his dochter on Bischop Caiphas.


Now have ye heard the Act[ i ]s honorabill
3975   Devysit in this present Parliament :
To Common-weill we think [ it ] agreabill
All faithfull folk sould heirof be content,
Them till observe with hartlie trew intent.
I wait nane will against our Acts rebell
3980   Nor till our law be inobedient,
Bot Plutois band, the potent prince of Hell.

*Heir sall Pauper cum befoir the King and say* :

   PAUPER
I gif yow my braid bennesoun
That hes givin Common-weill a goun :
I wald nocht for ane pair of plackis
3985   Ye had nocht maid thir nobill Actis.
I pray to God and sweit Sanct Geill
To gif yow grace to use them weill :
Wer thay weill keipit, I understand,

--------

degraithit *stripped*

It war great honour to Scotland.
3990 It had bene als gude ye had sleipit
As to mak acts and be nocht keipit;
Bot I beseik yow, for Alhallows,
To heid Dissait and hang his [fallowis],
And banische Flattrie aff the toun,
3995 For thair was never sic ane loun.
That beand done, I hauld it best
That everie man ga to his rest.

CORRECTIOUN

As thou hes said, it salbe done.
Swyith, sergeants, hang yon swingeours sone!

*Heir sall the Sergeants lous the presoners out of the stocks and
leid them to the gallows.*

FIRST SERGEANT

4000 Cum heir, sir theif, cum heir, cum heir!
Quhen war ye wont to be sa sweir?
To hunt cattell ye war ay speidie;
Thairfoir ye sall weave in ane widdie.

THIFT

Man I be hangit? Allace, allace!
4005 Is thair nane heir may get me grace?
Yit or I die, gif me ane drink.

FIRST SERGEANT

Fy, huirsun carle! I feil ane stink!

THIFT

Thocht I wald nocht that it war wittin,
Sir, in gude faith, I am [beschittin]—
4010 To wit the veritie gif ye pleis,
Louse doun my hois, put in your neis.

FIRST SERGEANT

Thow art ane limmer, I stand foird!
Slip in thy head into this coird,
For thou had never ane meiter tippit.

———

heid *behead*   widdie *gallows-rope*   feil *sense*
neis *nose*   tippit *collar*

4015 Allace, this is ane fellon rippit!

*Pausa*

The widdifow wairdanis tuke my geir,
And left me nether hors nor meir,
Nor earthlie gude that me belangit.
Now, walloway! I man be hangit!

4020 Repent your lyfis, ye plaine oppressours,
All ye misdoars and transgressours,
Or ellis gar chuse yow gude confessours,
 And mak yow forde;
For gif ye tarie in this land
4025 And cum under Correctiouns hand,
Your grace salbe, I understand,
 Ane gude scharp coird.
Adew, my bretheren common theifis,
That helpit me in my mischeifis:
4030 Adew Grosars, Nicksons and Bellis,
Oft have we run out-thoart the fellis;
Adew, Robsonis, [Hawis] and Pyilis,
That in our craft hes mony wylis;
Lytils, Trumbels and Armestrangs.
4035 Adew, all theifis that me belangs,
Tailyeours, [Erewynis] and Elwands,
Speidie of fut and wicht of hands;
The Scotts of Ewisdaill and the Graimis,
I have na tyme to tell your namis:
4040 With King Correctioun and ye be fangit,
Beleif richt weill, ye wilbe hangit!
    FIRST SERGEANT
Speid hand, man, with thy clitter-clatter!
    THIFT
For Gods saik, sir, let me mak watter;

---

fellon rippit *terrible fix*　wairdanis *wardens*
out-thoart *throughout*　wicht *strong*

Howbeit I have bene cattel-gredie,
4045 It schamis to pische into ane widdy.

*Heir sall Thift be drawin up, or his figour.*

SECOND SERGEANT
Cum heir, Dissait, my companyeoun!
Saw ever ane man lyker ane loun,
    To hing upon ane gallows?
DISSAIT
This is aneuch to make me mangit:
4050 Duill fell me, that I man be hangit!
    Let me speik with my fallows.
I trow wan-fortune brocht me heir.
Quhat mekill feind maid me sa speidie:
Sen it was said it is sevin yeir
4055 That I sould weave into ane widdie.
I leirit my maisters to be gredie.
Adew, for I se na remeid—
Luke quhat it is to be evil-deidie!
SECUND SERGEANT
Now in this halter slip thy [heid]—
4060 Stand still; me think ye draw aback!
DISSAIT
Allace, maister, ye hurt my crag.
SECUND SERGEANT
It will hurt better, I woid ane plak,
Richt now, quhen ye hing on a knag.
DISSAIT
Adew, my maisters, merchant-men:
4065 I have yow servit, as ye ken,
    Truelie baith air and lait.
I say to yow, for conclusioun,
I dreid ye gang to confusioun
    Fra tyme ye want Dissait.
4070 I leirit yow merchants mony ane wyle

---

duill fell *woe betide*   wan-fortune *misfortune*   crag *neck*
woid *wager*   knag *branch*   air *early*   wyle *trick*

Upalands wyfis for to begyle
    Upon ane markit day,
And gar them trow your stuffe was gude
Quhen it was rottin, be the Rude,
4075    And sweir it was nocht sway.
I was ay roundand in your ear,
And leirit yow for to ban and sweir
    Quhat your geir cost in France,
Howbeit the Devill ane word was trew.
4080  Your craft, gif King Correctioun knew,
    Wald turne yow to mischance.
I leirit yow wyllis many fauld :
To mix the new wyne and the auld,
    That faschioun was na follie ;
4085  To sell richt deir and by gude chaip,
And mix ry-meill amang the saip,
    And saiffrone with oyl-dolie.
Foryet nocht ocker, I counsall yow,
Mair than the vickar dois the kow
4090    Or lords thair doubill maill :
Howbeit your elwand be too skant
Or your pound-wecht thrie unces want,
    Think that bot lytill faill !
Adew, the greit Clan Jamesone,
4095  The blude royal of [ Couper toun ]—
    I was ay to yow trew :
Baith Andersone and Patersone,
Above them all Thome Williamsone,
    My absence ye will rew.
4100  Thome Williamson, it is your pairt
To pray for me with all your hairt,
    And think upon my warks :
How I leirit yow ane gude lessoun,
For to begyle in Edinburgh toun
4105    The Bischop and his clarks !

———

upalands *rustic*  sway *so*  ban *curse*  saip *soap*
oyl-dolie *olive oil*  doubill maill *double rent*  ocker *usury*
elwand *one-ell measure ( about 45 inches )*

Ye young merchants may cry 'allace!':
[Lucklaw, Welandis, Carruders, Dowglace]—
    Yon curst king ye may ban.
Had I leifit bot halfe ane yeir
4110 I sould have leirit yow crafts perqueir,
    To begyle wyfe and man.
How may ye merchants mak debait
Fra tyme ye want your man Dissait?
    For yow I mak great cair.
4115 Without I ryse fra deid to lyfe
I wait weill ye will never thryfe,
    Farther nor the fourth air!

*Heir sall Dissait be drawin up, or ellis his figure.*

FIRST SERGEANT
Cum heir, Falset, and mense the gallows:
Ye man hing up amang your fallows,
4120     For your cankart conditioun!
Monie ane trew man have ye wrangit—
Thairfoir, but doubt, ye salbe hangit,
    But mercie or remissioun.
FALSET
Allace, man I be hangit to?
4125 Quhat mekill Devil is this ado?
    How came I to this cummer?
My gude maisters, ye craft[i]s-men,
Want ye Falset, full weill I ken
    Ye will all die for hunger!
4130 Ye men of craft may cry 'allace!'
Quhen ye want me ye want your grace;
    Thairfoir put into wryte
My lessouns that I did yow leir.
Howbeit the commons eyne ye bleir,
4135     Count ye nocht that ane myte!
Find me ane wobster that is leill,
Or ane walker that will nocht steill—

———————

mense *adorn*   cummer *trouble*   bleir *blur*
myte *small amount*   wobster *weaver*

Thair craftines I ken ;
Or ane millair that hes na falt,
4140 That will nather steill meall nor malt—
Hald them for halie men !
At our fleschers tak ye na greife :
Thocht thay blaw leane mutton and beife,
That thay seime fat and fair,
4145 Thay think that practick bot ane mow,
Howbeit the Devill a thing it dow—
To thame I leirit that lair.
I leirit tailyeours in everie toun
To schaip fyve quarters in ane goun,
4150 In Angus and in Fyfe ;
To uplands tailyeours I gave gude leife
To steill ane sillie stump or sleife
Unto Kittok his wyfe.
My gude maister Andro Fortoun,
4155 Of tailyeours that may weir the croun,
For me he will be mangit ;
Tailyeour Baberage, my sone and air,
I wait for me will rudlie rair,
Fra tyme he se me hangit.
4160 The barfit deacon, Jamie Ralfe,
Quha never yit bocht kow nor calfe,
Becaus he can nocht steall ;
Willie Cadyeoch will make na plead,
Howbeit his wyfe want beife and bread,
4165 Get he gude barmie aill.
To the brousters of Cowper toun
I leife my braid black malesoun,
As hartlie as I may :
To make thinne aill thay think na falt,
4170 Of mekill burne and lytill malt,
Agane the market day ;

———

blaw *blow (see note)*  mow *joke*  dow *avails*
fyve quarters *a yard and a quarter*  stump *leg of a garment*
rair *roar*  barfit *barefoot*  barmie *frothy*
brousters *brewers*  burne *water*

[ 146

And thay can mak, withoutin doubt,
Ane kynde of aill thay call 'Harns Out'—
   Wait ye how thay mak that?
4175 Ane curtill queine, ane laidlie lurdane,
Of strang wesche scho will tak ane jurdane,
   And settis in the gyle fat—
Quha drinks of that aill, man or page,
It will gar all his harnis rage!
4180    That jurdane I may rew:
It gart my heid rin hiddie-giddie—
Sirs, God nor I die in ane widdie
   Gif this taill be nocht trew!
Speir at the sowtar Geordie [ Selly ],
4185 Fra tyme that he had fild his bellie
   With this unhelthsum aill!
Than all the baxters will I ban,
That mixes bread with dust and bran,
   And fyne flour with beir maill.
4190 Adew, my maisters wrichts and maissouns:
I have neid to leir yow few lessouns—
   Ye knaw my craft perqueir.
Adew, blak-smythis and lorimers;
Adew, ye craftie cordiners,
4195    That sellis the schone over deir.
Gold-smythis, fair-weill above them all:
Remember my memoriall,
   With mony ane sittill cast!
To mix, set ye nocht by twa preinis
4200 Fyne Ducat gold with hard gudlingis,
   Lyke as I leirnit yow last.
Quhen I was ludgit upaland
The schiphirds maid with me ane band,
   Richt craftelie to steill:
4205 Than did I gif ane confirmatioun

---

harns *brains*   curtill *sluttish*   queine *woman*
wesche *stale urine*   jurdane *chamber-pot*
gyle fat *fermentation vat*   baxters *bakers*
lorimers *harness-makers*   cordiners *shoemakers*
sittill *subtle*   preinis *pins*   gudlingis *guilders*

To all the shiphirdis of this natioun
    That they sould never be leill,
And ilk ane to reset ane [uder].
I knaw fals shiphirds fyftie [fuder]:
4210        War [all thair cawteills] kend,
How thay mak in thair conventiouns
On montans far fra ony touns,
    [God] let them never mend!
Amang crafts-men it is ane wonder
4215    To find ten leill amang ane hunder:
    The treuth I to yow tell.
Adew! I may na langer tarie—
I man pas to the King of Farie,
    Or ellis [strecht way] till Hell.

*Heir sall he luke up to his fallows hingand.*

4220    Wais me for the, gude Common Thift:
Was never man maid ane mair honest schift
    His leifing for to win:
Thair was nocht ane in all Lidsdaill
That ky mair craftelie culd staill,
4225        Quhair thow hings on that pin.
Sathan ressave thy saull, Dissait,
Thou was to me ane faithfull mait,
    And als my father-brother:
Duill fell the sillie merchant-men;
4230    To mak them service, weill I ken,
    Thaill never get sic ane uther!

*Heir sall thay festin the coard to his neck with ane dum
countenance; thairefter he sall say:*

Gif any man list for to be my mait,
Cum follow me, for I am at the gait:
Cum follow me, all catyfe covetous kings,

---

reset *shelter*   cawteills *exceptions*

4235     Reavers but richt of uthers realmis and rings,
         Togidder with all wrangous conquerours;
         And bring with yow all publick oppressours:
         With Pharao, King of Egiptians,
         With him in Hell salbe your recompence.
4240     All cruell schedders of blude innocent,
         Cum follow me, or ellis rin and repent;
         Prelats that hes ma benefeits nor thrie,
         And will nocht teich nor preiche the veritie,
         Without at God in tyme thay cry for grace,
4245     In hiddeous Hell I sall prepair thair place.
         Cum follow me, all fals corruptit judges:
         With Pontius Pilat I sall prepair your ludges.
         All ye officials that parts men with thair wyfis,
         Cum follow me, or els gang mend your lyfis;
4250     With all fals leiders of the constrie law,
         With wanton scribs and clarks intill ane raw,
         That to the puir maks mony partiall traine,
         Syne *hodie ad octo* bids them cum againe,
         And ye that taks rewairds at baith the hands:
4255     Ye sall with me be bund in Baliels bands.
         Cum follow me, all curst unhappie wyfis,
         That with your gudemen dayly flytis and stryfis,
         And quyetlie with rybalds makes repair,
         And taks na cure to make ane wrangous air:
4260     Ye sal in Hel rewairdit be, I wein,
         With Jesabell, of Israell the Queene.
         I have ane curst unhappie wyfe my-sell:
         Wald God scho war befoir me into Hell!
         That bismair, war scho thair, withoutin doubt,
4265     Out of Hell the Devill scho wald ding out!
         Ye maryit men, evin as ye luife your wyfis,
         Let never preists be hamelie with your wyfis:
         My wyfe, with preists scho [did] me greit onricht,
         And maid me nine tymes cuckald on ane nicht.

---

reavers *robbers*   rings *realms*   raw *row*
traine *trick*   flytis *scolds*   rybalds *rogues*
wrangous air *illegitimate heir*   bismair *whore*

4270 Fairweil! For I [mon] to the widdie wend;
For quhy, Falset maid never ane better end!

*Heir sall he be heisit up, and not his figure, and an craw or ane*
*ke salbe castin up, as it war his saull.*

FLATTERIE

Have I nocht chaipit the widdie weill?
Yea, that I have, be sweit Sanct Geill!
   For I had nocht bene wrangit,
4275 Becaus I servit, be Alhallows,
Till have bene merchellit amang my fellowis,
   And heich above them hangit!
I maid far ma falts nor my maits:
I begylde all the Thrie Estaits
4280    With my hypocrisie.
Quhen I had on my freirs hude
All men beleifit that I was gude:
   Now judge ye gif I be!
Tak me ane rackles rubiatour,
4285 Ane theif, ane tyrane or ane tratour,
   Of everie vyce the plant;
Gif him the habite of ane freir,
The wyfis will trow, withoutin weir,
   He be ane verie Saint!
4290 I knaw that cowle and skaplarie
Genners mair hait nor charitie,
   Thocht thay be blak or blew:
Quhat halines is thair within
Ane wolfe cled in ane wedders skin?
4295    Judge ye gif this be trew!
Sen I have chaipit this firie farie,
Adew! I will na langer tarie
   To cumber yow with my clatter,
Bot I will with ane humbill spreit
4300 Gang serve the Hermeit of Lareit,
   And leir him for till flatter.

———

heisit *hauled*  ke *jackdaw*  servit *deserved*
rubiatour *libertine*  genners *engenders, causes*
wedder *castrated ram*

*Heir sal enter Foly.*

FOLY

Gude day, my lords, and als God saine!
Dois na man bid gude day againe?
Quhen fuillis ar fow, then ar thay fane:
    Ken ye nocht me?
How call thay me, can ye nocht tell?
Now, be Him that herryit Hell,
I wait nocht how thay call my-sell,
    Bot gif I lie!

DILIGENCE

Quhat brybour is this, that maks sic beiris?

FOLY

The Feind ressave that mouth that speirs!
Gude-man, ga play yow with your feiris,
    With muck upon your mow!

DILIGENCE

Fond fuill, quhair hes thou bene sa lait?

FOLY

Marie, cummand throw the Schogait;
Bot thair hes bene ane great debait
    Betwixt me and ane sow.
The sow cryit 'guff' and I to ga,
Throw speid of fute I gat awa,
Bot in the midst of the cawsa
    I fell into ane midding;
Scho lap upon me with ane bend—
Quha-ever the middings sould amend,
God send them ane mischevous end,
    For that is bot Gods bidding.
As I was pudlit thair, God wait,
Bot with my club I maid debait:
Ise never cum againe that gait,
    I sweir yow be Alhallows!
I wald the officiars of the toun,

4305
4310
4315
4320
4325
4330

---

saine *bless*  brybour *rascal*  beiris *rattling noises*
feiris *companions*  cawsa *street*  midding *dung-heap*
bend *spring*  pudlit *in a puddle*

That suffers sic confusioun,
That thay war harbreit with Mahown
    Or hangit on ane gallows!
Fy, fy, that sic ane fair cuntrie
4335 Sould stand sa lang but policie:
I gif them to the Devill hartlie
    That hes the wyte.
I wald the Provost wald tak in heid
Of yon midding to make remeid,
4340 Quhilk pat me and the sow at feid—
    Quhat may I do bot flyte?
    REX
Pas on, my servant Diligence,
And bring yon fuill to our presence.
    DILIGENCE
That sall be done but tarying.
4345 Foly, ye man ga to the King.
    FOLY
The King, quhat kynde of thing is that?
Is yon he, with the goldin hat?
    DILIGENCE
Yon same is he; cum on thy way.
    FOLY
Gif ye be King, God [gif] yow gude day;
4350 I have ane plaint to make to yow.
    REX
Quhom on, Folie?
    FOLY
               Marie, on ane sow:
Sir, scho hes sworne that scho sall sla me,
Or ellis byte baith my balloks fra me!
Gif ye be King, be Sanct Allan,
4355 Ye sould do justice to ilk man;
Had I nocht keipit me with my club,
The sow had drawin me in ane dub.
I heir them say thair is cum to the toun
Ane king callit Correctioun:

———

at feid *in dispute*   dub *puddle*

4360   I pray yow tell me, quhilk is he?

      DILIGENCE

Yon with the wings : may [ thow ] nocht se?

      FOLY

Now, wallie fall that weill fairde mow !
Sir, I pray yow correct yon sow
Quhilk with hir teith, but sword or knyfe,
4365 Had maist have reft me of my lyfe !
Gif ye will nocht mak correctioun,
Than gif me your protectioun
Of all swyne for to be skaithles
Betuix this toun and Innernes.

      DILIGENCE

4370 Foly, hes thou ane wyfe at hame?

      FOLY

Yea, that I have, God send hir schame !
I trow be this scho is neir deid :
I left ane wyfe bindand hir heid.
To schaw hir seiknes I think schame :
4375 Scho hes sic rumbling in hir wambe
That all the nicht my hart overcasts,
With bocking and with thunder-blasts.

      DILIGENCE

Peradventure scho be with bairne?

      FOLY

Allace, I trow scho be forfairne :
4380 Scho sobbit and scho fell in sown,
And then thay rubbit hir up and doun ;
Scho riftit, routit and made sic stends ;
Scho yeild and gaid at baith the ends
Till scho had castin ane cuppill of quarts,
4385 Syne all turnit to ane rickill of farts ;
Scho blubert, bockit and braikit still,
Hir arsse gaid evin lyke ane wind-mill ;

---

skaithles *unharmed*   bocking *belly-rumbling*   sown *swoon*
riftit *belched*   routit *bellowed*   stends *leaps*
yeild *gave up*   rickill *stream*   blubert *sobbed*
braikit *farted*

Scho stumblit and stutterit with sic stends
That scho recantit at baith the ends;
4390 Sik dismell drogs fra hir scho schot
Quhill scho maid all the fluir on flot;
Of hir hurdies scho had na hauld
Quhill scho had tumed hir monyfauld!

DILIGENCE

Better bring hir to the leitches heir!

FOLY

4395 Trittill trattill, scho may nocht steir:
Hir verie buttoks maks sic beir
    It skars baith foill and fillie.
Scho bocks sik bagage fra hir breist
He wants na bubbils that sittis hir neist,
4400 And ay scho cryis, 'a preist, a preist!',
    With ilk a quhillie-lillie.

DILIGENCE

Recoverit scho nocht at the last?

FOLY

Yea, bot wit ye weil scho fartit fast!
Bot quhen scho sichis my hart is sorie.

DILIGENCE

Bot drinks scho ocht?

FOLY

4405    Ye, be Sanct Marie:
Ane quart at anis it will nocht tarie,
    And leif the Devill a drap!
Than sic flobbage scho layis fra hir,
About the wallis, God wait sic wair,
4410 Quhen it was drunkin I gat to skair
    The lickings of the cap.

DILIGENCE

Quhat is in that creill, I pray the tell?

FOLY

Marie, I have folie hattis to sell.

---

drogs *excrement*   on flot *afloat*   hurdies *buttocks*
bubbils *bubbles*   quhillie-lillie *penis*   flobbage *phlegm*
skair *share*   creill *basket*

**DILIGENCE**

I pray the, sell me ane or tway.

**FOLY**

4415 Na, tarie quhill the market day!
I will sit doun heir, be Sanct Clune,
And gif my babies thair disjune.
Cum heir, gude Glaiks, my dochter deir;
Thou salbe maryit within ane yeir
4420 Upon ane freir of [Tullilum].
Na, thou art nather deaf nor dum!
Cum hidder, Stult, my sone and air:
My joy, thou art baith gude and fair—
Now sall I fend yow as I may,
4425 Thocht ye cry lyke ane ke all day.

*Heir sal the bairns cry 'keck' lyke ane ke, and he sal put meat
in thair mouth.*

**DILIGENCE**

Get up, Folie, but tarying,
And speid yow haistelie to the King.
Get up! Me think the carle is dum!

**FOLY**

Now bum balerie, bum, bum!

**DILIGENCE**

4430 I trow the trucour lyis in ane trance!
Get up, man, with ane mirrie mischance,
Or be Sanct Dyonis of France,
    Ise gar the want thy wallet!
Its schame to se, man, how thow lyis.

**FOLY**

4435 Wa, yit againe! Now this is thryis:
The Devill wirrie me and I ryse,
    Bot I sall break thy pallet!
Me think my pillok will nocht ly doun—
Hald doun your head, ye lurdon loun!
4440 Yon fair las with the sating goun

-------

disjune *lunch*   Glaiks *from 'glaik', a foolish person*
Stult *from Latin stultus, a fool*   pallet *head*   pillok *penis*
sating *satin (these lines presumably refer to a woman in the
audience)*

Gars yow thus bek and bend.
Take thair ane neidill for your cace;
Now for all the hiding of your face,
Had I yow in ane quyet place,
4445    Ye wald nocht waine to flend!
Thay bony armis thats cled in silk
Ar evin als wantoun as any wilk:
I wald forbeir baith bread and milk
    To kis thy bony lippis!
4450  Suppois ye luke as ye war wraith,
War ye at quyet behind ane claith
Ye wald not stick to preife my graith,
    With hobling of your hippis!
[Be God, I ken yow weill annewch:
4455  Ye ar fane, thocht ye mak it tuich—
Think ye not on into the sewch
    Besyd the quarrell hoillis?
Ye wan fra me baith hoiss and schone,
And gart me mak mowis to the mone,
4460  And ay lap on your courss abone .....
    DILIGENCE
Thow mon be dung with poillis!]
Suyith, harlot, haist the to the King,
And let alllane thy trattilling!
Lo, heir is Folie, Sir, alreadie;
4465  Ane richt sweir swingeour, be Our Ladie!
    FOLY
Thow art not half sa sweir thy sell!
Quhat meins this pulpit, I pray the tell?
    DILIGENCE
Our new bischops hes maid ane preiching;
Bot thou heard never sic pleasant teiching—
4470  Yon bischop wil preich throch [all] the coast.
    FOLY
Than stryk ane hag into the poast,
For I hard never in all my lyfe

---

waine *think*   flend *flee*   graith *possessions*
sewch *ditch*   poillis *poles*   poast *tally post*

Ane bischop cum to preich in Fyfe !
Gif bischops to be preichours leiris,
4475 Wallaway ! quhat sall word of freiris?
Gif prelats preich in brugh and land
The sillie freirs, I understand,
Thay will get na mair meall nor malt ;
Sa I dreid freirs sall die for falt.
4480 Sen, sa it is that yon nobill King
Will mak men bischops for preiching,
Quhat say ye, sirs? Hauld ye nocht best
That I gang preich, amang the rest?
Quhen I have preichit on my best wayis,
4485 Then will I sell my merchandise
To my bretherin and tender maits
That dwels amang the Thrie Estaits ;
For I have heir gude chaifery
Till any fuill that lists to by !

*Heir sall Foly hing up his hattis on the pulpet and say* :

4490 God sen I had ane doctours hude !
REX
Quhy Folie, wald thou mak ane preiching?
FOLY
Yea, that I wald, Sir, be the Rude,
But eyther flattering or fleiching.
REX
Now, brother, let us heir his teiching,
4495 To pas our tyme and heir him raife.
DILIGENCE
He war far meiter for the kitching,
Amang the pottis, sa Christ me saife !
Fond Foly, sall I be thy clark,
And answeir the ay with 'amen'?
FOLY
4500 Now, at the beginning of my wark,

---

word *become*   brugh *burgh, town*   chaifery *merchandise*

The Feind ressave that graceles [ gane ] !

*Heir sal Folie begin his sermon, as followis:*

*Stultorum numerus infinitus.*
Salamon, the maist sapient king,
In Israell quhen he did ring,
4505   Thir word[ i ]s in effect did write :
The number of fuillis ar infinite.
I think na schame, sa Christ me saife,
To be ane fuill amang the laife,
Howbeit ane hundreth stands heir-by
4510   Perventure als great fuillis as I !

*Stultorum etc.*
I have of my genelogie
Dwelland in everie cuntrie :
Earles, duiks, kings and empriours,
4515   With mony guckit conquerours,
Quhilk dois in folie perseveir
And hes done sa this many yeir.
Sum seiks to warldlie dignities
And sum to sensuall vanities :
4520   Quhat vails all thir vaine honours,
Nocht being sure to leife twa houris ?
Sum greidie fuill dois fill ane box ;
Ane uther fuill cummis and breaks the lox
And spends that uther fuillis hes spaird,
4525   Quhilk never thocht on them to wairde.
Sum dois as thay sould never die :
Is nocht this folie, quhat say ye?

    *Sapientia huius mundi stultitia est apud Deum.*

Becaus thair is sa many fuillis

----

Stultorum numerus infinitus *'The number of fools is infinite'*
(*Ecclesiastes 1:15 ; see note*)   guckit *daft*   wairde *guard*
Sapientia ... Deum  *'For the wysdome of thys worlde is folyshnes
with God'* (*1 Corinthians 3:19*)

4530 Rydand on hors, and sum on muillis,
Heir I have [brocht] gude chafery
Till ony fuill that lists to by;
And speciallie for the Thrie Estaits,
Quhair I have mony tender maits,
4535 Quhilk causit them, as ye may see,
Gang backwart throw the haill cuntrie.
Gif with my merchandise ye list to mell,
Heir I have folie hattis to sell.
Quhairfoir is this hat, wald ye ken?
4540 Marie, for insatiabill merchant-men,
Quhen God hes send them abundance
Ar nocht content with sufficiance,
Bot saillis into the stormy blastis
In winter, to get greater castis,
4545 In mony terribill great torment,
Against the Acts of Parliament:
Sum tynis thair geir, and sum ar drounde—
With this sic merchants sould be crounde.

DILIGENCE

Quhom to schaips thou to sell that hude?
4550 I trow to sum great man of gude.

FOLY

This hude to sell richt faine I wald
Till him that is baith auld and cald,
Reddie till pas to Hell or Heavin,
And hes fair bairn[i]s sax or seavin,
4555 And is of age fourscoir of yeir,
And taks ane lasse to be his peir
Quhilk is nocht fourteine yeir of age,
And joynis with hir in mariage,
Geifand hir traist that scho nocht wald
4560 Rycht haistelie mak him cuckald—
Quha maryes beand sa neir their dead,
Set on this hat upon his head!

DILIGENCE

Quhat hude is that, tell me, I pray the?

———

castis *profits*   peir *mate*

FOLY

This is ane haly hude, I say the:
4565 This hude is ordanit, I the assure,
For sprituall fuillis that taks in cure
The saullis of great diocies
And regiment of great abesies
For gredines of warldlie pelfe,
4570 That can nocht justlie gyde them-selfe;
Uthers sauls to saife it settis them weill,
Syne sell thair awin saullis to the Devil—
Quha-ever dois sa, this I conclude,
Upon his heid set on this hude!

DILIGENCE

4575 Foly, is thair ony sic men
Now in the Kirk that thou can ken?
How sall I ken them?

FOLY

                    Na, keip that clois:
*Ex operibus eorum cognoscetis eos*!
And fuillis speik of the prelacie,
4580 It will be hauldin for herisie.

REX

Speik on hardlie: I gif the leife.

FOLY

Than my remissioun is in my sleife!
Will ye leife me to speik of kings?

REX

Yea, hardlie speik of all kin things.

[FOLY]

4585 Conforming to my first narratioun,
Ye ar all fuillis, be Cok[i]s passioun!

DILIGENCE

Thou leis! I trow this fuill be mangit!

FOLY

Gif I lie, God nor thou be hangit!
For I have heir, I to the tell,
4590 Ane nobill cap imperiell,

———

regiment *rule*   settis *fits*   Ex operibus … eos '*By their fruites
[ literally, works ] ye shall knowe them*' (*Matthew 7:20*)

Quhilk is nocht ordanit bot for doings
Of empreours, of duiks and kings,
For princelie and imperiall fuillis :
Thay sould have luggis als lang as muillis.
4595 The pryde of princes, withoutin faill,
Gars all the warld rin top ovir taill :
To win them warldlie gloir and gude
Thay cure nocht schedding of saikles blude.
Quhat cummer have ye had in Scotland
4600 Be our auld enemies of Ingland?
Had nocht bene the support of France,
We had bene brocht to great mischance.
Now I heir tell the Empreour
Schaippis for to be ane conquerour,
4605 And is muifing his ordinance
Against the nobill King of France ;
Bot I knaw nocht his just querrell
That he hes, for till mak battell.
All the princes of Almanie,
4610 Spainye, Flanders and Italie
This present yeir ar in ane flocht :
Sum sall thair wages find deir bocht !
The Paip with bombard, speir and scheild
Hes send his armie to the feild :
4615 Sanct Peter, Sanct Paull nor Sanct Androw
Raisit never sic ane oist, I trow !
Is this fraternall charitie
Or furious foly, quhat say ye?
Thay leird nocht this at Christis scuillis ;
4620 Thairfoir I think them verie fuillis.
I think it folie, be Gods mother,
Ilk Christian prince to ding doun uther—
Becaus that this hat sould belang them,
Gang thou and part it evin amang them !
4625 The Prophesie, withouttin weir,
Of Merling beis compleit this yeir ;

---

luggis *ears*  flocht *commotion*  oist *host, army*
Merling *Merlin, the wizard of Arthurian legend ( see note )*

For my gudame, the Gyre Carling,
Leirnde me the Prophesie of Marling,
Quhairof I sall schaw the sentence,
4630 Gif ye will gif me audience :
*Flan Fran resurgent, simul Hispan viribus urgent,*
*Dani vastabunt, Vallones valla parabunt,*
*Sic tibi nomen in a, mulier cacavit in olla :*
*Hoc epulum comedes .....*

DILIGENCE

4635 Marie, that is ane il-savorit [mess] !

FOLY

Sa be this Prophesie plainlie appeirs
That mortall weirs salbe amang freirs :
Thay sall nocht knaw weill in thair closters
To quhom thay sall say thair Pater nosters.
4640 Wald thay fall to and fecht with speir and sheild,
The Feind mak cuir quhilk of them win the feild !
Now of my sermon have I maid ane end :
To Gilly-moubrand I yow all commend,
And I yow all beseik richt hartfullie,
4645 Pray for the saull of gude Cacaphatie,
Quhilk laitlie drownit himself into Lochleavin,
That his sweit saull may be above the Heavin.

DILIGENCE

Famous peopil, hartlie I yow requyre,
This lytill sport to tak in patience.
4650 We traist to God, and we leif ane uther yeir,
Quhair we have failit we sall do diligence
With mair pleasure to mak yow recompence,
Becaus we have bene sum part tedious,

———

gudame *grandmother*   Gyre Carling *Hecate, as a horrible witch*
( *see note* )   Flan Fran ... comedes *This means something like*
'*Flanders and France will rise again, likewise Spain will use her*
*strength ; the Danes will lay [ you ] waste, the Welsh will yield the*
*ramparts. Such is your name in A, the woman crapped in a can ; you*
*dine at this feast ...*' ( *see note* )   Gilly-moubrand *a*
*sixteenth-century fool* ( *see note* )   Cacaphatie *also a fool's name*
( *see note* )

With mater rude, denude of eloquence,
4655 Likewyse, perchance, to sum men odious.
[Adew, we will mak no langar tary,
Prayand to Jesu Chryst, Oure Salviour,
That He be the requeist of His moder Mary,
He do preserve this famous awditour:
4660 Without that grittar materis do incure,
For your plesour we sall devyse ane sport
Plesand till every gentill creatour,
To raise your spreitis to plesour and confort.]

Now let ilk man his way avance:
4665 Let sum ga drink and sum ga dance.
Menstrell, blaw up ane brawll of France:
    Let se quha hobbils best!
For I will rin, incontinent,
To the tavern or ever I stent,
4670 And pray to God Omnipotent
    To send yow all gude rest.

*Rex sapiens eterne Deus genitorque benigne,*
*Sit tibi perpetuo gloria, laus et honor.*

———

awditour *audience*   incure *ensue*   brawll *intricate French dance*
stent *finish*   Rex ... honor *'Wise king, eternal God and*
*beneficent Creator, everlasting glory, praise and honour be to You'*

# Appendix

## PROCLAMATIOUN maid in Cowpar of Fyffe

[NUNTIUS]
Richt famous pepill, ye sall understand
How that ane prince richt wyiss and vigilent
Is schortly for to cum in to this land,
And purpossis to hald ane parliament.
5 His Thre Estaitis thairto hes done consent
In Cowpar toun into thair best array,
With support of the Lord omnipotent,
And thairto hes affixt ane certane day.

With help of Him that rewlis all abone,
10 That day salbe within ane litill space:
Our purpos is, on the sevint day of June,
Gif weddir serve, and we haif rest and pece,
We sall be sene in till our playing place,
In gude array abowt the hour of sevin.
15 Of thriftiness that day I pray yow ceiss,
Bot ordane us gude drink aganis allevin.

Fail nocht to be upon the Castell Hill
Besyd the place quhair we purpoiss to play:
With gude stark wyne your flacconis see ye fill,
20 And hald your self the myrieast that ye may.
Be not displeisit quhatevir we sing or say,
Amang sad mater howbeid we sumtyme relyie.
We sall begin at sevin houris of the day,
So ye keip tryist; forswth we sall nocht felyie!

———

stark *strong*  flaccconis *flagons*  howbeid *although*
relyie *make jokes*  tryist *appointment*  felyie *fail*

25 I salbe thair, with Goddis grace,
Thocht thair war nevir so grit ane prese,
  And formest in the fair,
And drink ane quart in Cowpar toun
With my gossep Johnne Williamsoun,
30  Thocht all the nolt sould rair.
I haif ane quick divill to my wyfe,
That haldis me evir in sturt and stryfe,
  That warlo! and scho wist
That I wald cum to this gud toun,
35 Scho wald call me fals ladrone loun,
  And ding me in the dust.
We men that hes sic wickit wyvis,
In grit langour we leid our lyvis,
  Ay dreifland in diseiss.
40 Ye preistis hes grit prerogatyvis,
That may depairt ay fra your wyvis,
  And cheiss thame that ye pleis.
Wald God I had that liberty,
That I micht pairt als weill as ye
45  Without the Constry law.
Nor I be stickit with ane knyfe,
For to wad ony uder wyfe
  That day sowld nevir daw!

NUNTIUS
War thy wyfe deid, I see thow wald be fane!

COTTER
50 Ye, that I wald, sweit Sir, be Sanct Fillane!

NUNTIUS
Wald thow nocht mary fra-hand ane uder wyfe?

COTTER
Na, than the dum Divill stik me with ane knyfe!
Quha evir did mary agane, the Feind mot fang thame,

---

gossep *companion*   nolt *cattle*   rair *roar*   sturt *vexation*
warlo *the Devil*   wist *knew*   ladrone loun *vile fellow*
ding *knock*   dreifland *living miserably*   fane *happy*   fang *seize*

Bot as the preistis dois ay, stryk in amang thame.
NUNTIUS
55 Than thow mon keip thy chestety as effeiris?
COTTER
I sall leif chest as abbottis, monkis and freiris.
Maister, quhairto sowld I myself miskary
Quhair I, as preistis, may swyve and nevir marry?
WYFE
Quhair hes thow bene, fals ladrone loun?
60 Doyttand and drinkand in the toun?
Quha gaif the leif to cum fra hame?
COTTER
Ye gaif me leif, fair lucky dame.
WYFE
Quhy hes thow taryit heir sa lang?
COTTER
I micht not thrist owtthrow the thrang,
65 Till that yone man the play proclamit.
WYFE
Trowis thow that day, fals cairle defamit,
To gang to Cowpar to see the play?
COTTER
Ye, that I will, deme, gif I may.
WYFE
Na, I sall cum thairto sickerly,
70 And thow sall byd at hame and keip the ky.
COTTER
Fair lucky dame, that war grit schame,
Gif I that day sowld byid at hame.
Byid ye at hame, for cum ye heir
Ye will mak all the toun asteir.
75 Quhen ye ar fow of barmy drink
Besyd yow nane may stand for stink!
Thairfoir byid ye at hame that day,

---

effeiris *is appropriate*   swyve *fornicate*
doyttand *behaving stupidly*   thrist *thrust*   cairle *fellow*
sickerly *certainly*   ky *cows*   asteir *astir*
fow *full*   barmy *frothy*

That I may cum and see the play.
      WYFE
Fals cairle, be God, that sall thow nocht,
80 And all thy crackis sall be deir coft.
Swyth, cairle, speid the hame speidaly,
Incontinent, and milk the ky—
And muk the byre or I cum hame!
      COTTER
All salbe done, fair lucky dame.
85 I am sa dry, dame, or I gae
I mon ga drink ane penny or twae.
      WYFE
The Divill a drew sall cum in thy throte!
Speid hand, or I sall paik thy cote—
And to begin, fals cairle, tak thair ane plate!
      COTTER
90 The Feind ressaif the handis that gaif me that!
I beseik yow, for Goddis saik, lucky dame,
Ding me ne mair this day, till I cum hame;
Than sall I put me evin into your will.
      WYFE
Or evir I stint thow sall haif straikis thy fill!

*Heir sall the wyfe ding the carle and he sall cry:*
*Goddis mercy!*

[COTTER]
95 Now wander and wa be to thame all thair lyvis,
The quhilk ar maryit with sic unhappy wyvis!
      WYFE
I ken foure wyvis, fals ladrone loun,
Baldar nor I dwelland in Cowpar toun.
      COTTER
Gif thay be war, ga thow and thay togidder:
100 I pray God nor the Feind ressaif the fidder!

———

crackis *jibes*   coft *bought ( see note )*   swyth *away*
drew *drop*   paik *thrash*   plate *blow*   stynt *stop*
wander *wonder*   baldar *bolder*   war *worse*   fidder *rest*

Wow! Mary, heir is ane fellone rowt!
Speik, schiris, quhat gait may I get owt?
   I rew that I come heir!
My name, schiris, wald ye understand,
105 They call be Findlaw of the Fute Band,
   A nobill man of weir.
Thair is na fyifty in this land
Bot I dar ding thame hand for hand;
   Se, sic ane brand I beir!
110 Nocht lang sensyne, besyd ane syik,
Upoun the sonny syd of ane dyk
   I slew with my richt hand
Ane thowsand, ye, and ane thowsand to:
My fingaris yit ar bludy, lo,
115    And nane durst me ganestand.
Wit ye, it dois me mekill ill,
That can nocht get fechting my fill,
   Nowdir in peax nor weir.
Will na man for thair ladyis saikis
120 With me stryk twenty markit straikis,
   With halbart, swerd or speir?
Quhen Inglismen come in to this land,
Had I bene thair with my bricht brand,
   Withowttin ony help
125 Bot myn allane, on Pynky Craiggis
I sowld have revin thame all in raggis
   And laid on skelp for skelp!
Sen nane will fecht, I think it best
To ly doun heir and tak me rest;
130    Than will I think nane ill.
I pray the grit God of His grace
To send us weir and nevir peace,
   That I may fecht my fill!

-------

fellone *terrible*   Fute Band *infantry company (see note)*
gait *way*   brand *sword*   syik *marshy stream*   peax *peace*
markit *deliberate*   revin *torn*   skelp *blow*

*Heir sall he ly doun.*

THE FULE
My Lord, be Him that ware the croun of thorne,
135  A mair cowart was nevir sen God was borne!
He lovis him self, and uther men he lakkis—
I ken him weill, for all his boistis and crakkis.
Howbeid he now be lyk ane captane cled,
At Pyncky Clewch he was the first that fled:
140  I tak on hand, or I steir of this steid,
This crakkand cairle to fle with ane scheip heid!

*Heir sall the Auld Man cum in, leidand his wyfe
in ane dance.*

[AULD MAN]
Bessy my hairt, I mon ly doun and sleip,
And in myne arme se quyetly thow creip:
Bessy my hairt, first let me lok thy cunt,
145  Syne lat me keip the key, as I was wount.
BESSY
My gud husband, lock it evin as ye pleiss:
I pray God send yow grit honor and eiss!

*Heir sall he lok hir cunt and lay the key under his heid: he sall
sleip and scho sall sit besyd him.*

THE COURTEOUR
Lusty lady, I pray yow hairtfully,
Gif me licence to beir yow cumpany.
150  Ye sie I am ane cumly courteour,
Quhilk nevir yit did woman dishonour.
MARCHAND
My fair maistres, sweitar than the lammer,
Gif me licence to luge in to your chalmer.
I am the richest marchand in this toun:
155  Ye sall of silk haif kirtill, hude and goun.
CLERK
I yow beseik, my lusty lady bricht,

---

mair *greater*    lakkis *disparages*    Clewch *steep ravine*
steir of this steid *leave this place*    lammer *amber*

To gif me leif to ly with yow all nicht,
And of your quoman lat me schut the lokkis;
And of fyne gold ye sall ressaif ane box!

FULE

160  Fair damessell, how pleiss ye me!
I haif na mair geir nor ye sie—
Swa lang as this may steir or stand
It sall be ay at your command.
Na! it is the best that evir ye saw!

BESSY

165  Now welcome to me aboif thame aw!
Was nevir wyf sa straitly rokkit;
Se ye not how my cunt is lokkit?

FULE

Thinkis he nocht schame, that brybor blunt,
To put ane lok upoun your cunt?

BESSY

170  Bot se gif ye can mak remeid,
To steill the key fra undir his heid!

FULE

That sall I do, withowttin dowt!
Lat se gif I can get it owte.
Lo! heir the key. Do quhat ye will!

BESSY

175  Na than, lat us ga play our fill!

*Heir sall thay go to sum quyet place.*

FYNLAW

Will nane with me in France go to the weiris,
Quhair I am captane of ane hundreth speiris?
I am sa hardy, sturdy, strang and stowt
That owt of Hell the Divill I dar ding owt!

CLERK

180  Gif thow be gude or evill I can not tell:
Thay ar not sonsy that so dois ruse thame sell!

---

quoman *female genitalia*   schut *shoot, open*   geir *property*
rokkit *(?) confined*   brybor *rascal*   remeid *remedy*
sonsy *lucky*   ruse *rouse*

At Pyncky Clewch I knew richt woundir weill
Thow gat na creddence for to beir a creill.
Sen sic as thow began to brawll and boist,
185 The Commoun Weill of Scotland hes bene loist.
Thow cryis for weir, bot I think peax war best;
I pray to God till send ws peice and rest,
On that conditioun that thow and all thy fallowis
War be the craiggis heich hangit on the gallowis,
190 Quha of this weir hes bene the foundament.
I pray to the grit God omnipotent
That all the warld and mae mot on thame wounder,
Or ding thame deid with awfull fyre of thunder.
    FYNLAW
Domine doctor, quhair will ye preiche to-morne?
195 We will haif weir, and all the warld had sworne!
Want we weir heir, I will ga pass in France,
Quhair I will get ane lordly governance.
    CLERK
Sa quhat ye will, I think seuer peax is best.
Quha wald haif weir, God send thame littill rest!
200 Adew, crakkar! I will na langar tary:
I trest to see the in ane firy fary.
I trest of God to see the and thy fallowis,
Within few dayis, hingand on Cowpar gallowis!
    FYNLAW
Now art thow gane; the dum Divill be thy gyd!
205 Yone brybour was sa fleit he durst not byid!
Be woundis and passionis, had he spokkin mair ane word,
I sowld haif hackit his heid af with my swerd!

*Heir sall the gudman walkin and cry for Bessy.*

[AULD MAN]
My bony Bessy, quhair art thow now?
My wyfe is fallin on sleip, I trow!
210 Quhair art thow, Bessy, my awin sweit thing,

———

creill *basket*  craiggis *necks*  mae *more*  seuer *sure, secure*
firy fary *great confusion*  fleit *frightened*

My bony, my hairt, my dayis darling?
Is thair na man that saw my Bess?
I trow scho be gane to the Mess!
Bessy my hairt, heiris thow not me?
215 My joy, cry keip! quhairevir thow be.
Allace for evir, now am I fey,
For of hir cunt I tynt the key!
Scho may call me an jufflane Jok;
Or I swyve, I mon brek the lok!
    BESSY
220 Quhat now, gudman, quhat wald ye haif?
    AULD MAN
No thing, my hairt, bot yow I craif.
Ye haif bene doand sum bissy wark?
    BESSY
My hairt, evin sewand yow ane sark
Of Holland claith, baith quhyt and tewch:
225 Lat pruve gif it be wyid anneuch.

*Heir sall scho put the sark ovir his heid and the Fuill sall steill
in the key agane.*

    AULD [MAN]
It is richt verry weill, my hairt.
Oure Lady lat us nevir depairt!
Ye ar the farest of all the flok.
Quhair is the key, Bess, of my lok?
    BESSY
230 Ye reve, gudman! Be Goddis breid,
I saw yow lay it undir your heid.
    AULD MAN
Be my gud faith, Bess, that is trew.
That I suspectit yow, sair I rew!
I trow thair be no man in Fyffe
235 That evir had sa gude ane wyfe.
My awin sweit hairt, I [hald] it best
That we sit doun and tak ws rest.

---

fey *doomed*  tynt *lost*  jufflane *fumbling*
sark *shirt*  tewch *tough*  depairt *separate*

Now, is nocht this ane grit dispyte,
That nane with me will fecht nor flyte!
240 War Golias into this steid,
I dowt nocht to stryk of his heid.
This is the swerd that slew Gray Steill
Nocht half ane myle beyond Kynneill.
I was that nobill campioun
245 That slew Schir Bews of Sowth Hamtoun.
Hector of Troy, Gawyne or Golias
Had nevir half so mekle hardiness .....

*Heir sall the Fuile cum in with ane scheip heid on ane staff
and Fynlaw sall be fleit.*

Wow! wow! braid benedicitie!
Quhat sicht is yone, schiris, that I see?
250 *In nomine Patris et Filii,*
I trow yone be the spreit of Gy!
Na, faith, it is the spreit of Marling,
Or sum scho-gaist, or Gyrcarling.
Allace for evir, how sall I gyd me?
255 God sen I had ane hoill till hyd me!
Bot dowt my deid yone man hes sworne;
I trow yone be grit Gowmakmorne!
He gaippis, he glowris—howt welloway!
Tak all my geir, and let me gay!
260 Quhat say ye, schir, wald ye have my swerd?
Ye, mary, sall ye at the first word
My gluvis of plait and knapskaw to!
Your pressonar I yeild me. Lo!
Tak thair my purss, my belt and knyfe.
265 For Goddis saik, maister, save my lyfe!
Na, now he cumis evin for to sla me!
For Godis saik, schiris, now keip him fre me!
I see not ellis bot tak and slae;
Wow! mak me rowme and lat me gae!

———

plait *plate-armour*    knapskaw *metal skull-cap*

270  As for this day, I haif na mair to say yow.
     On Witsonetysday cum see our play, I prey yow.
     That samyne day is the sevint day of June;
     Thairfoir get up richt airly and disjune.
     And ye ladyis, that hes na skent of leddir,
275  Or ye cum thair faill nocht to teme your bleddir;
     I dreid, or we haif had done with our wark,
     That some of yow sall mak ane richt wait sark!

———

disjune *have breakfast*  skent *shortage*  ledder *genitalia*
teme *empty*  wait *wet*

# Commentary

Throughout the Commentary, *B* refers to the text of *The Thrie Estaitis* in the Bannatyne manuscript, *C* to the 1602 quarto text printed by Henry Charteris; see Introduction, pp.xxxvi–xxxvii.

Reference is periodically made to the following previous editions of *The Thrie Estaitis*:

George Chalmers, in Lindsay, *Poetical Works* (2 vols, London 1806), II, 1–156

David Laing, in Lindsay, *Poetical Works* (3 vols, Edinburgh 1879), II, 1–363

David Hamer, in Lindsay, *Works* (STS, 4 vols, Edinburgh 1931–36), II, 8–404

James Kinsley, *Ane Satyre of the Thrie Estaitis* (London 1954)

Matthew McDiarmid (from the acting edition by Robert Kemp), *A Satire of the Three Estates* (London 1967)

Peter Happé, in *Four Morality Plays* (Harmondsworth 1979), pp.431–615, 663–75.

## PART ONE

| | |
|---|---|
| 4 | *B's* 'ransonit on the Rude' (ransomed on the Cross) is manifestly a better reading than *C's* unintelligible 'ranson rude'. |
| 5 | 'pretious' (B) preserves the alliterative and metrical structure of the line, lost in *C's* 'hart'. |
| 8 | 'save': *so B; C has* 'Gif', which lacks a direct object. |
| 12 | Diligence in his role as presenter addresses the audience with proper deference; *C*, which has 'soverane', loses the point of the line. |
| 21 | 'triumphant': *so B; C*, reading 'triumph and', separates the regular participial -*and* ending, to which the French adjective has been assimilated, from its root. |
| 26 | The *B* version of the line is better both metrically and syntactically than *C's* 'That innocentis bene broght on thair beiris'. |
| 28 | 'elderis': *so B; C has* 'elder', perhaps because the inflection of plural adjectives, never a regular feature of OSc., was becoming entirely obsolete by the early seventeenth century. |
| 38 | 'into his flouris' is derived from the Latin *in florenti* |

*aetate* ('in the full flower of his age').

64 'And': *so B; C* 'Als'.

80 'Eterne': *so B; C* 'Ever'.

81 The theological exactness of B's reading seems superior
to *C* more diffuse phrase 'Quha be great micht and':
the point that God, the Creator, is Himself uncreated is
emphasised in the Athanasian Creed, to which Lindsay
may be alluding.

94 The preoccupation with Christ's sufferings on the Cross
is characteristic of late medieval religious sensibility;
cf. the lyrics printed by Carleton Brown (ed.),
*Religious Lyrics of the XVth Century* (Oxford 1939),
pp. 131–62, and the discussion by Douglas Gray,
*Themes and Images in the Medieval English Religious
Lyric* (London 1972), pp. 122–45.

95 Perhaps responding to the loss of the unaccented
syllable -is, *C* gives 'the deidis', while *B*'s reading
makes better sense of the line.

125 *So B; C* 'nocht': it is likely that Charteris was
confused by the ambiguity of the obsolescent verb 'let'
(prevent) and the surviving 'let' (permit).

129 *So B and C (Selden and 1604); C (Gough and
NLS)* 'ye'.

132 beriall: *so B; C* 'buriall'.

142 Solace is the first of the comic vice characters to refer
to the audience on his entrance: this appears to be
a stock-in-trade of morality drama. It certainly suggests
a closer interaction than in the case of the other
characters, and may imply that Solace and others enter
from among the audience (cf. ll. 602, 'Mak roume,
sirs .....'; 658, 'Stand by the gait .....'; 2424, 'Out of
my gait .....').

147 'trebill': *so B; C* 'troubill'.

150 Such 'outrageous' fashions are frequently attacked
by medieval moralists; cf. G.R. Owst, *Literature and
Pulpit in Medieval England* (2nd edn, London 1961),
pp. 404–11, and Alexander Barclay, *The Ship of
Fools*, ed. T.H. Jamieson (2 vols, Edinburgh 1872),
I, 34–40.

152 *so B; C* shone.

156 *Peblis on the Grene* is evidently the title of a song,
sometimes, but almost certainly wrongly, identified
with the extant poem *Peblis to the Play*.

161 The point of this remark is that Besse lives in the town.
The allusion is quite general, as Hamer points out,
and could apply to any burgh; there may also be an
indecent meaning.

185-9   *C* reads 'fidder' and 'brother'; *B* preserves an
        originally perfect OSc. rhyme, although it is impossible
        to determine whether Lindsay would have used /i/ or
        /u/. A recognisable group of OSc. words is affected in
        this way: the most common are 'mother', 'brother',
        'other' and 'futher', any of which could in theory occur
        as /ud(d)/, /id(d)/, /uth/ or /ith/. *B* consistently
        uses /d/-spellings while *C* has a strong preference for
        /th/, although the preservation of /d/ at ll. 185, 3041
        and 4209 suggests that Lindsay himself would have
        used /d/. There is no reliable evidence for *idder* before
        the nineteenth century, and the frequent occurrence
        of *uder/uther* in rhyme therefore gives strong support for
        Lindsay's use of *uder* / *moder* / *bruder*, and this
        is corroborated by the set *bruder* / *Struder* / *moder*
        (3261-3), where *Stridder is not a possible form.
        But he was also willing to use /idd/ where rhyme
        required it, as the set *liddir* / *Balquhiddir* / *moder* (only
        in *B* = 3306-8) demonstrates, despite Bannatyne's
        rather inconsistent spelling. I have only emended *C*
        where it is necessary to restore a rhyme.

224     This image is found in Aristotle's *De anima*, III,
        iv, 430a, and was widely employed in the later Middle
        Ages. Lindsay's is the earliest use of the phrase
        in a vernacular British text, but cf. Richard Eden's
        translation of Peter Martyr's *Decades of the New Worlde*
        (1555): 'Rased or un-paynted tables are apte to
        receave what formes soo ever are fyrst drawen thereon'.

233-4   The phrase is proverbial; the earliest recorded
        occurrence is in the fifteenth-century English work
        *Dives and Pauper* (c. 1405-10), ed. P.H. Barnum
        (3 vols, EETS London 1976- ), I, 128, where
        we are told 'It is a common proverbe, yonge seint
        olde deuyl'. Almost exactly the same phrase occurs in
        a contemporary sermon in BL MS. Royal 18.B.xxiii,
        *Middle English Sermons*, ed. W.O. Ross (EETS,
        London 1940), p. 159; cf. Dunbar, 'The Merle
        and the Nichtingaill', 35, *Poems*, ed. James Kinsley
        (Oxford 1979), p. 61.

237     *C* has 'kirk', no doubt reflecting the institutional
        preoccupations of the beginning of the seventeenth
        century. But there is no evidence elsewhere in the play
        that Lindsay had moved so far, and there is an
        unequivocal reference to Sensualitie's success at 'the
        Court of Rome' at l. 286. *B* therefore seems to have the
        better reading.

249     '*In nomine Domini*' is a stock invocation, used

for example in the opening phrase of legal instruments drawn up by notaries public. Its use here is clearly blasphemous.

259 *so B; om. C*

261 Balmerino was a Cistercian house, about six miles north-east of Cupar. There is no reason to believe that monastic discipline there was worse (or better) than that anywhere else, but its defects would be well known to the 1552 Cupar audience.

267 *so B; om. C.*

269 This misuse of Scripture is a traditional trait of the wicked, found in Henryson's *Morall Fabillis* and elsewhere. St Paul, obviously, would not approve of this application of his advice.

271 Sensualitie's opening speech is full of the elaborate rhetoric of courtly amatory poetry: the repeated use of 'behauld', for example, is a particularly emphatic piece of *anaphora*, drawing attention to her presumably obvious physical attractions. She applies to herself the descriptive conventions normally applied by the lover to his mistress.

299 *B*'s reading is metrically preferable to *C*'s 'nocht', which is also less emphatic.

301 'Danger' is a courtly term from the tradition of the *Roman de la Rose*, and refers to the more-or-less obligatory stand-offishness of the lady. Lindsay's point is that such female behaviour is merely part of the courtly game.

312 Fund-Jonet (literally 'foundling Janet') has proved something of a problem to editors. Hamer suggests (IV, 175), presumably because the character takes the bass part and has instructed the ladies in sexual matters, that Fund-Jonet must be male; Jonet, however, is unmistakably a female name, and there really was a woman known by this nickname at the court of Mary of Guise in 1544–5 (*Treasurer Accts*, viii, 355). McDiarmid associates Lindsay's character with the Vekke or go-between of the *Roman de la Rose*.

318 *B*'s reading is metrically superior to *C*'s 'lernit'.

334 *so B; C* 'soverance'.

349 'Cok' is a common euphemism for 'Christ': such oaths, used throughout by the vices and other low characters, were much condemned in the later Middle Ages and were the subject of legislation in the 1552 Parliament, which noted that 'notwithstanding the oftt and frequent prechingis in detestatioun of the grevous and abominabill aithis, sweiring, execratiounis and

blasphematioun of the name of God, sweirand in vane
be His precious Blude, Body, Passioun and Woundis,
Devill stick, cummer, gor, roist or ryfe thame, and
sic uthers ugsume aithis and execratiounis aganis the
command of God, yet the samin is cum in sic ane
ungodlie use amangis the pepill of this realme, baith of
greit and small estaitis, that daylie and hourlie may
be hard amangis thame oppin blasphematioun of Godis
name and majestie, to greit contemptioun thairof and
bringing of the ire and wraith of God upone the pepill'
(*APS*, ii, 485). Cf. Hamilton's *Catechism*, ed. T.S.
Law (Oxford 1884), p. 64.

386    *C*'s 'And present hir with this same ring' is metrically
weaker, and loses the alliterative force of 'riche ring';
cf. *Squyer Meldrum*, 196 ('Ane riche rubie set in
ane ring') and 1004 ('Ane ring set with ane riche
rubie').

393    *so B*; *C* 'Gods goun'.

398    *so B*; *C* 'fetch'.

404    The colloquial phrase 'back or edge' has caused
some difficulty to commentators, but it appears to mean
'come what may', as in the line 'Well, fall back, fall
edge: I am ons att a poincte' (*Respublica*, 1467, ed.
W.W. Greg [EETS, London 1952], p. 50).

411    *so B*; *om. C*.

420    i.e. 'we have travelled as far as we are going'.

425    *so B*; *C* 'Quhilk'.

445    The inflected form 'makis' was still current in
Lindsay's lifetime: *C* amends to the more acceptable
seventeenth-century form 'do mak'.

452    The gambade (from French *gambade*, Italian
*gambata*), also known in Scotland as the gamond, was
a lively French dance; cf. Gavin Douglas, *Aeneid*,
XIII, ix, 107, ed.. D.F.C. Coldwell [4 vols,
STS, Edinburgh 1957–64], IV, 180: 'And gan do
dowbill brangillis and gambatis'.

461    St Bride or Bridget is frequently invoked in the play,
and was a popular saint in Scotland. She was depicted
with a cow, an allusion to her supposed origin as a
milkmaid.

469    Wantonnes' folly is represented by this piece of
business, in which he hurts his leg, presumably while
cavorting across the stage, and promptly forgets which
one is damaged.

478    Christ's Harrowing of Hell, described in the apocryphal
*Gospel of Nicodemus*, was a familiar elaboration
of the Easter story, and hence suitable material for a

blasphemous oath. For a serious version of the legend, cf. Dunbar's 'Done is a battell on the dragon blak', *Poems*, ed. Kinsley, pp. 11–12.

491–2    The idea is that the modesty of the lady might be preserved if her eyes are covered with the train of her skirt.

505    *B*'s reading is manifestly preferable to *C*'s 'dyosie'.

512    The dependence of kings on good advice and the dangers of young advisers are favourite themes in works of political advice; cf. for example Gilbert Hay's *Buke of the Governaunce of Princis*, *Prose Manuscript*, ed. J. Stevenson (2 vols, STS, Edinburgh 1899–1914), II, 152, and *The Thre Prestis of Peblis*, ll. 456–62, ed. T.D. Robb (STS, Edinburgh 1920), p. 28.

521    'Rolland into his rage' has the ring of an alliterative formula; the sense of 'rolland' is unclear, and it may be related to 'rolpand', 'roaring', as in Dunbar's *Flyting*, l. 142, 'Ramand and rolpand', *Poems*, ed. Kinsley, p. 81.

538–9    These lines are given to Sensualitie in *C*, but the sense demands that they be assigned to Hamelines, as in *B*.

539    The game of 'cap out' or 'cop out' apparently involved the competitors in draining a cup in turn; cf. *The Freiris of Berwik*, ll. 415–6, *Maitland Folio Manuscript*, ed. W.A. Craigie (2 vols, STS, Edinburgh 1919–27), I, 144.

540    'Batye tout' has puzzled previous editors: McDiarmid suggests that 'batty' means 'plump' and 'towt' a drink, but these senses are not attested before the nineteenth and eighteenth centuries respectively. Nevertheless, this is a more probable meaning than Hamer's desperate '? a drinking cup'.

543–5    Wantonnes now descends to obscene double-entendre: 'gumis' and 'justing lumis' both have obvious sexual reference. This lowering of the tone is characteristic of the scenes where Sensualitie reigns.

546    'rycht': *so B; om. C*.

548    'All': *so B; om. C*.

552    The point is surely that Wantonnes will take advantage of the King's preoccupation with Sensualitie: *B*'s 'he' therefore makes sense, but *C*'s 'ye' does not.

580–1    Since the assassination of James I at the age of 43, every Scottish king had died prematurely: James II at the siege of Roxburgh (aged 29), James III after Sauchieburn (aged 36), James IV at Flodden (aged 40), and James V after Pinkie (aged 30). All these catastrophes could credibly be ascribed, in one sense or another, to the want of good counsel; cf. *Testament and Complaynt of the Papyngo*, 430–520, *Works*, ed. Hamer, I, 69–71.

598     'that': *so B; om. C*.

601 s.d. The isle of May, 5 1/2 miles SE of Crail, provided the last safe anchorage in the Firth of Forth for ships venturing out into the North Sea.

603     'in': *so B; om.C*.

604     Wearing motley associates Flatterie with folly (he is 'your awin fule'), closely linked in medieval thought with the notion of sin; cf. the illustrations of sinners in cap and bells in the various versions of Sebastian Brant's *Narrenschiff*, one of the most popular books in Europe in the early sixteenth century and translated into English as the *Shyp of Folys* by Alexander Barclay (1509). It may be, as Hamer suggests (IV, 180), that Flatterie's storm-beaten ship itself falls within this tradition.

609     This is a hint of the traditional association of fools with Christmas, having its origins in the Roman Saturnalia; see below, l. 631.

620     It is difficult to choose between *B*'s *wy* and *C*'s *roy*: either might well be a misreading of the other. *Wy* (fellow) is more obviously applicable to Flatterie, but *roy* could refer to the tradition of the *Roy des Sots* (Hamer) or the Christmas custom of electing the King of the Bean (McDiarmid), or to both.

631     Here Flatterie associates himself with the riotousness of Yuletide festivities, in which order is ceremonially reversed. His arrival now, therefore, heralds a similar but unseasonal upsetting of order; cf. Alexander Scott's play with the same idea in relation to the lord of misrule / abbot of Narent tradition in his poem 'May is the moneth maist amene', *Poems*, ed. James Cranstoun (STS, Edinburgh 1896), pp. 23–5.

633     *B* preserves the rhyme, marred in *C*'s 'nocht fail'.

635     *C*'s 'wa sair the Devill' is difficult: Hamer keeps this reading, but later lists it as an error (IV, 69), while Kinsley gives 'fair'. But 'sair' may be a reduced form of *B*'s 'serve', a reading which seems as probable as the hypothetical confusion of /s/ and /f/.

642–3     'Quhen freindis meitis, hartis warmis' is proverbial, although this is the earliest authority for it; cf. Tilley, *Dictionary of Proverbs in English in the Sixteenth and Seventeenth Centuries* (Ann Arbor 1950), F758. 'Frelie fud' is a ME alliterative formula, while 'Jok' is, as Hamer points out, a conventional name for a fool.

| 672 | 'futher': *C* 'fither; cf. above, note to ll. 185–9. |
|---|---|
| 689 | 'fowll': *so B; om. C.* |
| 692 | This line is quite obscure as it stands. 'Howis' is the plural of 'houch' (although there may also be a hint of the sense of 'hollows' suggested by Kinsley); the difficulty is in 'with hoch' adjacent to the present participle 'hurland'. It seems to me that the only way to render this intelligible is to take 'hoch' as an exclamation. |
| 706–7 | These lines seem to look forward to the end of the play, where Dissait and Falset are indeed hanged, while Flatterie betrays them and escapes. |
| 723 | France, and especially Paris, was still an important training ground for the Scottish clergy, and a key centre of orthodox opinion, while those who were on the side of the Reformers had begun to prefer German universities. |
| 742 | 'to': *so B; om. C.* |
| 746 | 'hes lent to': *so B and C (1604); C* 'to hes lent'. |
| 753 | The tenderness of women, especially married ones, towards the mendicants was proverbial, and forms the basis of adverse comment in sermon and verse alike; cf. Chaucer's *General Prologue*, 208–24, *Complete Works*, ed. F.N. Robinson (2nd edn, Oxford 1957), p. 19. |
| 760–7 | The exact point of this complex and evidently derisive reference to the Carmelite house of Tullilum near Perth is not clear. Perhaps Dissait means that if one is hoping to gain credence by disguising oneself as a friar, there's little point in pretending to be a Carmelite; there is, however, no contemporary evidence that the friars of Tullilum were regarded as particularly corrrupt or delinquent. But the reference would, in the Cupar performance at least, have been a local one, and Lindsay may have been relying on the particular knowledge (or prejudices) of his audience. |
| 768 | 'Porteous': *so B; C* 'portouns'. |
| 771 | 'Freir Gill' is credibly identified by Anthony Ross OP with a figure of that name who occurs in the *Treasurer's Accounts* between 1526 and 1538, and with a Dominican called Friar Johannes Aegidii or Gyl, attested betwen 1491 and 1508 ('Notes on the Religious Orders', in *Essays on the Scottish Reformation*, ed. D. McRoberts [Glasgow 1962], pp. 185–240, at 203). If his name had become proverbial, however, there may have been some association with a sixteenth-century French farce about a lecherous friar called *Frere Guillebert*, |

*Ancien Théâtre François*, ed. M. Viollet-le-Duc (10 vols, Paris 1854–57), I, 305–27.

797     'in': *so B and C(1604); om. C.*

812     'yonder': *so B; C* 'yeoman'. 'he': *so B, om. C.*

826–7   These lines, included in the *B* text, were omitted from
and     *C*, probably because of their indecency. But Lindsay
832–9   carefully modulates the tone of the play according to
        the condition of his characters, and the crudity here is a
        kind of moral index, as is the blasphemous swearing
        of the other vices. There seems no reason to doubt the
        authenticity of the passages deleted by Charteris.

830     'And' (*B*) makes better sense than *C*'s 'Bot'.

853     'that': *so B; om. C.*

859     *so B; om. C.*

863     That Falset / Sapience has forgotten his new name
        is morally emblematic, but his route to 'Thin Drink'
        is carefully explained in the subsequent dialogue. He
        evidently connects his disguise with *sypins*, the lees of
        a wine barrel, and translates this into a form which
        no longer reflects the punning link. He subsequently
        explains his lapse as the absent-mindedness of true
        genius, an excuse which Humanitie unquestioningly
        accepts.

868     'me': *so B; om. C.*

897     Distilling the 'quintessence', the fifth element after
        air, fire, water and earth, was one of the principal
        objectives of the alchemists; alchemy and astrology
        were often linked in medieval thought as occult
        and questionable sciences, but astronomy was generally
        recognised as a more legitimate discipline, and formed a
        regular part of the university curriculum.

906–11 This list comically links the European conquests of
        a modern Arthur (Danzig, Denmark and Germany;
        Spain, France and Rome) with inappropriate
        references to 'Spittelfeild' (perhaps the village of
        that name in Perthshire), Renfrew, Rutherglen
        ('Rugland') and Corstorphine. The inference is once
        again that the King is too besotted (and flattered) to
        notice the incongruity.

989     'nocht': *so B; C* 'noch'.

1023    'To break buithis' was clearly a sixteenth-century term
        for shopbreaking: cf. the reference in the Edinburgh
        Treasurer's Accounts for 22 December 1555 to 'ane
        thef that brak ane buith' (*Edinburgh Burgh Recs.*, II,
        295).

1059    This commonplace of political literature is ultimately
        attributed to the Emperor Theodosius (378–95),

and is quoted from Claudian's *Panegyricus de Quarto Consulatu Honorii Augusti*, 302 by John of Salisbury, Vincent of Beauvais and other medieval writers; interestingly, it occurs in Walter Bower's *Scotichronicon*, v, iv, ed. J. Goodall (Edinburgh 1747–59), I, 247.

1088    Swearing by the bells and books of the Mass is part of a more general pattern of sacrilegious oaths; cf. *Ywain and Gawaine*, 3023, ed. A.B. Friedman and N.T. Harrington (EETS, London 1964), p. 81 and *The Awntyrs off Arthure*, 30, ed. Ralph Hanna III (Manchester 1974), p. 65.

1100    Many editions of several versions of the English New Testament – and, indeed, of the whole Bible – had been published by 1552; the earliest to be printed in England were versions by Thomas Matthew, based on the translation by Tyndale frequently published abroad from 1525, and by Miles Coverdale, both produced in 1538. Parliament legalised the reading of the vernacular Bible, despite the opposition of the prelates, in 1542 (*APS*, ii, 415, 425).

1126    The Lutheran influence on the early Scottish reformers was considerable, from the teaching of Patrick Hamilton and John Gau's early translations, through the hymns of the *Gude and Godlie Ballatis*. Only with the rising influence of Knox in the mid-1550s did Calvinism become the dominant strain; see James K. Cameron, 'Aspects of the Lutheran Contribution to the Scottish Reformation', *Records of the Scottish Church History Society* 22 (1984), 1–34.

1140    Remission of a criminal conviction, usually in return for a monetary payment, was a standard part of legal procedure, and frequently condemned as an abuse in the fifteenth and sixteenth centuries.

1168    The image of the 'sleep of God' as a figure of disorder is not uncommon in later medieval literature, and is ultimately derived from *Psalm* 43: 22–3; cf. Henryson's *Morall Fabillis*, l. 1295, *Poems*, ed. Fox, p. 53 and note, p. 262.

1184    The correct reference, as Hamer points out, is to *Isaiah* 59:14: 'Truth is fallen down in the strete, and ye thing that is plaine and open may not be shewed. Yea, the trueth is layde in pryson, and he that refrayneth hym selfe from evell, must be spoyled'.

1190    2 Timothy 4:4: '*Et a veritate quidem auditum avertent*' ('For the time wil come when they wil not suffer wholesome doctrine: but after their owne lustes shal they (whose eares ytche) get theym an heape of teachers, *and shall turne their eares from the truth*, and shall be geven unto fables').

1208   'to': *so B; om. C.*

1210   So B; C 'neid not to think shame'. The double negative is quite acceptable in OSc.

1213   B's 'Quha' is preferable to C's 'Quhilk'.

1233   There is an ambiguity here: if Chastitie is denied 'harberie' she will indeed suffer deprivation, but it will be 'caus of' (grounds for) deprivation in a more technical sense, in that the Priores will be liable to loss of her office for misconduct; this is, in fact, the primary meaning of the word in OSc. The thrust is, of course, ineffective.

1257   'hes': *om. C.*

1258   This is a most curious reading: the rhyme evidently demands 'bocht', for which 'coft' is a much less common synonym. It would seem to follow that the more difficult reading has, against all the normal assumptions of modern editors, been substituted for the more common one, but cf. the Cupar Proclamatioun, 79–80 (Appendix, p. 168), where *B* reads *nocht / coft*.

1304   C repeats 'play cap-out', but this is presumably a printer's error.

1319   'tumes': *C* 'turnes'; *B* 'temiss'.

1347   St Blaise, or Blasius, of Cappadocia was a fourth-century martyr, widely reverenced throughout Europe. There were altars dedicated to him at Dunblane, Dundee, Edinburgh, Perth and elsewhere.

1353   A bedstaff was, in Kinsley's words, 'a stick used in reaching to spread the coverings on a recessed bed'. Both Hamer and Kinsley seem to misread these lines quite perversely: the Sowtar's Wife regards her bedstaff simply as an offensive weapon, and surely not as a euphemism for her husband's (much less useful) penis!

1355   St Blane was an early Scottish saint traditionally supposed to have been bishop of Kingarth in Bute, and to have been buried at Dunblane.

1358   St Crispin, martyred at Soissons in 287, was the patron saint of shoemakers. Altars dedicated to him and his brother Crispinian and maintained by the shoemakers' craft were commonly a feature of burgh churches.

1360   'platt': *so B; C* 'flap'.

1375   'to': *so B; C* 'we'ill'.

1379   St Clone or Clune (l. 4416) is difficult to identify. Hamer suggests that 'St Cluanus' was a sixth-century

Irish abbot; his reference is apparently to St Mochua, whose other name, according to the *Acta Sanctorum*, I, 47–9, was *Cuanus*. One possibility is that 'St Clone' is a distortion of the name of either St Mochua of Cluain-Dobhtha or St Mochonna of Cluain-Airdne, both early Irish saints of great obscurity. 'Cluain' (meaning 'pasture') is a common Irish placename element and often occurs in the names of religious communities. Whoever he was, St Clone is also mentioned by Dunbar in 'Quhy will ye merchantis of renoun', l. 31, *Poems*, ed. Kinsley, p. 202.

1393
s.d.
There was apparently a small burn, known as Our Lady's Burn, running through the playfield on Castle Hill. But stage directions in other plays suggest that, in England at any rate, a ditch may have been used as a boundary of the playing area.

1393
s.d.
The pavilion was evidently a retiring-house adjacent to the stage; there are no clear grounds for supposing, as Richard Southern suggests (*The Medieval Theatre in the Round* [London 1957], pp. 133–4), that this was situated 'outside the action altogether'.

1402
The 'bar' is any barrier used to exclude unwanted persons, here perhaps referring to the barrier closing the entrance to a city.

1458
The theme of Constantine's responsibility for the corruption of the primitive Church recurs almost obsessively in Lindsay's works: its first occurrence is in *The Dreme*, 233 (*Works*, ed. Hamer, I, 11), and it is again taken up in the *Papyngo*, ll. 801–28 (ibid., I, 80) and the *Monarche*, l. 4410 (ibid., I, 330). According to medieval tradition, Constantine granted temporal possession of Italy to the Church in 330, when he was supposed to have moved the Imperial capital to Byzantium.

1513
'leddy': *so B; C* 'ladie'.

1555
'us': *so B; C* 'of'.

1577
B's 'na' may be a better reading than *C*'s 'ma', since no demands have actually been made.

1579
'wirth': *so B; C* 'with'.

1580
Matt. 5:6: 'Blessed are they whiche honger and thruste for righteousnes'.

1613
The doctrine that earthly kings are merely Christ's deputies is another commonplace of medieval political theory; cf. Ernst H. Kantorowicz, *The King's Two Bodies: A Study in Medieval Political Theology* (Princeton 1957), pp. 28–30 and *passim*.

1633
'yow': *so B; om. C.*

1649     'resset': *so B; C* 'resavit'. *Reset* is a term in general
use in Scots law for the harbouring of criminals and /
or stolen goods.

1705     Sardanapulus, king of Assyria was a familiar type
of the voluptuary; there is a longer account of him
in the *Monarche*, 3273–3380, which seems to be
derived ultimately from Diodorus Siculus, v. *Works*, ed.
Hamer, III, 245–6, 371–4.

1712     For the destruction of Sodom and Gomorrah, see
*Genesis* 18:19–19:29.

1725     Again, Lindsay invokes a familiar political motif:
the idea of the 'body politic', with the king as its
head, the knights as its arms, the peasantry as the legs
and so on, is at least as old as Cicero. Partly, no
doubt, because of 1 Corinthians 12:22, it is frequently
used by medieval political theorists such as John of
Salisbury (Policraticus, v, 2ff., ed. C.C.J. Webb [2
vols, Oxford 1909], I, 282–4), Thomas Aquinas
(*De regimine principum*, 12, *Selected Political Writings*,
ed. A.P. d'Entrèves [Oxford 1959], p. 66) and so
on. For a survey of the theme, see Kantorowicz, *op. cit*,
pp. 207–32.

1734     Proverbial: the earliest recorded occurrence is in
Henryson, *Morall Fabillis*, 512, *Poems*, ed. Fox, p.
23; cf. Alexander Scott, 'To luve unluvit it is a pane',
22, *Poems*, ed. J. Cranstoun (STS, Edinburgh 1898),
p. 74.

1758     'hier': *so B; om. C*, but required by the metre.

1769     The rape of Lucretia by Sextus Tarquinius, narrated
by Livy, *Histories*, I, 57–59 and Ovid, *Fasti*, II,
655–852, was widely invoked in the Middle Ages and
the Renaissance as a figure of oppressed chastity;
cf. Chaucer, *Legend of Good Women*, 1680–1885,
*Complete Works*, ed. Robinson, pp. 507–9.

1773     All copies of *C* except Gough read thus; Gough has
'regraidit'.

1777     'till': *so B; C* 't'inclyne'.

1778     'sa': *so B; om. C*.

1782     'consonabill': *so B; C*'s 'consociabill' is possible, but
metrically and semantically weaker.

1813     Hamer suggests, almost certainly correctly, that the
reading 'ferry myre', shared by B and C, is an
error, and that Lindsay's reference was to Ferny Myre,
situated 3 1/2 miles west of Cupar. There would,
of course, be no mussels at this inland location and
therefore no income from the tithes; hence the irony
of the King's grant. The local reference would have lost

its point outside the context of the Cupar performance, which no doubt explains the reading in the surviving texts, but the joke has been destroyed in the process.

1817     Diligence responds appropriately to the King's worthless gift, invoking the popular sixteenth-century tradition of *impossibilia* with his suggestion that he will benefit from it when (after Doomsday!) butter grows on broom bushes in the Tranent coal-mines. Dunbar uses the same device in 'The Birth of Antichrist', and there are several examples, generally applied to the supposed infidelity of mistresses, in the Bannatyne MS. (e.g. IV, 42–5). There is evidence that coal was produced in the Tranent area from the beginning of the thirteenth century; see *Reg. Newbattle*, p. 53.

1850     As Hamer points out, the doctrine of princely recreation was another commonplace of medieval political thought. For a fifteenth-century Scottish example, see Gilbert Hay's *Buke of the Governance of Princis*, in *Gilbert Haye's Manuscript*, ed. J.H. Stevenson (STS, 2 vols, Edinburgh 1898–1914), II, 96–8.

1853     'Hawking and hunting' were particularly approved as princely recreations; cf. such compilations as Edward, duke of York's *The Master of Game*, ed. W.A. and F. Baillie-Grohmann (London 1904), and the discussion in Sir Thomas Elyot's *Book named the Governor*, ed. J.E. Lehmberg (London 1907), pp. 65–9.

1862     So *B*; *C* 'was nathing war'.

1874     Previous editions read 'thrifteously', but *B* and *C* agree that the correct reading (which makes better sense and is linguistically more probable) is 'thifteouslie'; cf. Hamer, IV, 199, where the error is corrected.

1877     St Mavane or Mevenna was a sixth-century Welsh or Cornish saint, founder of the abbey of St Meen in Brittany.

1883     Cf. Vulgate *Psalm* 100:10: *Initium sapientie timor Domini* ('The feare of the Lord is the beginnynge of wysdome').

1909     'A Hoyzes' is a rough-and-ready form of French 'Oyez',
s.d.     'hear ye', generally used to obtain silence for an official proclamation.

1927–8   These (evidently crude) lines seem to have been bowdlerized in *C*: 'quhislecaw' is difficult and otherwise unattested, but presumably refers to the effects of flatulence (? 'whistle-call'). *C* reads 'gif that your *mawkine* (companion) cryis quhisch'.

1955   Fillan, son of St Kentigerna, was an eighth-century
saint who was active mainly in Glendochart, Perthshire
and who was the subject of numerous dedications;
his cult is reflected in such placenames as Strathfillan
and Kilfillan. Several churches and altars in Fife were
dedicated to him.

1974   'Session' and 'senyie' refer respectively to the temporal
and ecclesiastical courts, the parallel systems of justice
which recur as a source of grievance from here to
the end of the play. The Session was the court operated
by the College of Justice, established by James V in
1532; 'Senyie' is strictly the Scots word for a synod or
ecclesiastical council, here acting in a judicial capacity.

1987   'hyne to': so B; C 'into'.

1993   The 'hyreild horse' or heriot, consisting of the
tenant's best beast, was customary in eastern Scotland
at least as early as the twelfth century' (A.A.M.
Duncan, *Scotland: The Making of the Kingdom*
[Edinburgh 1975], p. 338); cf. *Regiam Majestatem*,
ed. Lord Cooper (Stair Society, Edinburgh
1947), pp. 285–6. Its ecclesiastical equivalent, owed
to the vicar, was the *corspresent* (or 'cow'); cf.
*Monarche*, 4709–38, *Works*, ed. Hamer, I, 338–9.
There is a striking parallel to the Poor Man's story
in the case pursued before the official of Lothian by
Nicholas Wilkieson, vicar of St Cuthbert's, Edinburgh
against the widow of David Ravy on 7 December
1546; v. Simon Ollivant, *The Court of the Official
in Pre-Reformation Scotland* (Stair Society, Edinburgh
1982), pp. 82–3.

2002   Like the cow, the 'umest clayis' were a duty owed
to the vicar, consisting of the 'best upper garment' of
the de ceased; cf. *Monarche* 4711 and n., *Works*, ed.
Hamer, III,

2009   The teind (tithe) was a payment of one-tenth of
the year's produce due to the rector or parson, usually
in practice a member of a religious community far
removed from the parish itself; in the case of Tranent,
for example, the parish had been appropriated to the
Augustinian house of Holyrood.

2011   Refusal of the sacraments was the most immediate
consequence of excommunication, a punishment which
was not, under canon law, the prerogative of ordinary
clergy or intended to be used for such minor offences
as non-payment of teinds; cf. Hamilton's *Catechism*,

ed. Law, pp. 234–5. But it was not uncommon
for clergy to petition the official's court for the
excommunication of parishioners; cf. Ollivant, *op. cit.*,
pp. 77–80.

2012    'ye': *so B; C* 'he'.

2023    St Geill (Giles) was the patron saint of Edinburgh,
a hermit greatly reverenced in France and, to a lesser
extent, in Scotland.

2027    'for': *C* 'fra'.

2051    The Pardoner's alliterative name might imply
'anyone travelling to Rome for religious reasons'
(McDiarmid), but it equally suggests someone who
rakes together a hoard, for or in the name of
Rome. Pardoners were frequently the subject of sharp
criticism, not only by poets and preachers, but
also by the Church authorities; cf. for example the
edict issued by Pope Boniface IX in 1390 and
quoted by J. Jusserand, *English Wayfaring Life in the
Middle Ages*, trans. Lucy Toulmin Smith (London
1890), pp. 443–4. There is little evidence of activity
by pardoners in Scotland: Lindsay's portrait in
many ways resembles, and was probably influenced by,
that of the Pardoner in Chaucer's *General Prologue*,
669–714, *Complete Works*, ed. Robinson, pp.
23–4; cf. for his name the cryptic reference in *Piers
Plowman*, VI, 148 to 'Robert Renne-aboute' (*Piers
Plowman: The B-Text*, ed. George Kane and E. Talbot
Donaldson [London 1975] p. 357), identified
by Owst with the Pardoner (*Literature and Pulpit*, pp.
372–3). A remarkably close parallel to Sir Robert's
treatment of the Poor Man is found in a sermon
in Bodleian MS. 95, f. 14r: 'Perdoners and fals
prechours, wyth othyr suche, that, yif a man have but
on peny, they wol have hyt, though he schuld [lack]
bred and watur, and al hys howsehold' (quoted by
Owst, *ibid.* p. 373). And cf. the suggestion (n. to ll.
2105–6) of an underlying French source.

2055    'prevelage': *so B; C* 'pilgrimage'. Pardoners derived
their claimed authority from privileges granted by the
Pope.

2058    For publication of the English Bible, see above, l.
1100. Access for all literate laypeople to the vernacular
Scriptures was an important objective of all Reforming
sects.

2078–9    The Pardoner attacks three of the most prominent
members of the first generation of Reformers, Luther,
Heinrich Bullinger, Zwingli's successor at Zürich, and

Philip Melanchthon, an important associate of Luther's and compiler of the Augsburg Confession (1530).

2082 He now widens the attack to include St Paul, whose views on the early Church formed a model for the Reformers. This assault on the Bible itself is clearly intended to make the Pardoner condemn himself in the eyes of all reasonable Christians, as Chaucer's Pardoner does in the *Canterbury Tales*, *Complete Works*, ed. Robinson, pp. 148–9.

2088 As in Dunbar's 'Fenyeit Freir of Tungland' (*Poems*, ed. Kinsley, pp. 161–4), the Muslim territories of Tartary are equated with the realm of Satan; infernal names and those of Islam are constantly conflated in the Middle Ages. *C* reads 'Caue', *B* 'Can'; Hamer was correct in suggesting that the intended sense was 'Khan', but was misled by a mistaken reading of *B* as 'Cam'.

2094 The Pardoner's list of (most secular!) relics begins with the jawbone of Fionn Mac Cumhaill, leader of the legendary *Fianna*, who was a prominent figure in the shared literature of Ireland and Gaelic Scotland. There is a heavy emphasis on poems in this tradition in the early sixteenth-century *Book of the Dean of Lismore* (NLS MS. Advocates 72.1.37), written by a group of scribes in Perthshire; some of these texts are unquestionably of Scottish authorship. Cf. *Heroic Poetry from the Book of the Dean of Lismore*, ed. Neil Ross (SGTS, Edinburgh 1939) and *Scottish Verse from the Book of the Dean of Lismore*, ed. William J. Watson (SGTS, Edinburgh 1937).

2096 Who Colin was, why his cow should be remembered for its martyrdom in Balquhidder in Perthshire and, indeed, who MacConnal was are all mysteries, and may have been even to Lindsay's audience (though Dr John Durkan has suggested to me that a reference to the Campbells, among whom Colin was a common Christian name, may have been intended). But the burlesque of authentic saints' relics is clear enough, and Balquhidder was no doubt remote enough for almost anything to be possible; cf. l. 3307 below.

2100 Johnny Armstrong, a notable Border reiver, was hanged at Carlenrig, Roxburghshire in July 1530 as part of a general attempt to crack down on lawlessness in the region; v. the B version of Robert Lindsay of Pitscottie's *Chronicles*, ed. J.G. Dalyell (2 vols, Edinburgh 1814), II, 342–3. A contemporary ballad, sympathetic to Armstrong, is recorded in F.J.

Child's *English and Scottish Popular Ballads* (5 vols, New York 1882–98), III, 362–72.

2105–6 St Bride's association with cows has already been noted; St Anthony is generally portrayed with a pig and a bell for reasons which are obscure. Perhaps, as Hamer suggests, the pig represents the subduing of the flesh. But the reference probably echoes *La Farce d'un Pardonneur*, 106–7, *Ancien Théâtre François*, ed. Viollet-le-Duc, II, 54 (see Introduction, p.xlii).

2115 The right to give divorces was confined to the ecclesiastical courts, and then only on very restricted grounds: according to the canonist William Hay, divorce from the marriage bond could only be granted if the marriage itself was unlawful, while divorce from cohabitation (which did not permit re-marriage) might be granted on grounds of adultery, attempted murder or leprosy, v. William Hay, *Lectures on Marriage*, ed. John C. Barry (Stair Society, Edinburgh 1967), pp. 56–75. Hay also specifies (pp. 63–6) the requirement of a competent judge, which did not, of course, include pardoners.

2170 According to the theory of the humours, 'cold and dry' were the characteristics of a melancholic temperament, one of the attributes of which was impotence; cf. Henryson, *Morall Fabillis*, 519, *Poems*, ed. Fox, p. 24.

2185 Belial occurs in the Old Testament as a Hebrew word meaning 'worthless, wicked' (cf. the Matthew Bible's gloss to *1 Samuel* 2:12: 'The Hebrew worde is Belial, which is as much in English as unthriftye, frowarde or wicked'); but in later Judaic texts and the New Testament it has come to be a name for the Devil (cf. *2 Corinthians* 6:15).

2201 As Joanne S. Kantrowitz points out (p. 53), only the archbishop of St Andrews, John Hamilton, held this title in Scotland at the time the play was performed.

2212 Christian Anderson appears from the context to have been a well-known whore (? in Cupar), but there is no evidence to support the inference.

2256 *Totiens quotiens* is not, as Hamer suggests, a nonsense phrase, but two terms often balanced in Latin and meaning 'as often as ... so often'; see, for example, Virgil, *Aeneid*, XII, 483–5, and Livy, *Histories*, VI, 15, 7.

2258 'leddy': *so B; C* 'lady'.

2272 The doctrine of Purgatory is one of the few theological issues raised by Lindsay (see Introduction, p.xviii); it was, of course, integrally linked with

the sale of indulgences and could hardly be avoided
here. While condemning indulgences, Luther and
Melanchthon generally avoided any outright rejection of
Purgatory itself, although even some late medieval
Catholic theologians were inclined to interpret the
concept spiritually rather than literally; Zwingli, on
the other hand condemned the doctrine in unambiguous
terms.

2281    'this': *so B; C* 'his'.

2292    'on': *so B; C* 'in'.

## PART TWO

2322    The association of each of the vices with one of
s.d.    the Estaitis is here made explicit. Dissait is 'counsallour
    to the merchand-men' (l. 655) and Flatterie
    is particularlie linked with Spiritualitie; perhaps, then,
    Falset is the vice of the Temporalitie.

2381    For the history of the notion of the body politic, see
    Note to l. 1725.

2396    There is a reference to a 'John Dempster, dempster
    of Parliament' in the parliamentary record for 1483
    (*APS*, ii, 151–2).

2433    'maid': *so B; C* 'cumde'.

2437    This is presumably the burn which featured in
s.d.    the business at l. 1391, here functioning as a natural
    boundary of the playing-area proper.

2466    'Thou': *so C; B* reads 'How', which may be
    the original reading, but which is not overwhelmingly
    superior to the printed text.

2478    'Lord': *so B; C* 'Lords'.

2489–    *C* reads 'laird or laid' (2489), 'spur-gaid' (2490) and
93    'skap skyre skaid' (2492), but it seems clear that *B* gives
    the correct rhymes. 'Gawd' is the past participle, with
    /l/-vocalisation, of 'gall', to vex or irritate; 'skawd' is
    similarly derived from 'scald'; while 'skyre' (from Latin
    *scirrhus*) is a cancerous piece of hard tissue.

2533    'bot': *so B; om. C.*

2561    Gude Counsall invokes the traditional custom of calling
    together a host in times of military need.

2565    'lo': *C* 'to'.

2579    Lindsay here comments on the first stages of
    the process of enclosure, by which lords took over the
    land of their tenants and turned it over to pasture.
    For similar comment on the situation in England
    a generation earlier, see Thomas More, *Utopia*, ed.
    Edward Surtz SJ and J.H. Hexter (New Haven
    1965), pp. 60–71.

2586    'gud': *so B; C* 'ane'.

2587    'the': *so B; om. C.*

2604    'labour': *so B; om. C.*

2606    2 Thessal. 3:10: 'For when we were wyth you, this
we warned you of, that *yf ther wer any which woulde not
worcke, that the same should not eate.*'

2621    Augustinians, Carmelites and Cordeliers
(Franciscans) were among the most widespread
orders of friars; the fourth major order, which
Lindsay here omits to mention, was the Dominicans. It
may be that he was better disposed towards them:
in the *Testament of the Papyngo*, for example, he singles
out the Dominican convent of Sciennes for praise as a
virtuous house.

2633    Diogenes of Sinope (c. 400–c.325), founder of
the Cynic sect, was famous for his abstemiousness. The
fullest Classical account of his life is that by Diogenes
Laertius, *Lives of Eminent Philosophers*, VI, 20–81.

2644    There was a tradition that Mary Magdalene, after
the Crucifixion, travelled to Marseilles and subsequently
lived a life of poverty in the wilderness; see the Scots
version of her legend in Cambridge UL MS Gg.ii.6,
*Legends of the Saints*, ed. W.M. Metcalfe (STS, 3 vols,
Edinburgh 1896), I, 256–84.

2645    Mary the Egyptian who, after a life of sin
in Alexandria, was converted to Christianity and lived a
life of poverty in the desert, is the subject of another
of the Scottish saints' lives; Metcalfe, *ed. cit.*, I
296–339.

2646    Not the Apostle, but St Paul the Hermit, whose life,
by Jerome, claims that he lived for ninety years in the
desert.

2655    C reads 'infetching', which is certainly a more difficult
reading than *B*'s 'grit misusing'. Though not otherwise
attested in OSc., 'infetching' appears to be a synonym
for 'inbringing', which occurs quite commonly from the
later fifteenth century with the sense of 'collection of
taxes or fines'. Happé glosses 'infetching' as 'deceiving',
which does not seem probable.

2671    'pertiall': *so B; C* 'perpetuall'. It is clear that John is
protesting at the *bias* of the ecclesiastical courts.

2688    'Temporalitie': *so B; C* 'Spiritualitie'.

2692    'jynkyne': *so B; C* 'gearking'.

2757    'royaltie': *C* 'royallie', but the context demands a
noun.

2833    Lindsay here acknowledges explicitly the authority of
the Pope in ecclesiastical matters, since his consent is a

prerequisite for the abolition of the death duties. But
the immediate effect, of course, is to 'demonstrate' that
even this proviso is insufficient for the Spiritualitie.

2837    The notary public was a key figure in the legal
business of Scotland, copying and witnessing documents
and acting as clerk to courts, burgh councils
and to Parliament. A notarial instrument was a legally
authenticated document, and could therefore be used as
evidence in subsequent proceedings.

2841    Lindsay is apparently alluding to the legal maxim
'*Quod maior pars curiae effecit pro eo habetur ac si omnes
egerint* ('What is done by the majority of an assembly
is considered to be the same as if it had been
done by all'); cf. Gaines Post, 'A Romano-canonical
maxim, *Quod omnes tangit*, in Bracton and in
Early Parliaments', in *Studies in Medieval Legal Thought*
(Princeton 1964), pp. 163–238. This principle was
widely applied by both civil and canon lawyers, but
there is no direct evidence of its application in the
Scottish parliament.

2845    Scotland's historic position as *filia specialis* of the
Church meant that ecclesiastical preferment was to
a large extent controlled directly from Rome. The
innumerable references to Scottish petitions in the
Vatican Archives, now collected by the Department
of Scottish History at the University of Glasgow,
testify to the huge business which the Scots brought
to the Curia.

2860    Simony, from the name of the sorcerer Simon Magus
(see *Acts* 8:9–24) was the corrupt practice of
buying ecclesiastical preferments and other privileges,
or in the words of Hamilton's *Catechism*, 'a diligent will
to by or sel ony spiritual thing or ony uthir thing that
is annexit to spiritual thingis' (ed. Law, p. 99).

2874    The granting of the headship of religious houses
*in commendam* to non-members of the community, and
especially to bishops or even those who were
not priests, had developed in the later fifteenth century,
and was a central feature of royal policy by the middle
of the sixteenth.

2878    It was customary practice for Scottish (and other)
clerics to obtain dispensation from the theoretical ban
on pluralism, and it was not uncommon for bishops
and others to hold several benefices at once, including
abbacies held *in commendam*.

2913    The quotation which follows is from *1 Timothy*
3:1–3. The translation is not the same as that in

any of the available English versions; see Introduction, p.xxxviii

2938     The order of consecration of bishops included from the earliest times the holding (rather than binding) of the New Testament over the shoulders of the new bishop; for British examples, see *Pontificale Lanalatense*, ed. G.H. Doble (Henry Bradshaw Society, London 1937), p. 57, and *The Pontifical of Magdalen College*, ed. H.A. Wilson (Henry Bradshaw Society, London 1910), p. 73.

2965     David I (1124–53) was the founder of monastic houses at Selkirk (subsequently moved to Kelso), Melrose, Holyrood and elsewhere, and made substantial grants to Dunfermline and Coldingham; v. A.A.M. Duncan, *Scotland: The Making of the Kingdom* (Edinburgh 1975), pp. 145–51. Lindsay's lines are closely related to a stanza of the *Tragedie of Cardinall Betour*, ll. 414–20; it is more likely, as Hamer suggests (IV, 220), that the longer version in *Ane Satyre* is derived from the rhyme royal stanza of the *Tragedie*, and that the passage here is therefore to be dated later than 1546–7.

2989     James I (1405–37), to whom these words are ascribed in Bellenden's translation (1531) of Hector Boece's *Historia Scotorum* (1527): 'And thairfor King James the First, quhen he come to his sepulture at Dumfermeling, said that he was ane sair sanct for the Croune', ed. E.C. Batho and H.W. Husbands (STS, 2 vols, Edinburgh 1938–41), II, 185. The passage is not found in Boece, where the list of David's foundations occurs on f. 273ʳ. McDiarmid notes (p. 144) that the rest of Bellenden's expansion here provides a possible source for Lindsay's comments on payments to Rome.

3005     These lines are not assigned to Flatterie in *C*, but it is evident from the subsequent dialogue that he must be the 'holy father' addressed by Spiritualitie. He is, of course, still disguised as a friar.

3015     The four orders of friars were the Dominicans, Franciscans, Carmelites and Augustinians; see above, l. 2622.

3022     John responds by reciting the Apostles' Creed, a simple and theoretically uncontroversial basis for Christian belief. The vindication by Correctioun is a direct challenge, since John omits the key word *catholicam* from his definition of the Church and rejects the abuses of the Catholic Church.

3042    'Sanct Tan' is probably a 'metanalytic' form of
        'St Anne', created by the partial transfer of the final
        consonant of 'Sanct' to the following name (as in the
        Shakespearean form 'my nuncle'); it is, at all events,
        curious that Correctioun should use a blasphemous oath
        at this solemn moment. The identification is supported
        by the remarkable vernacular excommunication of
        Border reivers (1525), where 'Sancte Tan' is invoked
        along with Catherine, Margaret and Bride: v.
        *St Andrews Formulare, 1514–1546*, ed. G. Donaldson
        and C. Macrae (2 vols, Stair Society, Edinburgh
        1942–44), I, 269.

3069    Pluto, king of the underworld, here takes
        on some of the significance of Satan, an identification
        which is made explicit at l. 3981; this assimilation
        is widespread in the Middle Ages (see, for example,
        D.D.R. Owen, *The Vision of Hell* [Edinburgh/London
        1970], p. 147), but for a parallel tradition,
        cf. Dunbar's *Goldyn Targe*, ll. 125–6, *Poems*, ed.
        Kinsley, p. 33, where Pluto appears in fairy green,
        described as 'the elrich incubus'.

3073    Local quarries must have been a common feature of the
        medieval landscape; this story is quite different from
        that which Pauper told earlier, and presumably relates
        to an earlier phase of his career.

3076–   Lindsay weaves a string of technical terms from
91      canon law into the narrative, emphasizing the alienation
        of the process from the laypeople whose lives
        were increasingly subject to it. '*Citandum*' is the
        opening word of a summons; '*lybellandum*' refers to
        the first statement of plea and '*ad opponendum*' to
        the reply; '*interloquendum*' is an interim decree; '*ad
        replicandum*' is the plaintiff's response to his opponent's
        '*ad opponendum*'; '*hodie ad octo*' means 'a week
        today' (constant delays were a notorious feature of the
        legal system); while '*pronunciandum*' commences the
        court's final judgment.

3097    The balance between secular and ecclesiastical courts
        in France had indeed shifted in favour of the former,
        largely as a result of the edict of Villers-Cotterets
        (1539), which restricted the power of consistory
        courts over laymen; subsequent legislation even gave
        lay courts some responsibility in matters of heresy.
        Cf. J.H.M. Salmon, *Society in Crisis: France in the
        Sixteenth Century* (London 1977), pp. 83–4.

3162    Cf. the Prologue to Hamilton's *Catechism*: 'And
        brevely, as he is nocht worthy to be callit ane craftis

man quhilk kennis nocht quhat belangis to his craft, na mair is ane man or woman worthy to be callit ane Christin man or ane Christin woman gif he or sche wil nocht ken quhat belangis to thair Christindome.' (ed. Law, p. 26).

3183   Diligence raises (forlornly, perhaps) the possibility of finding a virtuous, competent friar, singling out the Franciscans. The Provincial of the Conventual Franciscans at this period was John Ferguson, while the province of the stricter Observant order was presumably either Ludovic Williamson or John Paterson; v. W. Moir Bryce, *The Grey Friars in Scotland* (Edinburgh/London 1909), and John Durkan, 'The Observant Franciscan Province in Scotland', *Innes Rev.* 35 (1984), 51–7.

3196   The problem of the marriage 'markit' mentioned by Temporalitie is a recurring one, for which Lindsay's proposed solution is a startling form of marital *apartheid* (see ll. 3958–73). There was a reference in the 1540 Linlithgow interlude to the clergy's 'over bying of lordis and Barrons eldeste sones to thair Doughters, where thoroughe the nobilitie of the blode of the Realme was degenerate' (Hamer, 11, 5), and Alexander Scott raises the same issue in his *New Yeir Gift to the Quene Mary* (1562), 65–6, *Poems*, ed. Cranstoun, p. 3.

3205   St Allan or Elia was a sixth-century Cornish or Breton saint, sometimes confused with St Hilary.

3226   Eusdaill or Ewesdale is the valley of the Ewes Water, north of Langholm. This was reiver country, and Langholm was the centre of operations of Johnny Armstrong (see above, l. 2100).

3250   George Leslie, earl of Rothes (c. 1495–1558) was a notable Fife magnate, sheriff of the county from 1540 and perhaps, as Hamer suggests, a member of the Cupar audience. He would have been a receptive member: some of the Leslies were certainly members of Lindsay's party. The earl's brother, John, assassinated Beaton in 1546, and his son and heir, Norman, was also one of those who occupied St Andrews Castle on that occasion. The earl himself was charged with complicity and acquitted; v. *Fourth Report, Historical MSS. Commission*, p. 504.

3256   'Ewis durris' is the name of a pass between Teviotdale and Ewesdale.

3261   Dysart Moor lies on the direct route from Leslie House, seat of the earls of Rothes, to the nearest ferrry

crossing of the Forth, at Kinghorn. Thift has his
escape-route planned.

3263 Struthers Castle, just south of Cupar, was the seat of
the Lindsay earls of Crawford.

3268 As Laing first pointed out, the Annat Burn runs a
little north of Doune, taking a horse thief into the hilly
country of southern Perthshire.

3276 'with': *so B; om. C.*

3293 Liddesdale was another secluded valley in
Dumfriesshire, south-east of Langholm; cf. Sir
Richard Maitland of Lethington, 'Of Liddisdaill the
commoun theiffis', *Maitland Folio Manuscript*, ed.
Craigie, I, 301–3; *The Maitland Quarto Manuscript*,
ed. W.A. Craigie (STS, Edinburgh 1920), pp.
6–9.

3293 These lines are found in *B*, but omitted from *C*.
s.d.– There is no reason to doubt their authenticity, and no
3309 apparent reason for their exclusion from the printed
text.

3307 Balquhidder is again a suitably remote area, south-west
of Loch Tay in Perthshire.

3320 The Merse, in SE Berwickshire, was a fertile farming
area, a fruitful source of plunder for Border reivers.

3339 'Licents-men' were holders of a Master's degree from
a medieval university, which was in effect a licence
to teach. The licence in theology was normally taken
after four years' study in Arts and about eleven
in theology; cf. John Durkan and James Kirk, *The
University of Glasgow 1451–1577* (Glasgow 1977),
pp. 115–22.

3402 'for til': *om. C*, clearly making the line metrically
defective.

3429 The three vows of poverty, chastity and obedience were
generally regarded as the fundamentals of monasticism,
although they do not correspond exactly to the
vows of 'stability', conversion of habits and obedience
required by the Benedictine Rule; cf. Cuthbert
Butler, *Benedictine Monachism* (London 1919), pp.
122–45.

3440 'Catch', apparently derived from MFlemish *caetsespel*
('chasing game'), was a widespread Scots term for
[hand-] tennis. Cf. *Ratis Raving*, l. 1245, ed.
R. Girvan (STS, Edinburgh 1939), p. 35; and
*Treasurer Accts*, I, 277, recording a payment of £2.14s.
to James IV 'to play at the cach' (June 1496). At the
same time a boy was paid 2s. for the balls.

3445 The exchange of round caps for 'four-nuikit'

ones would be a fashionable move: the ecclesiastical authorities repeatedly emphasised the need for proper clerical garb, including the round biretta. An act to this effect was passed by the provincial council of 1549, v. *Statuta Ecclesiae Scoticanae*, ed. J. Robertson (2 vols, Edinburgh 1866), II, 89.

3465   'Inglisch' was still used in the sixteenth century, now alongside 'Scottis', as a term for the Lowland vernacular, contrasted with 'Ersche' (Gaelic). For a discussion of this terminology, see J.D. McClure, 'Scottis, Inglis, Suddroun: Language Labels and Language Attitudes', in *Proceedings of the Third International Conference on Scottish Language and Literature (Medieval and Renaissance)*, ed. Roderick J. Lyall and Felicity Riddy (Stirling/Glasgow 1981), pp. 52–69.

3474   Lindsay is perhaps thinking of *Ephesians* 2: 3–8: 'But God whiche is ryche in mercye, thorow his great love wherewyth he loved us, even when we were dead by synne, hath quyckened us together in Chryst (for by grace ye are saved) and hath raysed us up together and made us sytte together in hevenlye thinges thorowe Chryste Jesus, for to shew in tymes to come the excedynge riches of his grace, in kyndnes to us warde in Chryste Jesu. For by grace are ye made safe thorow faythe, and that not of youre selves.'

3524   Lindsay is conflating, in the manner of the medieval preacher, three passages from *Matt.* 22:37–40.

3535   The Doctour repeats his text, adding a '*Dei*' ('of God') which does not occur in the Vulgate version.

3594   A similar remark, using the same rhyme, occurs in *The Monarche*, which Lindsay was writing at about the same time that he completed *The Thrie Estaitis*. From the use of the present tense in both passages, they appear to refer to the Smalkaldic War of 1551–3, which included hostilities in Parma between Pope Julius III and Henry II of France (May 1551– April 1552). Hamer objects that Francis was in fact the aggressor, but Lindsay's view would presumably have been different, and instinctively anti-Papal. News of the truce of 29 April 1552 would have taken some time to reach Scotland; see Introduction, p.xiii.

3609   No speaker is identified for the response to Diligence in *C*, but it must be either the First (as in Hamer) or Second (as in Kinsley) Licent.

3647   A 'chaplarie', or scapular, is part of the habit of some monastic orders, a sleeveless top garment worn over the tunic. The cowl is a ceremonial vestment, characterised by wide sleeves and a hood.

3708    i.e. by producing food through physical labour, by ploughing and harrowing.

3712    B's 'fallowis' is demanded by the rhyme; C reads 'fellowis'.

3714    C does not allocate this speech; B gives it, correctly, to Flatterie.

3723    'he': *so B; C* 'ye'.

3823    The protection of the Church was reaffirmed by every medieval Parliament. The implications of 'the Kirk of Christ' are (no doubt deliberately) vague; the usual Parliamentary formula in Scotland was 'the prevelegis, libertes and fredomes of Haly Kirk', which had, of course, originally been uncontroversial.

3840–1    This is the first substantive measure, formalising the decision of Correctioun (2688–94) that temporal lands should be set in feu. The development of the system of feu-ferm, whereby lands were granted in return for an initial lump-sum payment and fixed annual feu-duty, dates back to the twelfth century, but it had expanded considerably in the century before 1550. Modern historians take the view that the spread of feuing, often with duties much higher than the previous rent, was a source of poverty rather than a remedy (cf. Ranald Nicholson, *Scotland: The Later Middle Ages* [Edinburgh 1974], pp. 570–2), but Lindsay was not the only contemporary writer to hold the opposite: cf. John Major, *History of Greater Britain*, trans. Archibald Constable (SHS, Edinburgh 1892), pp. 30–1. There is some evidence that tenant farmers in northern France, where ground-rents were relatively low, were in a much more favourable situation; cf. Emmanuel Le Roy Ladurie, *The French Peasantry 1450–1660*, trans. Alan Sheridan (London 1987), pp. 60–8, 171–81.

3848–9    Again, a decision by Correctioun (2679–80) is repeated, this time in a more explicit form. Lindsay has turned to the administration of justice, and he begins by making lords responsible for wrongdoers among their dependents. This was a traditional principle of medieval law, if unevenly applied in practice.

3857    This is new to the play: Lindsay proposes the establishment of a second College of Justice to serve the more remote parts of the kingdom. Delays in the execution of justice were commonplace in the sixteenth century, and greatly exacerbated by problems of distance and poor communications.

3863– Two different measures are here neatly (if somewhat
86    confusingly for the modern reader) conflated.
      Lindsay is conscious of the poor financial base of the
      existing College of Justice; at its foundation in
      1532, James v had intended that it should be endowed
      by contributions from the clergy, but these were never
      consistently paid. There was a serious crisis in 1549,
      when Senators of the College complained that their
      stipends were years in arrears; v. *APA*, pp. xxxii-xlv.
      It is in this practical context that Lindsay proposes
      the abolition of the nunneries and the application of
      their revenues to the maintenance of his two Courts of
      Session. The measure is not, *pace* Hamer, muddled; it
      is a neat attempt to solve two problems at once, and to
      justify the more contentious in terms of the
      other.

3888– The expanded jurisdiction of the consistory courts
90    was a frequent source of discontent; cf. Gordon
      Donaldson, 'The Church Courts', in *An Introduction
      to Scottish Legal History* (Stair Society, Edinburgh
      1958), p. 363: 'A clerk or spiritual man might – and
      often did – appear as a pursuer in a secular court;
      but as a defender he commonly claimed successfully
      that the suit should be heard before an ecclesiastical
      tribunal.' The principle which Lindsay here enunciates
      was, however, the theory upon which the parallel
      systems were supposed to operate.

3895–6 The Act on the consistory courts forms a bridge
      to the next group of measures, all of which deal with
      ecclesiastical abuses. The first, which is fundamental to
      what follows, is that all benefice holders should be
      properly qualified. The same theme emerges strongly
      from Hamilton's *Catechism*, where the prefatory letter
      quotes Augustine to the effect that 'Ignorance the
      mother of al errours suld maist of al be eschewit in
      preistis, quhilk hes ressavit the office of teching amang
      the christin pepil', ed. Law, p. 5.

3908–9 Similarly, schoolmasters and other teachers are to be
      of proper clerical standing and the necessary erudition.
      Parliament here instructs the bishops on ecclesiastical
      matters!

3925  The main thrust of the Twelfth Act is against
      pluralism, an important grievance of the Reformers;
      cf. *Statuta Ecclesiae Scoticanae*, ed. Robertson, 11,
      109, invoking the constitution *De multa* of the Fourth
      Lateran Council (1215), and *ibid.* 11, 113, citing

constitution VII,ii (3 March 1547) of the Council of Trent.

3929–30  The destructive power of these rights has, of course, been demonstrated by the story of the Poor Man; see above, ll. 1993 ff.

3934  The alleviation of the tax burden takes in temporal duties as well.

3940–1  Absenteeism (a natural corollary of pluralism, but also a consequence of the political role of many senior clergy) was another favourite topic of the Reformers.

3945  This is as near as Lindsay comes to challenging the authority of the Pope: no theological arguments are advanced, but preferment is here seen, with the notable exception of Archbishoprics, to be a purely Scottish matter.

3955  Although no break with Rome is overtly advocated, a unilateral abolition of clerical celibacy would presumably have made it inevitable. Clauses to this effect were in reality included in, for example, the ordinance of the Diet of Odense (1527) and the Augsburg Confession (1530); for Luther's view on clerical marriage, v. *Vom ehelichen Leben* (1522), *Werke* (62 vols, Weimar 1883–1986), 10 (2), 267–304.

3962  This is perhaps the most remarkable of all the Acts; cf. 3194–3213.

3972  Ananias is described as the father-in-law of his fellow high priest Caiaphas (John 18:13); together they were responsible for the condemnation of Christ, and Lindsay places them in Hell in *The Dreme* (217–8), *Works*, ed. Hamer, I, 11.

3976  'it' *om. C.*

3981  Cf. above, l. 3069 and note. In the context of the play, of course, 'Plutois band' are proved to be the spirituality.

3993  'fallowis': *so B; C* 'fellows'.

4009  'beschittin': *so B; C* 'bedirtin' (an obvious bowdlerization).

4030–8  These are principal reiving families: the Armstrongs, Scotts and Grahames are the most familiar, but most of the others occur in various contemporary documents about disorder in the Marches. A list of families which had been sworn to support Edward VI of England for at least a year before January 1553, for example, includes the Lytles of Eskdale, Ewesdale and Wauchopdale, the 'Elwoddes' (Lindsay's Elwands) and the Nixons of Liddesdale, the Irwins and others

(*Calendar of Scottish Papers*, I, 191–2); and the
Crosars and Nixons were required by the Privy Council
to give 'plegis for gud reull' on 20 February 1553
(*APC*, I, 138). The names clearly gave Charteris'
printers some difficulty: the 'Hansles' which occurs at
l. 4032 in some copies of *C* should read 'Hawis' (*so
B*), and 'Curwings' at l. 4036 should be 'Erewynis'
(*so B*).

4094–
4100
Although these are all common surnames, they do
appear to have a particular reference to Cupar, and *B*'s
reading of 4095 is better than *C*'s 'The blude royal of
Clappertoun'. The Jamiesons were a prominent burgess
family: David and Alexander Jamieson had just served
as commissioners for Cupar at the convention of royal
burghs on 4 April 1552 (*Records of the Convention
of Royal Burghs*, I, 1–2), and Alexander was Dean
of Guild three times between 1549 and 1553. Thomas
Williamson was a burgess by 1542, and served as baillie
in 1549. For a useful summary of this evidence, v. A.J.
Mill, 'Representations of Lyndsay's *Satyre of the Thrie
Estaitis*', *PMLA* 47 (1932), 636–49, as amended
*ibid.*, 48 (1933), 315–6.

4107
*C* omits this further list of Cupar names found in *B*,
substituting the ineffective 'For wanting of your wonted
grace'. These were presumably cut because the names
were generally less familiar elsewhere in Scotland, but
all were well-established burgess families in Cupar.

4117
Dissait's curse echoes the repeated Old Testament
curse 'to the third and fourth generations' (cf. *Exodus*
20:5, 34:7; *Numbers* 14:18; *Deuteronomy* 5:9.
For the locution 'to the [thrid] air', see *The
Thre Prestis of Peblis*, l. 94, ed. T.D. Robb (STS,
Edinburgh 1920), p. 7.

4143
It was apparently a common piece of sharp practice to
inflate the cellular membrane of meat in order to make
it more attractive to the customer.

4154
The Fortunes were another burgess family in Cupar;
an Andrew Fortune, who occurs as a servant in the
Burgh Court minutes for 1530–2, may be Lindsay's
tailor (Hamer, IV, 146–7).

4157
A John Banerache occurs as a servant in 1549, and is
party to an assize in 1551.

4160–5
No James Ralph occurs in the sixteenth-century
records, as the deacon of a craft or in any other
capacity, nor is there a William Cadyow. The Cadyows
were a well-established burgess family in Aberdeen by
the middle of the fifteenth century.

4184    'Selly': *so B; C* 'Sillie'. Not traced.

4200    Ducats and guilders were Italian and Netherlandish
        gold coins respectively.

4208–9  'uder', 'fuder': *so B; C* 'uther', 'fidder'.

4210    C's 'War thair canteleinis kend' is nonsense.

4213    'God': *so B; C* 'To'.

4219    'streicht way': *so B; C* 'the rycht'.

4261    Jezebel, wife of Ahab, king of Israel, was a worshipper
        of Baal and a vigorous persecutor of the prophets,
        attempting to bring about the death of Elijah (1 Kings
        16:31–21:23). Her death is described in *2 Kings*
        9:30–7; cf. the list of those excluded from grace at
        the Last Judgement, *Monarche*, 5696–5889 (Hamer,
        I, 367–72), where Jezebel occurs at 5824.

4268    'did': *so B; C* 'doith'.

4270    'mon': *so B; C* 'am'.

4294    The image of the wolf in sheep's clothing is ultimately
        derived from *Matthew* 7:15, but was widespread in
        medieval literature. Lindsay's reference to 'ane wedderis
        skin' perhaps recalls Henryson's fable of 'The Wolf and
        the Wedder', where the wether disguises himself as a
        sheepdog and chases a wolf.

4300    The shrine of Loreto, near Musselburgh, East Lothian,
        was established about 1533 by Thomas Douchty, who
        set up a chapel dedicated to the Virgin; the grant of
        the land was confirmed on 29 July 1534 (cf. David
        McRoberts, 'Hermits in Medieval Scotland', *Innes Rev.*,
        16 (1965), 199–216, at 209–12). Douchty
        was known as the 'hermit of Loreto'; for a vitriolic
        attack on him, composed by the Earl of Glencairn,
        see Knox's *History of the Reformation, Works*, ed. David
        Laing (6 vols, Edinburgh 1846–64), I, 72–5.
        Alexander Scott refers to the popularity of Loreto as a
        pilgrimage-centre in 'May is the moneth maist amene',
        ll. 56–60, *Poems*, ed. Cranstoun, p. 25.

4315    B has 'Bony Gait', referring to part of the
        main east-west axis of Cupar. 'Schogait' (Shoe Street)
        is more difficult to place, but there was a street of this
        name in Perth.

4318    'And I to ga' is an idiomatic use of the infinitive
        expressing speed of movement; cf. Henryson, *Morall
        Fabillis*, 295–6: 'Thay taryit not to wesche, as I
        suppose / Bot on to ga ...', *Poems*, ed. Fox, p. 15.

4349    'gif': *so B; om. C.*

4361    It is apparent from this allusion that Correctioun
        takes the form of an avenging angel, possibly similar
        in appearance to St Michael, who was commonly
        portrayed in armour and wielding a sword.

| 4420 | Cf. the earlier derogatory reference to Tullilum, 767; *C* has 'Tillilum'. |
|---|---|
| 4432 | St Denis or Dionysius, the third-century bishop of Paris, who was the patron saint of France. |
| 4454–61 | These lines, present in *B*, are omitted from *C*, but as in other comparable cases there is no obvious reason for their inclusion. They are probably genuine. |
| 4501 | 'gane': *so B; C* 'grim'. |
| 4502 | The Latin comes from the Vulgate text of *Ecclesiastes* 1:15. All vernacular versions from Luther on follow the Hebrew and Septuagint texts in reading this verse quite differently (the Matthew Bible, for example, has 'the fautes can not be nombred'); but the quotation was widely used in folly literature; cf. Barclay, *The Ship of Fools*, ed. Jamieson, I, 12: 'Thus is of Foles a sort almost innumerable'. |
| 4531 | 'brocht': *so B; C* 'bocht'. |
| 4539 | Foly now begins a catalogue of types of fool, beginning with merchants who, through greed, send ships out in winter. For a discussion of this and the following passages, see Introduction, p.xxxi. |
| 4546 | Chalmers (*Works*, I, 60) suggests that this is an allusion to the act of 7 June 1535, reaffirming legislation of 1466. This is possible, though Chalmers' inference that the play must therefore be contemporary with this act is hardly warranted. |
| 4552 | The type of the aged husband is a stock figure of ridicule in medieval literature; cf. the Cupar Proclamation, ll. 142 ff. |
| 4566 | Foly reverts to the dominant theme of the play, the abuses of ignorant and worldly clerics. |
| 4600 | The reference is to the Anglo-Scottish war of 1542–50, during which French forces supported the Scots against invading English armies. |
| 4603 | The Emperor Charles V was indeed preparing for war in the course of the summer of 1552, mounting a counter-campaign against the French attack on his Burgundian territories. He moved against Henry II in August, but his siege of Metz was unsuccessful. Lindsay's picture of diplomatic and military disorder is a fairly accurate version of the situation in 1552, which was not resolved until the Peace of Augsburg (1555); for a further discussion of this aspect of the play's topicality, see Introduction, p.xiii. |
| 4613 | Julius III's involvement in the Parma campaign of 1551–2 is discussed above, ll. 3593–6. |

4625-6 Various prophecies attributed to Merlin and others
circulated in the Middle Ages. For a general review of a
tangled and partly unpublished tradition, see the lists
provided by R.H. Robbins in *A Manual of the Writings
in Middle English 1050–1500*, V, 1519–34.

4627 The Gyre Carling was a popular names for Hecate,
conceived of as a grotesquely horrible witch. Lindsay
claims (*The Dreme*, 45) to have told the child James
V of 'the Reid Eitin' and 'the Gyre Carling': the
latter *may* be identical with the poem preserved in the
Bannatyne manuscript (ed. W. Tod Ritchie [4 vols,
STS, Edinburgh 1927–33], III, 13–14), which
features 'ane grit gyre carling ... That levit vpoun
christiane menis flesche'.

4631-4 The first two lines are reasonably close to some versions
of a fifteenth-century prophecy, which also occurs
as part of 'the Scottes prophecie in Latine' printed
by Waldegrave in *The Whole Prophecie of Scotland*
(1603); cf. *A Collection of Ancient Scottish Prophecies*
(Bannatyne Club, Edinburgh 1833), p.40. They
appear to mean: 'Flanders and France will rise again,
likewise Spain will use her strength; the Danes will
lay [you] waste, the Welsh will yield the ramparts'.
The latter part, which is indeed an ill-savoured mess,
can be translated as 'Such is your name in A, the
woman crapped in a can; you dine at this feast ...'

4638-9 Kantrowitz (pp. 17–21) convincingly relates these
lines to the controversy in St Andrews over whether
the Pater noster should be directed solely to God
(as the English Dominican Richard Marshall argued in
a sermon in St Andrews, probably in 1551) or
might also be addressed to the saints. The latter view
was defended on 1 November 1551 by the Franciscan
Andrew Coutts, and the matter was resolved with the
publication of Archbishop Hamilton's *Catechism*, which
declared only that the prayer should be addressed
to God. For a vivid if partisan contemporary account of
the controversy, see John Foxe, *Actes and Monuments*
(London 1570), pp. 1450–2. Tellingly, Foxe cites
a pasquil, 'set on the Abbay Churche', which
anticipates Lindsay's rhyme: 'Doctors of Theologie, of
four score of yeares / And old wyise (?) Lupoys
the bald gray Friers / They wouldbe called Rabbi and
Magister noster / And wot not to whome thay say their
Pater noster'.

4643 Gilly-moubrand was a sixteenth-century fool, mentioned
in the *Treasurer's Accounts* for 25 April 1527 (V, 320).

Hamer suggests that he may have been an itinerant
fool.

4645    Cacaphatie may also have been a well-known fool; his
name was apparently derived from Greek *kakemphaton*,
the name of two figures of rhetoric, one 'a disagreeable
and inharmonious composition of sounds' (Joannes
Susenbrotus, *Epitome troporum ac schematum et
grammaticorum et rhetorum* [Zurich 1541], p. 36), the
other 'the employment of language to which perverted
usage has given an obscene meaning' (Quintilian,
*Institutio Oratorica*, VIII, iii, 44): both references are
cited by Lee A. Sonnino, *A Handbook to Sixteenth
Century Rhetoric* (London 1968), pp. 166, 198. Cf.
George Puttenham, *The Arte of English Poesie*, ed.
Gladys Doidge Willcock and Alice Walker (Cambridge
1976), pp. 253–4, where the figure is defined
as 'unshamefast or figure of foule speech which our
courtly maker shall in any case shunne'. Mill draws
attention to a reference in the *Exchequer Rolls* for
1537–8 to a payment for the expenses of a 'bard
callit Cacopety', ('Representations', 641, citing *Exch.R*,
xvii, 143).

4650    Diligence clearly suggests that the play will be repeated
next summer.

4656–    These lines are omitted from C, probably because of
63    their Marian content.

4666    The brawl (from Fr. *branle*) was an intricate
French dance; cf. *The Complaynt of Scotlande*, ed.
A.M. Stewart (STS, Edinburgh 1979), p. 52: '...
it vas ane celest recreation to behald ther lycht
lopene, galmouding, stendling ..... pauuans, galyardis,
turdions, braulis and branglis ...'

4672–3    'Wise king, eternal God and beneficent Creator,
everlasting glory, praise and honour be to You.'

PROCLAMATIOUN MAID IN COWPAR OF FYFFE

50    St Fillan is also invoked in the play proper, l. 1955;
see note, p.191 above.

79–80    For this *nocht* / coft rhyme, where one would expect
*nocht* / bocht, see above, ll. 1256–8, and the note,
p.187.

105    A 'fute-band' appears in the records of the
royal household within a few years of the destruction of
the Scottish feudal host at Flodden; the *Treasurer
Accts* in 1517 (V, 155–7) contain various payments
to 'Capitane Glennyis futband' and to that of Sir
John Hamilton. Scattered references turn up throughout

the century; Fynlaw may, however, be a Highland mercenary rather than a member of the royal guard (see Introduction, p.xxxiv).

125    The battle of Pinkie Cleuch, east of Edinburgh, was fought on 10 September 1547, and was a huge defeat for the Scottish army at the hands of the Earl of Somerset's English forces. . The repeated references here to the retreat of the Scots indicate the continuing awareness of this military disaster.

202–3    The Clerk's prayer is a clue to the identity of Fynlaw, who was presumably played by an actor who would be among the vices hanged at the end of the Thrie Estaitis.

224    Holland cloth was a fine linen fabric, imported as its name suggests from the Netherlands.

240    'Golias' is Goliath, the Philistine warrior overcome by David (*1 Samuel* 17). This form of the name is, as Hamer notes, Chaucerian.

242    For Sir Gray Steill, a gigantic knight, see *Eger and Grime*, ed. J.R. Caldwell (Cambridge, Mass. 1933).

245    *Sir Bevis of Hamptoun* is a thirteenth-century romance which was widely known in the later Middle Ages.

251    The ghost of Guido or Guy of Alet featured in a popular late medieval pious tale, of which there were at least three English verse versions. For the most significant, known as *The Gast of Gy*, see the edition by Gustav Schleich, *Palaestra* I (Berlin 1898); there is a study of the relationship between the Latin original and the various English versions in R.H. Bowers, *The Gast of Gy*, Beiträge zur Englische Philologie 32 (Leipzig 1938).

253    For the Gyre Carling, see the note, p.xli above.

257    Gowmakmorne is Goll mac Morna, like Fionn mac Cumhaill a leader of the *Fianna*. He, too, is prominent in the texts recorded in the Book of the Dean of Lismore.

271    The Tuesday after Whitsunday fell on 7 June (l. 11) in 1552, thus providing a basis for the dating of the Cupar performance; see Introduction, p.xii.